Yani and the Knapper

The Journey

Cherie Coon

For all those who yearn to travel, even if only in their imaginations.

Forward:

The inspiration for this book came from my time spent as a volunteer in archeological villages in Europe. I have modeled my villages after ones I visited during my twenty-three years living and working in Germany. Yani's village, as well as several others, was patterned after the Museumsdorf Dueppel in Berlin, and the Knapper's home village after Biskupin in the Poland. The chalk cliffs and beech forest were inspired by the Island of Ruegen on the northern coast of Germany. The book is not meant to be an accurate depiction of life during the Stone Age but rather a gentle fantasy in a land I loosely patterned after Europe.

Part One
The Journey Begins

Chapter One

The leather strap of her carrying basket cut into Yani's forehead as she trudged along the trail. Her back itched between her shoulder blades where the sweat had caused her woolen dress to stick to her back. She twisted her shoulders trying to use the basket to scratch the itch. She reached up and inched the strap up a bit higher on her forehead. When the strap was settled in place again, her hand started to move automatically to the burned skin of her scalp where her hair was separated by the part. She stopped herself just in time. The last time she had scratched the tender skin her hands had come away red with blood from where the blisters had broken. It seemed like she had been walking forever but from the shape of the pale moon hanging low in the east, she knew it had only been the length of time that it takes for the thin new moon to grow fat again. Her body had toughened in that time but her feet were still sore from the stone bruises she had collected the first day on the trail. As she plodded along, her mind again took her back to her last day in the village that had been the only home she had ever known.

The first flowers of the spring had been opening in the fields around the meadow where the new lambs were frolicking, learning to use their spindly legs. She had spent the day looking for early dandelions and dreaming of the warm summer days to come. She had been grateful that the winter was nearly over. It had been such a terribly hard one. The hardest anyone in the village besides the Old Grandmother could remember. The snow and ice had kept the People confined to their hearths for much of the time. Food had run short, and her father had had little success in his hunting. Twice he had missed a kill simply because his blade had not been sharp enough to allow the spear to penetrate deeply, reaching a vital organ. The wounded animal had bounded off and although he had followed it for the three days demanded by the spirit of the animal, he had been too late. The wolves had found it before he could end its suffering and appease its spirit. It was said in the village that the spirit of this deer had cursed her family, which probably explained the terrible luck her family had had all winter. Perhaps that was also why she was here trudging along this path with her back and legs aching and the sun beating down on her head.

When she had come in from the meadow that day with her basket of dandelion greens, she had sensed the excitement in the village even before she saw the flint knapper. She too had caught the excitement thinking of the stories that would be told around the hearth fires that night. First they would hear the news of the other villages of the People, who had had new babies over the winter, who had made the journey to the Otherside, who had chosen a lifemate. More importantly, there would also be new blades to barter for. Men were already collecting furs they could trade with the Knapper for his fine, strong hunting points. Women were collecting the last of their dried berries and roots to trade for knives, burins, and scrapers. Yani's mother had been saving a beautiful pair of moccasins she hoped to trade for the new spearheads her father needed, as well as a new skinning knife and a scraping blade. They were decorated with the quills Yani had collected from the dead porcupine she had found in the woods during the Gathering Moon. She had carefully collected the quills and helped her mother dry and dye them. They had sewn them to the soft deer hide of the moccasins forming a bright Sun Spirit pattern. It was a pattern of interlocking circles of yellow, orange and red surrounded by lines of black and white. She was sure the Knapper would be only too happy to trade the lovely moccasins for the few blades her family needed.

The Knapper was resting against the log wall around the well in the center of the village when she walked across the common area to her house. She was not surprised that the Knapper was resting by the well. It was the pride of the village. The water was cold and sweet. Even in the driest season it never ran dry. Her father loved to tell the

7

story of how the well had been dug. How the men had first set the two posts that held the long pole that lowered and raised the basket into the depth of the well to bring up the water. They had used it in the beginning to bring up the baskets of dirt as they dug the hole deeper reaching down to the water below. Yani was always happy to hear the part about the digging of the well and how the men had been able to go so deep. She did not like the part that her father seemed to enjoy telling the most. He always laughed, seeming to be bragging about the beating his father had given him for putting his little sister in the basket and lowering her into the half finished well. Her screams of terror had brought the women of the village running who then quickly put a stop to his cruel fun. He had to rely on others to finish the story of the digging of the well because after his dangerous prank with his sister he had been banned from the commons until the strong log wall surrounding the well could be completed.

The sting of nettles on her bare legs jarred her out of her day dream and back to the present. The path was lined with the stinging weeds. Resisting the temptation to touch the stinging spot on her calf, she searched the edge of the trail for the shiny green leaf that would ease the sting. She knew that the plant the children called Fairy Jewels because of its bright leaves and pretty yellow and orange flowers should be close by. They almost always grew near where nettles grew. The juice from that plant would stop the sting. Seeing a nice clump at the edge of the trail, she grabbed a handful, crushing them, she quickly rubbed them over the place the nettles had touched. Just as a precaution she slipped a few leaves into her pocket too. She hurried to catch up and soon settled into her day dream again.

In her mind she pictured her house, going over each detail as if she were afraid she would forget them. First, there were the low circular walls made of woven willow twigs and covered with a mixture of clay and straw to keep out the winter's wind and the summer's heat. Inside

8

was the fire pit in the heart of the house around which her family gathered to eat and work. Above it all was the high thatched roof that shed the rain and snow making her home warm and snug. The door into the house was inset back from the edge of the roof making a small alcove where you could shake the rain or snow off before entering the living area. In this protected area, the family could leave their farming tools during the summer months.

As she had entered through this door the day the Knapper had come, she had been met with the wonderful smell of stew. As she had waited for her eyes to became accustom to the gloom after the bright spring sunshine, her nose had told her that there was meat in the stew. If her mother had added the last of their dried meat to the pot, it must mean that her mother had hoped the Knapper would take his evening meal with them. She had let out a small gasp causing her mother to look up from her cooking. They were not an honored family. Why would he choose them? Her mother had turned a sad knowing smile toward her daughter. It was rare for her mother to smile at all let alone at her. Remembering, she had wondered if her mother had known what was to come? Had her mother sensed more than that the Knapper would eat his evening meal with them. Had she known they would not be together much longer? It had been said by some in the village that her mother had the gift of the Sight but she had never given it much thought. She had sat down by her mother and had begun to clean the dandelions she had gathered. A few of them could be added to the stew making it even more special. A stew with meat and fresh greens not just the porridge made of the acorns the woman had gathered, leeched and ground during the Moon of Falling Leaves.

When she had finished with the dandelions, she had given them to her mother who had put a small handful into the stew then had put the rest into a storage basket. These would be made into the spring tonic much needed by her family after a winter of dried meat, acorn meal and not much else. The pumpkins that they had stored for the winter had rotted soon after her father had missed the deer adding to the rumor of the curse. After that the squirrels had chewed through the thatch of the roof and carried off almost all the nuts she had gathered. It had been a very bad winter.

As she walked along the trail in her mind she continued her mental inventory of the inside of her home. On the opposite side of the large room was a wider sleeping bench that her parents shared. Over the top of their bed was a loft that was used to store the families food supply and extra belongings. There were hides to be worked into moccasins and cloaks. There was still some wool to be carded with the teasel burrs and spun on the drop spindle. Most of it had been spun into yarn already and had been ready to either weave into cloth or make into mittens and socks using a deer horn needle to chain the threads together. The beams that made up the warp-weighted loom were also there. Her mother would be setting it up in the corner soon to begin weaving now that the majority of the wool had been spun. The wool too had added to the curse story since all winter they had raced with mice intent on destroying it before she and her mother could get it spun. They had had to put the precious spun wool into the bed with them to protect it from the mice.

Also in the loft were the farming tools her father would use to break the ground in the garden plot behind their house. Each family had a garden where they grew herbs, leeks, rutabagas and pumpkins. The men helped with the first breaking of the soil. Then the responsibility of the garden was that of the women. That is as it should be, for the men needed to hunt and fish to provide the meat for the stew pot.

The village also had a small flock of sheep that provided the wool her mother treasured. Wool was warmer and more comfortable than hides. Yani loved the small gray sheep with their soft curly wool. She loved the smell of the new fleece when it was just off the sheep.

And the slick feel of the oil in the fleece that made her hands so soft and healed the cracks in her feet after the cold winter. Shearing time was her favorite time of the year. Since the flock had grown so over the last few years, her family would be given three more fleeces for their share this season. That would be seven fleece that she would help her mother spin, while her sisters opened the locks and carded the wool to make it ready. She loved those times when they sat around the fire on late summer evenings or snugly in the house in the winter working the wool. They would whisper and laugh, gossiping about their friends in the village. They often speculated on who would next leave to find a husband and to which village of the People they would go.

But that was all in the past. Her face darkened as she thought of that night, the one that should have been so enjoyable, The one that had turned into a nightmare for Yani. The Knapper had come to their house just as the sun was setting. The time of day when the people ate their evening meals. He had set his heavy pack at the door and had shuffled with his lopsided walk into the room to take his place on the three-legged stool by the fire. It was the only stool the family owned and the one usually reserved for her father. The evening had begun pleasantly enough. He had brought word from her mother's sister that a new baby would be added to the family at the end of the summer, always a thing to rejoice about. He had also said her younger brother had taken a wife. Her mother's people were from a clan that lived in the south at the base of the Mountains That Are Always White, the mountains so high snow never melts off the peaks. Yani tried to imagine such mountains but having never gone more than a short distance from her village- just into the woods to look for nuts and berries or perhaps to the lake on the far side of the big meadow- the idea of mountains that seemed to go up and touch the clouds was beyond her. If she were a boy, she thought for the thousandth time, she would go see those mountains when she grew up. But she was only a girl so she know that the only other place she would

11

see would be the village she would go to when a man came to take her as his life mate.

The evening meal had been served as usual. As the men had eaten the stew, Yani, her mother and her sisters had listened to their talk, waiting for them to eat their fill before filling their own wooden bowls. It was only right for the men to eat first. They must keep up their strength for the hunt or the whole family would go hungry.

When the men at last had finished, the women had filled their bowls with what was left over and had settled themselves on one of the benches to listen to the bartering. Yani's father had spread a piece of raw deer hide on the rushes that covered the hard packed dirt floor. On this he had laid the lovely moccasins with the quill design, three wooden bowls he had carved and then polished with creek sand until they glowed softly, and several pouches of dried herbs and berries. The Knapper had unpacked a wide variety of flint blades from his pack and had laid them out on the deer hide he had spread on the floor. Then the negotiations had begun.

As Yani had scooped the tasty stew from the bowl with her fingers she had watched the Knapper. He was a very old man - he must have seen at least forty summers. Her father, who was not nearly so old, had just seen his thirtieth summer the year before. The Knapper had long reddish hair streaked with gray. His eyes were an icy blue but had a kind of distant look to them. He was tall, although when he walked it did not seem so because he was so stooped from the years of carrying his heavy pack. He had a strange gait caused by his crippled foot. She had heard several stories about how he had come to have such a deformity, not from the Knapper, of course, but from the village gossips. It was said by some that the gods had hit his mother with a bolt of lightning the week before he was born, making the foot shrivel up and die. Others said he had been held by that foot when he had been carried off by the cave bear that had raised him like her cub. Yani didn't

12

really believe any of the wild stories, but she could see his foot was badly deformed which explained why he was a Knapper and not a hunter. He would not have the speed for the chase, and his shuffling walk would alert the animal long before he could make a kill. He was strong though for an old man. The fact that he traveled such great distances was proof of that.

By the time she had finished her stew, the bargaining had been fully under way. Her father had examined all the blades offered and had decided on two beautiful flint spearheads and a knife blade for her mother. But, for some reason, the Knapper had showed little interest in the items offered for trade. He had picked up each and then had laid it back in the same spot her father had placed them. Had he been interested in the item, he would have moved it nearer to his side of the deer hide or even placed it on his hide indicating he had accepted it as part of the trade.

Silently, so as not to disturb the men, Yani got up and began collecting the empty eating bowls to take to the lake to wash. As she had bent down to pick up the Knapper's bowl from the ground beside him, he had gently laid his hand on her head. She had been so stunned to think that she had disturbed the men that she had frozen. Her father would be furious with her. She would be lucky if he only made her sleep with the sheep for a few nights. More likely she would get a beating. Fearing to look at her father, she had looked instead toward the trading hides. She had been shocked to see that with his other hand the Knapper had taken three other blades from his pack and had added them to the ones her father had selected. Yani had watched the look of understanding pass between the men. Bewildered, she had watched her father pick up the blades and carry them to his storage pouch hanging from the peg above his bed. Looking to her mother for an explanation Yani had seen only the top of her mother's bowed head. When her mother had raised her tear streaked face to look at Yani, she had

13

realized what had happened. She was to be the payment for the blades. She belonged to the Knapper.

Even now the tears stung Yani's eyes as she remembered the hard look that had replaced the sorrow on her mother's face when she had turned to her with pleading eyes. She had always known one day she would leave the village to join a hearth in another village, but had not dreamed it would happen this way. She was only ten summers. She was not yet a woman. But her mother had closed her mind to Yani and she had known it was done. Not that her mother could have done anything to change the situation once her father had agreed to the trade. She knew she would leave the next day when the Knapper continued his journey. Perhaps this, too, was the price demanded by the spirit of the deer the wolves had taken. His spirit was demanding that she walk this long trail behind the Old Knapper. She just hoped that her suffering would remove the curse from her family. Maybe life would be better for her little sisters then.

Chapter Two

On the spring morning he arrived, the old man had first noticed the girl as he crossed the meadow between the woods and the village. Emerging from of the pine forest into a sun-lit field, he had sensed her movement before he had actually seen her. He had turned toward the movement, and there she had been, dancing in a circle, her arms stretched high toward a cloud of tiny yellow butterflies. He had stopped and watched for a while as she had frolicked around the grassy field. Then suddenly, as if she had sensed his presence, she had stopped, looking embarrassed by her childish play. She had returned to her basket and kneeling down had picked more dandelions. He had stepped back into the forest and had waited a while, hoping the butterflies would once again tempt her into her childish dance. When instead she had busied herself with her gathering, all the time moving toward the far end of the meadow, he had once again emerged and had crossed unnoticed to the village. As he had rested by the well and had drowned his thirst with its sweet cool water, he had seen her enter the village. He had watched closely to see which of the houses she would enter.

The Knapper had lead a lonely life never having taken a life mate. It is true that he had been in love once as a young man. His Mati had been much like this young girl when he had first met her so many years ago. They were only children at the time, smiling across the fire when he had gone with his father to visit his father's sister in the village by the Rushing River. He knew from the first moment he had seen her, he would one day return to claim her. Over the next few years they had grown and undergone the rituals of adulthood. He was planning to present her father with the mating gifts at the next clan gathering. But that had been before the accident with the aurach. His foot had been whole then and he could run as swiftly as any of the young men of the People. Then had come the hunt when his dreams had all died. He had

15

been lucky though since in most villages he would have become an outcast. A village could not support a cripple who could not contribute. The old Knapper, who lived in his village, had offered him a way of life that was almost as honorable as that of a hunter. He had learned the trade of turning flint to blades. When the old Knapper had died several years later he had taken up his solitary life in the Knapper's hut continuing as the village's new knapper. But that was long ago and Mati had since married, bore children and died. Had he married Mati, he imagined their daughter would have been much like this butterfly dancer with her pale yellow hair blowing around her face.

As he had moved from fire pit to fire pit bartering his blades for the few things he needed, he had subtly asked questions about the girl and her family. That had been when the idea had come to him. He was getting old, and each year it became more difficult to carry his pack from village to village on his two-year circle from the Northern Sea to the Mountains That Are Always White in the south and back. It was time now to move northward to his summer camp and begin his work collecting and chipping flakes from the flint nodules he found there. Perhaps this year he would not make that trip alone.

The village gossips, men as well as women, had been only too glad to supply him with all he needed to know about the girl. He had learned her name was Yani and that her father, Gret, had had a very bad hunting year. Gret had blamed his blades for the misfortune and since he was still a strong man and had always been a good hunter, most had been inclined to believe that this was the case. The girl, Yani, was the oldest of three daughters. Although a dreamer, the women all felt she would someday outgrow this. But they also agreed they were glad she wasn't their daughter. She was not the kind of girl that mothers wanted for their sons. Too independent and unpredictable. Why hadn't Kari seen her in the woods one time trying to kill a squirrel with a stick she had sharpened. Who ever heard of a girl behaving so? The next thing

16

you know she would want to be going on a hunt with the men. Gret and his wife, Suti, had no sons, and they were fast approaching the age when it would be too late. Perhaps the younger daughters would be more reliable and they would care for their parents in their old age. But that Yani, she did not hold much promise. Marrying her off to a man from a distant village was what they would do if she were their daughter. Preferably to an older man who could control her. The women clucked and speculated on who this might be as women of the People do.

So the Knapper had decided to take the chance. He would offer the father the best of his blades in hopes that he would agree to the trade. He would have this smiling girl as his daughter to take care of him in his old age and the father would be rid of a strong willed daughter plus the blades needed to provide for the rest of his family. And it had worked. But he had not expected the girl to react as she had. He had seen the look cross between the mother and daughter as the father had agreed to the deal. Then the sunshine had gone out of her face and had been replaced by emptiness. But he felt sure this would pass and she would regain her brightness.

Feeling sorry for the mother, he had given her a very beautiful scraping knife as payment the girl's carrying pack. At first she had protested but when the father had gruffly ordered her to take it she had, lowering her head in thanks.

The next morning, Yani had begun to cry as she had placed her few personal items into her carrying basket before loading the bartered goods of the Knapper that she was to carry. The tears had continued as they had left the village and lasted well into the morning. The soft weeping had torn at the Knapper's heart with each step. He had to keep telling himself that she was young and would adjust.

Chapter Three

When they stopped to rest at noon, he had tried to reassure her, but he could still read the fear in her eyes. He had opened the package of dried meat and had offered her a piece. She had held it, quietly watching as he ate. He was puzzled by her actions since she had to be hungry after the long walk, then he remember the women had not eaten until after the men when he had visited their village.

Softly he said to her, "Your life is different now, and I have different ways. When I eat, you must also eat. There is always enough food at my fire pit for the both of us." Then he continued to chew thoughtfully on the jerky and gazed off at the distant hills they must cross before dropping down to the plain that stretched to the sea.

Shyly, as if testing him, she took a small bite of the jerky. Her eyes never left him. He looked up and smiled his approval. This seemed to reassure her since she quickly took a larger bite. When he finished his jerky, he walked over to the stream and drank deeply. Then he stretched out on the mossy bank and closed his eyes. He listened to her movements as she finished the meat and then came to the stream to drink also. He heard her lower herself to the moss and in minutes he knew from her breathing that she was asleep. He would let her sleep awhile before they resumed their journey. It did not matter if he reached his northern camp next week or the week after that. She needed the time to accustom herself to the walking..

He dozed himself, content with the bartering he had done this season. He had enough dried meat to last until they reached camp and for all the days when they were not able to fish. He ate very little anyway and although he knew a growing girl would eat more than he did, he was still sure that she would have enough to eat.

When he opened his eyes he could tell by the location of the sun that he had slept longer than he had planned. When he looked over at the girl, he saw that she was still sleeping soundly. So as not to frighten her, he called her name softly. When she did not move, he gently touched her shoulder calling her name again. She started up opening her eyes. He saw fear and confusion but was pleased to see that fade as he smiled at her.

"Yani, do you feel better now? It is time that we push on. I would like to reach the base of those hills by nightfall," he asked gently.

She quickly sprang to her feet planning to run and fetch her pack. Instead, she winced in pain when her feet hit the ground. The old man saw this and knew her feet would be even more tender in the morning.

"Slowly," he chuckled. " I am an old man and can't move as fast as you." She turned to see if that was a rebuke, but seeing his smile, shyly returned one of her own.

They had reached the hills as the last rays of the sun light faded to twilight. She had not cried during their afternoon walk, but she had not spoken either. Several times he had tried to engage her in conversation, but she had only answered in as few words as possible. He had heard her described by the village gossips as a chatterbox, so this silence puzzled and alarmed him. He had hoped for company on his long journeys. *Oh well, give her time,* he thought.

They stopped for the night in a clearing at the base of the hills. There was a large tree for shelter and a stream for water. When they had dropped their packs, Yani began instinctively to gather twigs and branches to make a fire. While she had gathered the wood, the Knapper built a firepit. First, choosing a flat area, he scraped away the dried leaves into a small pile at one side. After that he had placed some large smooth rocks from the stream bed around it in a ring. He carefully arranged the twigs to form a pyramid in the center of the ring over some of the dried leaves. Near the pyramid of twigs he placed two round, smooth rocks he had brought from the nearby brook. As Yani broke the

19

branches into smaller pieces, the Knapper opened his pack and removed a piece of flint and a firestone. He leaned over the fire pit and sharply struck the fire stone with the flint. Sparks jumped into the leaves and he gently blew on them coaxing them to burn. They caught and blazed up brightly igniting the pyramid of twigs. When they were burning well, he added some of the larger branches Yani had stacked beside the pit. She continued to bring wood until he told her that he thought they had enough for the night. Kneeling beside him, she opened her pack and removed the tightly woven-cooking basket that had been sealed with pitch, and went to the stream, filling it half-full of water. By the time she got back the Knapper had removed several pouches from his pack. She saw one held dried berries, another acorn meal. She set the basket next to the fire and waited while the fire burned merrily. After a time the Knapper used two sticks to gingerly lift one of the rocks he had placed in the circle from the fire. He carefully put it in the basket of water. Steam rose from the basket as the hot rock came in contact with the cold water. He waited a few minutes and then, using his hand, had reached in and removed the rock returning it to the fire. Then he used the two sticks to place the other rock in the water, being careful to blow the ashes off before he did. He repeated this process two more times, and when he tried to reach in for the rock the last time, he changed his mind and used the sticks to remove it.

Into the now hot water he dropped a hand-full of dried berries and two handfuls of acorn meal. Using one of the sticks he had been picking up the rocks with, he began to stir the mixture. As he stirred, he smiled at Yani and asked, "Do you know how to make acorn meal?"

The frightened look was back on her face as she shook her head "No".

"That is alright, Child, I will teach you. It is not a hard thing to learn."

When the mush was smooth, he took a bowl from his pack and scooped half of it into the bowl and handed it to her.

"I will eat from the cooking basket," he said. "That is, until I can trade for another bowl."

They ate in silence then, and when they had finished, the night had closed in. The fire glowed in the darkness and the surrounding woods began to come to life with the sounds of the night creatures. Yani took the deer hide cloak her mother had made for her from the pack and wrapped it around her. Then she lay down by the fire. Although she was tired, she did not go to sleep immediately. She lay there by the fire and watched the old man through half-closed eyes.

The Knapper took his cloak from his pack, but instead of going to sleep sat down by the fire and removed a pair of old, worn moccasins from his pack. He then took out a deer antler awl and a small flint blade. The last thing Yani remembered seeing before she finally dropped into an exhausted sleep was the Knapper using the blade to remove the lacing from the toes of the moccasins.

Chapter Four

The next morning Yani awoke to the sound of birds singing and the glow of the early morning sun peeking through the trees. The Knapper was stirring the coals of the fire and adding fresh wood. Yani stood up and immediately winced with pain. Her feet felt like someone had pushed thorns into them. She sat back down quickly and looked at the Knapper in fear. *Will he leave me here in the forest alone if I can't walk today? I have never been this far from my village and have no idea how to find my way back home. And would my family even take me back if I were able to get home?* But the Knapper was looking at her with a look of concern on his wrinkled face. He picked up the moccasins he had been working on the night before and began stuffing them with moss. Yani saw that the toes had been trimmed off, remaking them small enough to come close to fitting her feet. He carried them to her and knelt beside her. He picked up each bare foot and examined the bottom.

"You were not careful of where you placed your feet yesterday. The soles are bruised from the stones you stepped on. These will help." And with that, he placed the moccasins beside her. As he walked away, she pulled the moccasins on her feet. She stood up and found that although her feet still hurt, the moss cushioned the bruises and it was not as painful.

"Will you be able to walk today?" asked the Knapper when he saw her standing in the moccasins.

"Yes," whispered Yani. Then she limped off to the spring to drink.

After a breakfast of jerky and dried berries, they shouldered their packs and started on their way again. The second day was harder since they began to climb almost immediately. The strap from Yani's carrying pack cut into her forehead as she leaned into the hill. The

Knapper led the way up a rocky, winding path that he must have traveled many times since he was so sure of the way. Yani thought, as she climbed, she would not have been able to tell where the path was if she had not had him to follow.

At noon they stopped at the top of the ridge to have a lunch of jerky. This time Yani did not sleep. Even if she had wanted to, there was no comfortable moss as the day before. There was only the rocky, windswept ridge. They were soon chilled from the wind, so rested only long enough to eat, then began the steep decent to the valley below. As she walked, she could see where a river formed a narrow gap through the rest of the hills. The Knapper had told her that this was the only high hill they would have to climb on this journey so she decided the route they would follow was through that valley.

She had not expected the downhill climb to be as tiring as the uphill one had been, but she soon learned that it was almost as difficult. The heavy pack kept pushing her forward and soon the fronts of her shins were aching with the strain of holding herself and the pack back. Finally, just before sunset, they reached a sheltered glen at the foot of the hill. The Knapper set his pack down and, with a sigh, Yani did the same. She began to gather the firewood as the Knapper built the fire, and soon they were again sharing an evening meal of acorn mush. After she had washed the bowl and basket, she again wrapped herself in her cloak and was asleep almost immediately.

The next day in the late afternoon, the river valley they had been following opened onto a wide plain that stretched endlessly toward the horizon. Seeing the vast expanse, Yani began to wonder how much farther they would have to walk to reach their destination. It seemed to go on forever. She had not known there could be so much land.

For three days they walked across the plain, always keeping the morning sun on their left and the afternoon sun on their right. Toward noon on the fourth day, they came to a large marsh. Yani could see what looked like a village in the center of the sea of reeds. Skirting the edge of the marsh, the Knapper walked slowly, seemingly looking for something. Finally, he found what he had been seeking, for he turned and walked into the marsh toward the village. Yani watched in wonder, as he appeared to be walking across the top of the watery bog. After a few steps he turned and said, "Come, child, just be sure to walk where I walk."

Reluctant to risk sinking into the marsh, but more afraid to be left behind, Yani stepped into the water. To her surprise she found that just below the muddy water was a causeway of logs that provided a safe passageway for those who knew the path. She followed closely behind the Knapper as he navigated the twists and turns of the causeway. When they finally arrived at the village, the Knapper was greeted with friendly cries and waves.

That night she would sleep again in a house on a sleeping bench much like the one she had slept on all her life. The Knapper had spent the afternoon bartering his blades for things that he thought they might need. He had traded for fishing nets, a wooden bowl, a sleek otter pelt and more dried meat and berries. He had hoped to get a pair of new moccasins for Yani but none had been offered. He knew he could have asked to have a pair made but he did not want to linger that long. There would be enough time for that on the return trip in the Moon of Falling Leaves.

Their evening meal had been taken with the family of the village shaman, and Yani had waited patiently as the men had finished their meal. The son of the shaman had killed four ducks that day. The first of the year, as the ducks had only just returned the week before from the south. Yani watched the two men and the son eat two whole ducks without any indication that they were getting ready to stop. She was beginning to think that there would be none left for the wife, the two daughters and herself. But half way through the third duck, they had

24

stopped, wiped the grease from their beards and belched. That was the signal they were done and the woman could now eat. Yani loved duck, especially when it was roasted slowly over a beech wood fire. She controlled her hunger though, and ate slowly, savoring every bite. As the women ate, the men talked of the past winter and the coming summer. Yani ate until the last of the duck was gone and then helped the women clean up the bones. The older daughter carried the basket of bones to the door and shortly, Yani heard a splash.

"We throw the bones in the lake to appease the spirit of the duck. My father says that we must do that or the ducks will not return to our marsh. But secretly, I think we do this so that the bones won't smell up our village and the fish will grow fat eating the bones," whispered the Shaman's younger daughter. Yani guessed they were about the same age although Yani was taller and thinner. She was shocked to hear the daughter of a shaman speaking so irreverently about the spirits. *But,* she thought, *I have to agree with her. Her idea makes more sense.*

That night she shared a bed with the girl. As they lay beside each other on the narrow bench, the girl had whispered that her name was Lamu, and that someday she would marry a chieftain's son. As she used her fingers to comb out the tangles in Yani's long blonde hair, she asked how Yani had come to be traveling with the old Knapper. The need to tell the story overcame Yani, and her new friend drifted off to sleep listening to the hushed whisper of Yani unburdening herself.

As dawn broke, the travelers repacked their carrying baskets and were soon on their way. They retraced their steps across the sunken causeway and when they reached the shore, turned north. As the day progressed, Yani noticed that the earth beneath her feet was becoming more and more sandy. When they stopped for their noon day meal, she watched as a group of strange looking birds soared low overhead. They had large awkward heads and sacks hanging from their beaks. When the Knapper notice Yani watching them he said, "They are pelicans. We are nearing the northern sea and will soon be at the end of our journey. Have you also noticed that we have seen more and more sea gulls today? The large noisy white and gray birds?"

"Are we going to cross the sea?" asked Yani, her shyness overcome for the moment by curiosity.

"No, but we will camp at its edge for the summer. We don't have far to go now. We shall reach the cliff by late tomorrow afternoon."

And so, as the last day on the trail came to a close, with Yani reliving the beginning of her journey, she remembered the fear and uncertainty. Along the way, she had come to trust the Knapper but now that she was approaching the summer camp and her new life, she wondered if he would still be kind.

"We will soon be there," said the Knapper bringing Yani back to the present. Ahead of her she saw a wall of huge silver barked beech trees stretching as far as the eye could see in either direction. Since the start of her journey, the forests had gradually changed from the lightly leafed bright green of early spring to the darker green that comes with full foliage. When they entered the gloom of the trees, it was with relief to be out of the sun. But that soon changed as the huge beech trees closed around her blocking the light. Her apprehension heightened as she heard the sounds of animals scurrying through the leaves that blanketed the forest floor. Several times she thought she could see eyes of larger animals watching her in the dark foreboding gloom. They seemed to walk on forever in the eerie half-light. Then up ahead, out of the corner of her eye, she caught a flash of light. *Did I imagine it?* she thought. *No, there it is again.* Bright flashes like fire danced through the trees.

She realized the forest was not as dark. She could see small patches of sky up ahead. There were clusters of low bushes where the light penetrated the beech trees. Abruptly, the forest ended and, so it seemed, did the earth. What had seemed like dancing fires was really the sun's reflection off the sea. They had come to a high chalk cliff overlooking the sea. The Knapper turned south here and began to follow the edge of the cliff until he came to a narrow ravine. Stepping down into it he walked toward the edge of the cliff and disappeared from sight. Yani was terrified. *Has he fallen to the ground far below leaving me to fend for myself?* Then his smiling face reappeared and beckoned her to follow. She cautiously stepped into the ravine and walked towards him. As she did so, she realized he had stepped onto a ledge that ran at an angle down the cliff to the beach below. Carefully, she jumped down onto the ledge and hugging the wall of the cliff followed the old man downward. Only once did she risk a peek over the edge, but the dizzying height convinced her to keep her eyes firmly fixed on the trail and nothing else.

When they reached the beach she saw that it was littered with countless flint nodules. The beach, which lay at the base of a dazzling white chalk cliff, was not a wide one. It was only broad enough to allow them to walk side by side. The Knapper pointed to a small cove up ahead and said, "That is our summer camp."

As she walked along beside him, she marveled at the vastness of the sea. She had heard travelers describe it many times but never dreamed it could be so big. So much water all in one place. It would be so easy to fetch since it was only a few steps away. All of a sudden she was very thirsty from the day's travel. Dropping her pack, she ran to the water's edge and scooped up a handful of water.

"Wait, Yani, don't...." but the Knapper's warning had come too late. He laughed as Yani spewed the salty water out of her mouth.

"It is salty!" she cried. "What are we to drink? All this water and it is salty!"

The Knapper began to laugh. That was the most he had heard her say since they had left her village. "Don't worry, Little One, I have a sweet spring that trickles out of the cliff just a few feet from my camp. Come, I think you could use a drink of that water now."

When they arrived at the cove, the Knapper walked to a long vine that was hanging down from a shelf cut into the cliff just above his head. He began to pull on the vine, and soon a long pole started to protrude out over the edge of the shelf. As he walked backwards pulling on the vine, the pole inched forward and started to tilt downward. When the majority of it was extended out over the edge, it dropped with a thud onto the beach. The Knapper moved the lower end of the pole back nearer the base of the cliff. The upper end rested against the shelf above them. Yani noticed it had branches sticking out from opposite sides every foot or so. When it was firmly in place, the Knapper indicated that she was to climb up to the shelf. Placing one hand on the highest branch she could reach, she placed her foot on the lowest branch and began to climb. When she reached the top she pulled herself over the edge. She looked around and saw the shelf was really a shallow cave that had been scooped out of the soft chalk cliff providing shelter from the wind and the rain. Out of sight from the beach and the top of the cliff was a snug summer home. There was a fire pit near the front, which allowed the smoke to drift away rather than collecting in the shelter. In the back was a sleeping bench with storage baskets underneath. A short distance from the shelter was a narrow ledge leading to a spring that trickled out of the cliff forming a miniature waterfall. Yani laid her pack down and walked to the spring and drank deeply.

"Well, Yani, this is our home for the summer. How do you like it?" asked the Knapper.

She turned to him, a smile lighting up her face.

Chapter Six

Yani awoke with the first pale light of the dawn. She rolled over so she was facing the sea and watched as the sky turned from purple to deep rose to pink before fading into a dazzling blue as the sun crept higher. She had slept soundly, being lulled to sleep by the rhythm of the waves lapping on the beach below. She watched as a gull circled and dipped on the air currents and then it dove straight down into the water, coming up with a silvery fish. She could tell by his breathing that the Knapper was still asleep. Carefully so as not to wake him, she slid from under her sleeping cloak where she had spread it on the ground the night before, and tiptoed to the spring to drink. After she had drunk her fill, she went to where the Knapper had laid the ladder when he pulled it up the night before. She eased it to the edge of the shelter and lowered it until it was firmly seated on the ground below. Then she climbed down to the beach.

Curiosity led her to the water's edge. The tide was at it's lowest leaving shallow tidal pools, in which she began to wade in. A sudden movement to her left caught her eye, and when she leaned down to look, she found a strange looking creature. It had a round body with two large pincers held in front of it like fists. Being careful to keep an eye on it so she would not lose it, she waded to the edge of the pool and picked up a piece of driftwood. Coming back to the strange animal, she touched it lightly with the stick. It scurried backward so quickly that she, too, jumped back. Giggling at her reaction, she again closed on the creature. This time she used the stick to herd it into a corner of the pool. To her surprise, the creature left the water and went scurrying across the beach and into a smooth round hole.

Having lost this playmate, she went back to the pool to see what other creatures she could find. She found dozens of black oblong shells attached to a rock just below the water line. She had once been given one of these shells by a traveler who had stopped for the night at her village and was amazed to see so many in one place. She bent down to pick one off the rock only to find that they were stuck fast to it. She looked around until she found a large piece of shell and used that to pry one of the black shells loose. She held it up and examined it in the morning sunlight. She saw there was a thin crack all around the shell dividing it into two halves. As she was trying to decide how best to pry it open so she could see what was inside, a voice behind her said, "They make very good eating but you must not open them before you cook them. If you pry them open it will kill the creature inside."

She turned to see the Knapper sitting on a large rock behind her. She smiled at him and said, "What is this thing called?"

"That is a mussel. They attach themselves to the rocks near the low tide mark. When the water goes out like it is now, we can take a knife and cut them loose. Then we can steam them on a bed of seaweed until they open."

"And the creature with the fists that runs backwards? What is its name?"

The Knapper laughed, "I have never thought of it that way but that is a good description. That is called a crab."

"The sea has many interesting things," said Yani.

"True, but not all are friendly. You must let me know when you leave the shelter in the future."

Yani hung her head from the rebuke. Tears stung her eyes and she whispered, "I am sorry."

"You needn't cry, Yani. I am not angry. I am only telling you so you will be safe. When you have learned what can bring danger then you may roam the beach freely.

"Come, it is time we had our breakfast. Then you will begin to learn about the sea. I can see you will be good at catching our food."

They turned and walked side by side back to the bottom of the cliff. The Knapper waited as Yani climbed the pole ladder and then he followed behind.

The Knapper took a pouch from a basket under his sleeping bench and laid it by the firepit. He removed both of the wooden bowls from the pack, the one he had had the first night on the trail and the new one he had traded for at the Village in the Marsh. Into each of the bowls he placed a handful of the dried berries which he also took from his pouch. He carried the bowls to the spring and filled them with a little water. Into the mixture he sprinkled a small amount of the powder from a pouch he took from under his sleeping bench. Yani watched with interest as he stirred it all together with his finger and handed it to her. She noticed that he had given her the new bowl. Tipping the first two finger of her right hand into the bowl, she scooped up a dollop of the mixture and placed it in her mouth. It had a sweet nutty taste that she could not identify. She looked her question to the Knapper. He had been watching for her reaction so he answered immediately. "It's made from the nuts of the beech tree. They are very small, so it takes most of a day to gather enough to make into meal. Then I roast them by the fire and grind them between two rocks. The gathering can be your job when the Moon of Golden Leaves is here."

She nodded and went back to her meal. They ate in silence, listening to the waves on the beach below and the mewing of the gulls. When the Knapper finished, he looked up to find Yani gazing thoughtfully at him. When she caught his eyes on her, she asked, "What am I to call you?"

"Well," he smiled, "most people call me Knapper."

He could tell by her expression that that was not the answer she wanted, so he continued. "My mother named me Knut after her brother. You may call me that if you would like."

This seemed to please her and she stood and walked to him. "I will wash the bowls now, Knut." And with that picked up the bowls and carried them to the spring to wash.

Knut walked to his bench, and squatting down, pulled a tightly woven basket of willow fronds from under it. In it was an assortment of flint nodules. He began to pick through them until he found one that pleased him. He spent several minutes examining the stone from all angles. When he was satisfied with what he saw, he picked up a rounded stone of granite and began to hammer on the flint. After several small chips had flown off, he gave the flint one sharp blow breaking off a razor sharp sliver of flint the length of his hand. He lay that aside and continued chipping off flakes until he had a half dozen of them. Then he placed the flint core back in the basket. Picking up a deer antler chisel and hammer stone, he began to shape the flakes, breaking off small chips along the edges. When he was satisfied with the edges, he used the deer antler to shape one end of the blade with a notch on each side. Yani saw that he had created a spearhead, a notched one that could be tied fast to the shaft with deer sinew.

"Come, I want to teach you how to choose a good flint for me to work." With that he stood up and walked to the ladder and began to climb down. Yani followed and they began walking along looking at the stones that littered the ground. After a short time the Knapper stooped down and picked up a nodule for a closer look. It was evenly shaped with one end slightly flattened. "Look, Yani, at the shape. See how one end is flat and the other is rounded. That is very good. And the color is important too. If it is all one color it is less likely to have weak places in it to cause the blades to break."

She looked at it closely as he searched the ground for another. When he had shown her several good nodules and explained why they were good, he said, "Now, Yani, you try to find one."

He moved to a rock at the water's edge and watched the sea as she scampered over the beach in search of a usable nodule. She chose and rejected several before running to him with the one she had selected.

"That is very good," he nodded in approval. "You will now be my legs and eyes on the beach. When you find good stones you will bring them to the shelter and put them by the basket." She smiled at his praise and sat down on the beach beside him. Together they watched the water lap the rocks.

"Why are there no little pools on the beach this afternoon?" Yani asked.

"They will be here later in the day. Right now the tide is high. See the beach is not as wide as it was when you first came down this morning."

She looked up and down the beach and nodded. Turning to face him, she simply asked, "Why?"

Chuckling the old man replied, "That I cannot tell you."

Again she nodded, acknowledging some things are mysteries. Rising from the rock, the old man said, "Come, we will get the nets and set them. When the tide goes back out we may catch some nice fat fish for our supper."

They walked back to the shelter together. The Knapper told Yani to climb the ladder and drag the nets from under his sleeping bench. When she had pulled them to the edge, he told her to throw them down. She pushed the heavy nets over the edge and climbed back down to join him. He picked them up and carried them to the water's edge.

"Now, run and find some strong pieces of drift wood about as long as your arm and as big around as your wrist."

When she had found several pieces the right size, she returned with them. The Knapper took one from her and threaded it through the holes at one end of the net. Then he pushed the stick deep into the sand

33

at the water's edge. Handing her the other end he said, "Now wade out until the water is to your knees, then walk parallel to the beach until I tell you to come back in."

Yani stepped into the cold water and waded out. Suddenly she stopped and turned to the Knapper. "What if I step on one of the big fisted creatures?"

Laughing the Knapper replied, "They will stay out of your way, don't worry."

Still uncertain, she waded gingerly deeper, watching the water and placing her feet carefully. When the water reached her knees she turned and began to wade away from the Knapper, following the line of the beach. As she walked she trailed the net behind her and the waves picked it up, carrying it seaward.

"Now come back in but be careful not to drop the end of the net," called Knut. When she reached the beach, he took the end from her and staked it in the sand anchoring it firmly. The net now formed a wide arc extending into the surf.

"Now let's set the other net and all we have to do is wait for our supper."

They repeated the procedure with the other net a little further down the beach. Then he turned to the girl and said, "You must gather wood for a fire to cook the fish we catch. Then we will climb to the forest and cut fresh green branches to use to hold them over the fire. If we catch enough, we can also smoke some for when the catch is not so good."

Yani turned and started up the beach looking for wood. She soon had an armful, so she returned to place it near the cliff. Since the Knapper was gathering his tools to go to the woods, she returned to the beach and soon had another load to add to her pile. When Knut climbed down and saw the wood supply, he smiled and placed his hand on her head. She smiled back, happy to have pleased him.

Chapter Seven

They climbed the pathway to the top of the cliff and began looking for long straight branches among the bushes that grew at the edge of the woods. When they found a suitable branch, Knut took a blade from the pouch around his shoulder and, using the shape edge, cut through the branch. He stripped the small twigs from it and finally trimmed the narrow end back to where the twig was about the size of his smallest finger. He handed Yani the branch and began to cut another. When he had a half dozen, he indicated that they were done by turning and heading back along the cliff's edge toward the path leading down to the beach. When they got to the path, he surprised Yani by turning into the woods rather than climbing down the slope. "There is a place I want to show you," he said. "Remember the way well, for there may come a time when you will need to use this place."

Mystified, she followed him as he left the path and entered the leafy green gloom of the beech trees. They had only gone a short way when he stopped in front of a large tree. At the base of the tree was a hole. It was partly hidden by a cluster of fern fronds, but when he parted them Yani could see that it was big enough to allow a person to crawl inside. He stooped down and crawled in motioning for Yani to follow. When she had joined him, she saw the inside of the tree was completely hollow. The opening ran high up into the giant beech and then broke through at the top, allowing sunlight to filter down providing just enough light to see.

"Someday you may need this hiding place," said Knut. "Remember it well. If the time comes that you need it you may not have time to search for it."

Yani felt a tremor of fear go down her back. *What could there be to fear here,* she thought. But Knut did not say more. After a moment the Knapper again knelt and crawled out of the tree. Yani followed after

35

him noting the way back to the trail. She felt sure she would be able to find the tree again.

Late in the afternoon Yani noticed more of the nets were visible on the beach. Then she saw that the sea was alive with silver flashes where the arc in the net was. Seeking out the Knapper at his work place at the base of the cliff, she asked him, "Knut, what are those silver flashes I see in the water?"

Looking up, the Knapper smiled. "It is time to pull our nets in," he told her. "That is our supper." Picking up the large basket he had brought down from the shelter, he headed toward the nets.

Together they took hold of one end of the net and began to pull it toward the shore. They worked facing each other across the net. Reaching hand over hand, they slowly hauled the net into the shallow water left by the receding tide. When the outer edge of the net was almost to the shore, Yani saw them, hundreds of shiny fish trying to swim back to sea through the holes in the net. The smallest ones made it through the holes but the ones that were too big to swim through were being dragged up onto the beach.

"Get the basket," he called to Yani as he hooked the net around the drift wood stake. "Put it here on the beach, wade out and catch the fish in your hands. When you have caught one, throw it in the basket, like this." And with that he waded into the water and began scooping up the frantic fish and tossing them into the basket behind him. Yani followed him but catching the fish was not as easy as he made it look. After several tries she caught one but it quickly wiggled out of her hands and flipped through the air, landing on the outside of the net. The Knapper laughed at the look on her face.

"You will soon learn how to do it," he assured her. "Just keep trying."

"But I lost that fish," she cried.

"Yes, but look at all the others."

After dropping three more fish, all on the inside of the net this time, she finally managed to get one into the basket. After that she got most of her fish in, only losing one or two. When they had this net emptied, they moved off to the other net. By the time they were finished they had a basket full of gasping fish.

"Now we must clean them and get them ready to smoke," said the Knapper. He picked up the basket and moved to the pool made by the spring as it trickled down the cliff from their shelter. Here was a large flat rock. He set the basket down and removed a blade from his pouch. Picking up one of the fish he quickly ran the blade along the belly and removed the contents. These he tossed over his shoulder onto the beach. He laid the fish on the rock and using the edge of the blade scraped the scales from the fish. He handed the fish to Yani to thread onto the willow branches that they had cut on the cliff earlier. Reaching for another fish, he repeated the process. Soon they had several sticks full of fish ready to smoke over the fire to preserve them for the days when the sea was too rough to fish or the fish did not come to the shore where they could catch them.

They carried them down the beach toward the pile of firewood Yani had gathered earlier, scattering the sea gulls that had gathered to feast on the entrails the Knapper had thrown away. The gulls dived and squabbled for the best and biggest pieces, their cries echoing off the cliff. Leaning the sticks full of fish carefully against a large rock, the Knapper had built a long firepit from some of the flatter rocks, making it several layers high. They had also gathered some dried seaweed from above the high tide line. Placing it in the middle of the pit, he made a small pyramid of the smallest of the pieces of driftwood. He picked up a piece of flint and holding it near the seaweed sharply struck it with another rock until the sparks caught in the seaweed. Blowing the sparks into a flame, he soon had the fire started. As Yani protected their catch from the sneak attacks of the sea gulls, the Knapper fed more wood onto the flames until he had a large fire going.

"Now, I will guard the catch. You take the fish basket and gather some fresh wet seaweed. We will need it as soon as the wood has burned down some," he said to the girl.

Yani picked up the basket and walked to the water's edge. As she started down the beach, she stopped to scoop up any seaweed that had drifted onto the shore. She soon had the basket full and carried it back to the fire. When she got there the Knapper was using a stick to spread the glowing coals over the length of the fire pit. He took the basket from her and began to cover the coals with a thin layer of damp seaweed. As soon as clouds of smoke started to rise up from the firepit, they began to place the spits of fish over the fire by sticking one end into the ground at an angle.

"I will protect our fish from the gulls while you gather more wood. We must be sure that the fish are thoroughly dried or they will not keep long."

Yani again started down the beach, collecting wood until she had a large pile beside the fire. When she had enough wood, she picked up the basket and again filled it with seaweed. She had noticed that the seaweed on the fire was starting to dry, too, and small flames were licking at the edges. The Knapper smiled his approval as she walked away. When she got back he was carefully feeding more wood into the fire. As soon as it caught and was burning well, they again covered it with the damp seaweed.

Soon the smell of cooking fish mixed with the smoke, making Yani's mouth water. When some of the fish were partially dried, the Knapper slide one off and handed it to her. It was warm and smelled delicious. Hungrily, she picked the succulent meat off the bones then sucked every bit of favor from them before tossing them to the gulls.

As the sun was setting, the fish were dry enough to place in a storage basket to carry to the shelter. There they would finish the drying process by laying them in the sun for several more days, always being careful to collect them again before the evening mists began to rise up from the sea. When they were finally dry enough, they would pack them into baskets to be stored in the back of the shelter.

Chapter Eight

Yani spent the lengthening days of early summer exploring the new world of the seashore. She collected shells, and the Knapper showed her how to make them into necklaces by boring holes into them and stringing them on rawhide thongs. Each day she collected what driftwood there was to add to the fuel supply. If she found a usable flint nodule, she would carry it to the Knapper for his final inspection. In the evenings they would watch the night sky, and the Knapper would tell her stories of the stars that twinkled there. As the days went by, Yani settled into her new life and found it suited her.

One morning a few weeks after they had arrived at the cliff, as she was gathering firewood, she noticed that the Knapper had come to the edge of the shelter and was staring out to sea. Suddenly, he turned to the back of the shelter and reappeared carrying her sleeping cloaks and a food pouch. Throwing them down to the beach, he called to her, "Yani, quickly take these and go to the hiding place."

Frozen by the sudden harsh command, she stood looking up at him as he began to clamber down the ladder. Realizing she had not moved he called over his shoulder to her, "Now! Quickly!"

Seeing the look on his face, a look of fear, she began to move. She gathered up the things and raced to the trail up the cliff. When she reached the top she turned, expecting to see the Knapper laboring up behind her, but instead he stood at the water's edge looking out toward the open sea. She let her gaze follow his and saw a strange object out on the horizon. It seemed to be a huge fish that was skimming on the top of the water. Moving back from the edge, she hid in the bushes so she could watch to see what this creature would do. When it came closer she could see that it had many long legs on either side extending out into the water. They moved in unison, taking long steps that moved the creature forward. As Yani and the Knapper watched, the creature continued to close on the cove where the shelter was. More puzzled than frightened, Yani was disturbed by the strange urgency she had heard in the Knapper's voice as he commanded her to climb quickly and go straight to the hiding place. The next time she looked the creature had come nearer to the shore. She could now see that there were men riding on its back. Also, the legs were not legs but long poles held by the men and used to propel it through the water. When it drew near enough for her to see the men clearly, she began to understand the Knapper's fear. These men were frightening, with wild unruly hair. Their faces were streaked with lines of blue and red. *Why did the Knapper not run to join me? Is he safe?* Her thoughts were mixed with fear for his safety and the panicked thought of what would become of her if he were to be killed by these fierce looking men.

But he stood his ground, and when the creature came close enough that she could see it well, she saw that it was made of wood and not a living thing. The Knapper extended his hand above his head in the traditional greeting. The man standing in the front of the creature... *No, that is not right, but what is it?* The man returned the gesture. This reassured Yani for Knut's safety but fear for her own returned, and she softly crept backwards into the woods before turning and running to the hiding place. When she reached the hollow tree, sweaty and out of breath, she knelt and pushed her bundle through the hole. She scrambled in behind it and squatted on the cool, damp earth, puzzling over the strange sight on the beach. Trembling with fear she thought, *Who are these men? Why is the Knapper afraid of them? Will he be safe?*

When she had caught her breath and her heart had slowed its beating, she opened the bundle and spread her cloak on the ground. She sat down on it and prepared to wait until the Knapper came for her. *But what if he does not come? How long should I wait?* The chatter of the birds in the trees reassured her that all was well. The gentle rustle of the

41

wind though the leaves soothed her and soon she found herself dozing. Giving into her fatigue, she curled up on the deer hide cloak and fell asleep. Sometime later, she was not sure how long, she came fully awake with a start. What was it that had disturbed her? She lay quietly and listened. It was not what she heard now that frightened her, but what she did not hear. The sound of the birds was missing. Then she heard another sound, that of a large animal moving through the leaves. But it was not the irregular sound of a forest animal, rather the regular pacing of a man. The sound came closer to the tree. She could tell it was not the Knapper. She knew his shuffling loop-sided gait too well to mistake this steady walk for his. Had the strange men in the "thing" on the water seen her run to the top of the cliff? But how could they? They were so far away that she had not even known there were men in it. She remained frozen in the same position in which she had awakened, afraid that the slightest movement would give her hiding place away. The man had stopped not far from her tree when she heard the voice of another man calling. The words were strange. She could not understand the meaning though she could hear him clearly. But the nearer man must have understood for he answered in the same strange talk. Then the first man began to move away from the tree and toward the sound of the other man.

Yani dared not move for the longest time. Her stomach started to rumble telling her she had not eaten since early morning. Finally she gave in to her stomach and silently sat up. Loosening the string on the pouch Knut had given her, she opened it and looked inside. It contained a strange mixture of a white greasy substance and dried berries. She scooped out a small finger full and smelled it. It had a rich fatty smell that made her mouth water. She popped it into her mouth and found it delicious. She must ask Knut what it was since she had never tasted anything like it before, she decided. As she ate another larger fingerful of it she wonder where he had gotten it. Maybe he had gotten it from the Seapeople. Then she closed the bag and prepared again the wait.

Chapter Nine

As the hours stretched by, the light faded from the hole in the top of the tree and the night sounds of the forest began. Yani became more and more anxious but she knew she dared not leave the tree. The strange men might still be in the forest. She was terribly thirsty and wished she had a cool drink of water from the brook she knew was only a short distance away. Did she dare venture out for a drink? But her fear kept her locked in the hollow tree until she finally lay down and rolled herself in the cloak and slept.

Suddenly a bright light was shining in her eyes. The strange men were holding a burning torch in her face. She was trying to run away in the now huge confines of the hollow tree. She knew that if she could just get to the other side of the tree she would be safe. But no matter where she looked the torch was shining in her eyes and blinding her. One of the strange men had hold of her shoulder. He was shaking her and calling her name.

"Yani, Yani!" he kept saying her name, but how did he know what her name was? "Yani, wake up! You are dreaming!"

She opened her eyes to see Knut smiling at her and the morning sun shining through the hole in the top of the tree. So had she dreamed the strange men? But no, she was in the hollow tree so that part had been real.

"Come, Child, they are gone and it is safe to come back." With that he backed from the tree and waited for her to join him.

She rolled up her cloak and put the pouch of berry mixture around her neck and crawled through the opening to join him. When she had emerged from the tree, he said, "You must be thirsty. Let's go to the brook first then we will return home."

When they reached the brook, she drank her fill of the clear sweet water. She stood up and looked at the Knapper. His face looked tired and strained. She smiled at him, truly glad to see the old man. For the first time she realized how fond of him she had become in the weeks since she had come to this place.

"Who were the men and what was that strange thing they came in?" she asked him.

"They were the People of the Sea. They live across the water and are strange fierce people. I am never sure of them, but they come at least once each summer to barter for my blades. It is said that they steal women and children from the villages near the sea. That is why I had you hide. They sometimes only stay for a short time and then move on. But other times they have stayed for several days. Two of the men came to the forest in search of herbs to sooth the fever of one of the men with them. He had cut his hand on the sharp spine of a fish they catch in the open sea and it had festered. They wished to make a poultice. It was late when they had applied the poultice and so stayed the night on our beach but they have gone now. They left at first light as the tide was going out and have disappeared over the horizon. Come, let's go home."

Yani nodded and together they walked through the forest to the cliff's edge. They climbed down the path to the beach she had climbed with so much fear what seemed such a long time ago. This time she smiled for she was going home.

Chapter Ten

After the scare with the Seapeople, Yani was more watchful when she wandered the beach. She would frequently look out toward the sea, scanning the surface for a boat shaped form. *Boat* was what Knut had said the thing that the men rode in was called. She hoped never to see that shape on the horizon again, but if she did she was ready this time. She had taken out her carrying pack when she got back to the shelter that day and filled it with things she might need for a long stay. As soon as she was satisfied she had what she needed she climbed the cliff and stowed it in the hollow tree. Now she was searching the dunes far from the cliff shelter, hoping to find a gourd vine that had some ripe gourds she could use to make a water vessel. She did not like the idea of being there for long periods of time without water. She and Knut had agreed if she were to see the boat when she was away from the shelter, she would go straight to the hiding tree. Since then, she had found several other ways up the cliff to the forest. She made sure of her escape route before she turned to the foraging she was intent on at the moment. This one had been easy. The cliff dropped away to the sea here, so she had only to run away from the sea a short distance and she could climb the slope leading to the top and the safety of the hiding tree.

Again she stepped to the highest point of the dune she was searching and, using her hand to shade her eyes, scanned the sea. Suddenly she froze. Her heart raced. Was that a boat? It was too big to be any bird or fish. And it was so close. How had she not have seen it before this? Had she been daydreaming long enough for it to have slipped up on her? It had to be a boat since nothing else she had seen was that huge. Turning on her heels she raced toward the trail leading to the forest and safety. Running for all her worth she quickly reached the path along the edge of the cliff. Stopping to check on the location of the boat again, she was amazed to see that it had disappeared.

Thinking she must be looking in the wrong place she searched the horizon but there was no sign of it. As she stood puzzling over the boat that was no longer there, a huge black object rose up out of the sea where the color changed indicating deep water. It looked like a fish but Yani could not imagine one that huge. As she watched, to her total amazement, from the top of its head a stream of water shot up into the air. Then with a flip of its monstrous tail, it dove back into the sea.

As the water settled back to the gentle surf, Yani sprang into motion. She retraced her steps to the base of the cliff and raced up the beach toward the shelter. When it came into view she began calling to the Knapper.

"Knut! Knut! Quickly! A monster!" she called long before he could hear her words.

Glancing up from his work, he saw the girl racing toward him. She was calling and pointing toward the sea but the wind was blowing her words away. Fearing that the Seapeople had returned, he pulled himself onto his feet and looked out toward where the water met the sky. He searched the sea the length of the horizon but could see nothing. Looking back toward the girl, he saw that she was almost to the shelter. She tried to call to him again but she did not have enough breathe to get the words out. Scrambling up the ladder she tumbled on to the floor of the shelter and raised to her knees.

"There......was....huge..." she gasped between gulps for air.

"Was it the Seapeople?" asked the Knapper. When she shook her head, he continued. "Then wait a moment and catch your breath."

She nodded and sat back on her heels gulping in the air. When her breathing at last had calmed, she began again, "There was a huge fish. It was bigger than the boat the Seapeople come in. And it shot water high in the air from a hole on the back of its head and then dove back into the sea. It was very close to the land," she glanced at him apprehensively. "I really did see it," she added remembering the

47

scolding her mother had given her so often when, as a little girl, she had come in from playing to tell about the imaginary playmates she had created.

To her surprise, the Knapper broke into a fit of laughter. He laughed so hard he had to walk to the sleeping bench and dropped down on to it. Yani could only watch in amazement. This was certainly turning out to be an unusual day. First the huge fish and then the Knapper's strange behavior. She had only heard him chuckle in the past at things that she thought to be extremely funny. When the fit seemed to pass, he wiped the tears from his eyes and took a deep breath.

"What you saw, Child, *was* a great fish. I have heard it called by some a Whale Fish. The people that live much further north hunt it and it provides much of their food. One of these fish can feed a whole village for months. The Seapeople told me of this on a visit when they stayed for several nights to repair their boat. The berry mixture you took with you when you hid from them was made from the fat of a Whale Fish."

"Then it is real," she whispered in awe.

Yani turned to look out to sea again hoping to catch another glimpse of the Whale Fish. For the rest of the day she sat on the edge of the shelter gazing out to sea but the monster had moved on to other feeding ground. She saw nothing more of it that day.

Chapter Eleven

As the days began to shorten, the leaves on the beech trees turned from the bright green of summer to the dull dark green of early autumn. One morning the Knapper said, "Come, Yani. We must find some sea oats to make some new baskets." Gathering up two flint knives and placing them in his pouch, he hobbled to the ladder and climbed down.

As they walked along the beach in silence, Yani noticed that today the Knapper limped more than he had for some time. Gathering her courage to ask him a personal question, she said in a low voice, "Does your leg hurt more today?"

Turning to look at her, he smiled, "Yes, it does. How did you know?"

"The way you are walking," she said looking down at her feet blushing.

"It is the weather. I think perhaps we will have a storm tomorrow."

They continued to walk in silence until they reached the high rolling dunes to the south, where the cliff fell away to meet the sea. Here they took their knives out and began cutting the tall stems of the sea oats that grew there. As they cut them, they striped the leaves, leaving only the bare stems. These they laid in piles until they had a large cluster. They took one of the leaves and tied the bundles together to make them easier to carry. They worked in silence cutting, stripping and tying until they had a dozen bundles. They collected these and began to retrace their steps up the beach. It was the middle of the afternoon when they got back to their shelter. They carried the bundles a few at a time up to the ledge. Yani took one of the bundles over to the pool by the spring. She opened the bundle and placed the reeds in the water. She returned to the Knapper who had opened the basket that held

49

the smoked fish. He removed three fish, giving two to Yani and keeping the remaining one for himself. As they slowly chewed the salty fish he said, "Tomorrow we will spend the day in the shelter making baskets. It will storm. That is why we went to collect the reeds today. In a few days it will be time to go to the other side of the forest to pick berries, and we will need new baskets to put them in."

Yani smiled at this. She loved picking berries. Unlike the other children in the village, she actually got more berries in the baskets than in her mouth. When she would come back with a basket full, her mother would place them in the sun on a woven mat to dry. Her mother was proud that her family always seemed to have more berries than the other families in the village.

All of a sudden, a wave of homesickness swept over Yani. It had been days since she had thought of her family and the village, but now she longed to see them all again. She especially missed her little sisters. She wondered if they missed her too. Who was telling them stories at night? Who comforted them when they had nightmares? Who kissed their skinned knees when they fell? Tears filled her eyes and she turned to face the sea so the Knapper would not see them.

But she had not been quick enough for he had seen her eyes begin to glisten. She had not mentioned her home since they started on their journey north together. At first she had cried often in the night when she thought he was asleep, but lately her nights had been peaceful. Before he could find words to comfort her, she jumped up and hurried to the pool where the reeds were and turned them to make sure they were getting wet through and through. As she busied herself, he thought, *Activity is the best thing to keep her mind off of her home.*

When she returned, the tears were gone and, seeing the look of concern on the old man's face, she smiled.

The old man took a flake of flint and the deer antler chisel from his workbasket. Using his hammer rock, he began to shape the flake into a point to be used as a knife. Yani stretched out on her sleeping cloaks and watched the gathering clouds as she waited for the reeds to be soft enough to work into a basket. The rhythmic sound of the hammer stone on the deer antler soon lulled her to sleep.

She awakened with a start not knowing where she was or what had disturbed her. Sitting up she saw black storm clouds scudding across the sky. Then the clouds brightened as a flash of lightning streaked from cloud to cloud. Seconds later an ear splitting crash of thunder roll along the cliff. So that is what had awakened her. Smiling, she watched more lightning dance across the sky.

The Knapper watched her reaction with interest. Most children he had known were terrified of the flashes of light and noise of a thunderstorm. But here Yani sat just far enough into the shelter to stay dry, smiling like a child listening to a storyteller.

"Doesn't the storm frighten you, Yani?" he asked.

Smiling at him, she shook her head, "No, I think it is beautiful. When the other children in the village would run and hide under their beds during a storm, I would slip to the edge of the village and huddle under the roof of a house so I could watch the lightning."

"Child, you amaze me," he smiled and shook his head.

As the clouds gathered, Yani went to the pool to collect a handful of the reeds so she could begin making a basket. To start the basket she placed six reeds that were about the same thickness on the ground in front of her so that each crossed the other in the middle. The ends radiated out like the spokes of a wheel. Reaching up and pulling a long hair from her head she used it to tie them. Carefully she wove the hair around the reeds, securing them in place. She took another reed and began to weave it over and under around the circular pattern formed by the original six. Soon she had made several passes around the circle and had a round disk of reeds about the width of her hand. Taking a knife, she trimmed twelve more reeds so that they were the same length as the

51

spokes made by the original six reeds that now stuck out on all sides of the woven circle. Carefully, she inserted the twelve shorter reeds between the lacing of the circle and made another round or two securing them in place. She now had the base made, and began shaping the basket by pulling the reeds tighter as she wove so the sides would turn upwards. As she ran out of reeds, she would make a trip to the pool to fetch more until she had used most of the reeds softening in the water. When she had used most of this bundle, she placed a new bundle in the pool insuring that she always had a supply of soften reeds. Soon she had the basket as big as she wanted it. Carefully trimming the upright spokes of the basket, she tucked them into the weaving, securing the ends and finishing her basket.

By the time she had completed two baskets, it was getting dark and the storm had settled into a steady rain. They wrapped themselves in their sleeping cloaks and, adding a little wood to the fire to ward off the chill, were soon peacefully sleeping lulled by the sound of the sea and the falling rain.

They woke the next morning to find the sea blanketed with a heavy fog. The rain had slackened to a steady mist. After building up the fire and cooking some breakfast, they settled down to spend the day at their tasks; Yani to weaving her baskets and the Knapper to making his points. As they worked, the Knapper told her tales of the villages he visited on his annual rounds and of the adventures he had had along the way. As the day wore on, Yani became more and more fascinated by all he told her.

Finally, after hearing his description of the high mountains to the south, the ones that are so tall that the snow never leaves them even in the summer, she cried, "Oh, I wish I could see those beautiful, white mountains!"

The Knapper looked up in surprise, "But, Yani, you will. That is where we will spend next summer. In a few more weeks when the leaves are turning colors, we will pack our baskets and begin the winter journey to the south. Next summer we will be there and the summer after back here. I thought you understood that you will be going to all the places I have been telling you about."

Yani became very quiet for a few minutes as she digested the information. It was frightening but terribly exciting to think she would see all the places the Knapper had told her about. Then she looked up at the Knapper and smiled. Perhaps the deer had not demanded such a heavy sacrifice after all.

Chapter Twelve

The next day dawned sunny and bright. They now had several sturdy well-woven baskets to use for gathering berries. With the rest of the reeds Yani had made mats to use as drying mats and rugs in the cave-like shelter. She planned to use the mats also to cover their belongs they would leave in the shelter against their return in two years. After they finished their breakfast, the Knapper gathered up the baskets and motioned for Yani to follow him. They climbed the cliff path and soon were deep in the cool shade of the beech trees. In the peaceful coolness, Yani marveled that she had ever thought this beautiful forest was frightening. Now it seemed to offer safety and comfort. She listened to the warbling "dee-dee-lit, dee-dee-lit" of a goldfinch in a nearby tree. In the distance a cuckoo called. After the days with the constant lapping of the waves, the peaceful quiet of the forest was a welcome change.

As they emerged into the sunlight of meadow at the other edge of the forest, Yani had the urge to dance in the soft grassy meadow. Thinking that the Knapper might object, she started toward the nearest berry bramble with her basket. But when she saw a cloud of butterflies rising over a patch of buttercups, she could not contain herself. Dropping her empty basket to the ground, she ran to them and began to circle around reaching to catch them. The old Knapper watched as she frolicked. His old heart warmed at the sight. He knew then that he would end his life happily with this sunny, young girl to lighten his heart as well as his heavy load.

He began to pick the berries that grew in clusters throughout the meadow and at the edge of the forest. Soon Yani noticed he was working while she played and, embarrassed by her childish fun, ran to pick up her basket and began to pluck the fat juicy black berries from the vines.

"I'm sorry," she murmured when she rounded the brambles so that she was picking near the Knapper.

Looking at her with a puzzled looked on his old face, he asked, "What are you sorry for, Child?"

"Why, I left you to work while I was dancing like a hare in the full moon!"

The Knapper laughed his rolling laugh that seemed to start at his toes and echo clear through his body. "You were bringing me more pleasure than you will ever know. You never have to be sorry for being happy and letting it show. We have plenty of time to pick berries."

They picked in silence for a while. Yani felt the Knapper's eyes on her and when she looked up at him, he said, "Do you realize that the first glimpse I had of you was in a meadow much like this chasing a cloud of butterflies?"

Yani thought back to the day the Knapper had bartered for her and remembered the butterflies and the dandelions she should have been gathering.

"Yani, when I saw you that day I thought you looked like the girl I have always imagined my daughter would have looked like, had I married and had one. Do you mind so terribly now being my daughter?"

Tears stung Yani's eyes. She had never thought of it that way. She had come to feel close to the Knapper but to think of him as her father? She must think about this some before she answered. Turning away so he could not see her tears, she busied herself picking berries as she thought over how to answer him.

He is kind, that I know. He has never been cross with me as my father had been. But, I also have been very careful not to do things that are wrong to make him cross. I have what I need to eat, often more to eat than with my own family. He is taking me with him on his journey where I will see many wonderful things. No, she decided, *I do not mind at all. As a matter of fact, I am very happy. But will I be happy forever? Will I become lonely with only the Knapper for company? But, for now I can honestly tell him I am happy to be with him.*

Crossing the meadow to where he was stooped over picking berries, the warm sun making the silver in his hair glisten, she touched his arm. He looked up with as start. He had not heard her approach, he was so deep in thoughts of his own.

"I am glad you came for me. I will be very happy to be your daughter," she said in a hushed voice. Then to her surprise he put the basket on the ground and wrapped his arms around her thin shoulders and pulled her close to him. He hugged her and stroked her hair for a moment, then holding her at arm's length, smiled into her serious face. "Daughter, you have made an old man very happy."

As the sun hung low in the west, they gathered up their full baskets and, with equally full bellies, began the trek back through the woods to the shelter.

The next morning, after they had laid the berries to dry in the sun on the newly woven mats, the Knapper took the otter pelt he had traded for at the Village in the Marsh from the storage place under the bed.

"Are you good with an awl and needle?" he asked Yani.

"I have made moccasins and can do needle weaving to make socks and mittens from wool yarn but I have never worked with a fur before. It is too valuable for Mother to have let me yet," she replied.

"No matter," he answered. "I will direct your hands. I have the knowledge."

Taking a knife, an awl and an antler needle from the basket under the bed, he took the pelt and placed it over Yani's head with the fur side down. Yani giggled when the silky fur tickled her nose. Using a soft chalky rock, the Knapper marked the pelt at a point just above her eyes. Then marked again at about the same level all around her head.

"Wouldn't it be too small?" she asked. "Your head is larger than mine is."

"No," he chuckled. "This should be just right. There is nothing like otter pelt to keep off the wind and snow of winter."

After he had marked the pelt, he placed it on the ground and showed her how to use the blade to cut the excess, making a round piece of fur. Then he showed her where to make two slits at an angle toward the center. These he joined together at their point, bringing the circle into a bowl shaped hat. Yani then took the awl and, using a stone as a hammer, punched two holes in the end of each flap. Using deer sinew she laced the flaps together. Soon she had shaped the fur into a rounded hat. When she had finished, she handed the hat to the Knapper, more certain than ever that it would be much too small for him. Her concern was written all over her face as he examined her handy work.

"It is too small," she wailed. "Now I have ruined the pelt." She thought. *Will he become angry and beat me?* She knew her father surely would. She stood trembling waiting for the Knapper to speak.

"No," he replied. "I would say it is a perfect fit." Then he reached down and placed the hat squarely on Yani's head. "This should keep the snow and wind off as we travel this winter. You know this journey of ours is also dangerous and can be very difficult at times. If a sudden storm catches us between villages we will need all the fur we have to keep us warm. Are you still excited about this adventure?"

Thinking for only a minute, Yani smiled a shaky smile and whispered, "Yes." She had hardly heard the Knapper's discouraging words. She was so awed to think that this hat of otter fur was for her. She had never had such a valuable belonging in her life. This time it was Yani who hugged the Knapper. She threw her arms around his waist and gave him a shy, quick hug, babbling her thanks before pulling away and stroking the soft fur on her head.

As the summer days dwindled and the leaves on the trees began to show the telltale colors of the coming fall, the Knapper and Yani began their preparations for the winter journey. The Knapper sorted the blades and flakes he planned to take with him, placing them carefully in his carrying pack. Yani filled deer skin pouches with dried fish, berries and the meal she was making from the freshly fallen beechnuts. Each day she would go to the forest and gather a basket of the tiny nuts. She would scatter them around the edge of the firepit as close to the blaze as possible without actually being in the fire. When the shells split open, the tiny nuts would be roasted and crisp. Yani would peel away the soft shells and extract the tasty kernel. When she had a small mound of kernels on the flat rock they used as a millstone, she would pound them with a rounded pestle until they were crushed into a coarse meal. By the time she had the nuts all cracked and ground it would be time to sleep.

One night she awakened to the honking of wild geese as they made their autumn journey to the warmer shores of some southern sea. As she listened she knew it was time for them to leave their seaside home and follow the geese toward the villages to the south.

Part 2
Wolf

Chapter One

The leaves on the beech trees had turned to a golden yellow, when the Knapper and Yani shouldered their packs and started on the winter journey to the south. As they took the path again through the forest and into the meadow of the black berries beyond, Yani bounced with anticipation of the adventures to come. She smiled at every bird and flower she passed along the way. But, soon the novelty of the trail began to wear thin and by midday when they stopped to eat she was more than happy to lower her pack to the ground and drop down beside it.

As she chewed on the jerky they had packed for the trail, she remembered the trek from her village to the sea. She recalled her bruised feet and the aching muscles at the end of the first day. She was glad she had thought to line her moccasins with moss from the woods. Looking at her feet now she found no bruises. Perhaps this would not be as difficult as the trip from her village had been. After a short rest they resumed their journey and when evening found them, they were within sight of the Village in the Marsh.

They crossed the sunken causeway and entered the village, Yani coming a few steps behind the Knapper. As they walked along the path between the houses, Yani heard a squeal of delight and then someone called her name.

"Yani! Over here!"

Turning toward the voice, Yani spotted Lamu and her older sister sitting on a bench behind one of the houses. Lamu was sitting with her arms bent at the elbows, holding up her hands so her sister could wind the yarn from a drop spindle off into a skein that was forming around Lamu's out stretched hands. Yani looked back at the Knapper who smiled and nodded. Yani hurried over to where the girls were sitting and, dropping the pack to the ground, slid onto the bench beside Lamu.

"So what has happened to you since you were here last spring?" asked the ever noisy Lamu, without prelude.

"Hush, Magpie," warned her sister. "Mother would feed you to the Marsh Monster if she heard you talk so."

Lamu only laughed, "Oh, Honi, I stopped believing in the Marsh Monster years ago! Yani and I are friends. Friends don't have secrets from each other." She smiled at Yani and winked. "Besides you are just as curious as I am. Admit it."

Honi had to smile at that and after a moment she said to Yani, "Well, are you going to tell us what has happened, or not?"

Yani smiled and settled more comfortably onto the bench. From habit she picked up the teasel burrs and a hand full of wool and began teasing the locks of wool, opening and straightening the fibers as she did so. As she worked she told of her summer. "We live in a cave shelter in the most beautiful white cliff at the edge of the sea. Behind us on the top of the cliff is an ancient beech forest. The trees are ghostly silver and the leaves form a shelter that is so thick it is like green night when you walk through it."

"I know forests. What I want to know is, what is the sea like?" interrupted Lamu.

"The sea is wonderful. Imagine a lake so wide you can not see across it. And even on fair days, it has waves like a lake has on a windy day. Only the waves can be much higher than any that I have ever seen on a lake. It is never the same two days in a row. One day it's gray and angry with waves crashing on the shore. Other days it is so smooth and still that sunlight reflecting off it nearly blinds you. It is like looking at the sun on the snow. And there are strange and wonderful animals that live in it. One is a small round-bodied creature that has fist hands with pinchers on them. Knut says they are called crabs."

"Who is Knut?" asked Lamu.

"Knut? That is the name of the Knapper," replied Yani surprised that Lamu didn't know. "But the most wonderful thing is the Whale Fish. It is as big as a house and shoots water into the air from a hole in its head."

"Oh, Yani, now you are telling stories. You and Honi are just alike. Whale fish and Marsh Monsters," laughed Lamu.

"No, there are Whale Fish. I saw it one day and thought it was the Seapeople returning. I was almost to the top of the cliff when I looked again."

And so Yani entertained the girls with the stories of her summer as the sky faded to the pinks and purples of dusk before turning to twilight. When the light was too weak for the girls to see, they gathered their spinning and rounded the house to the doorway. They entered the dwelling to find Lamu's mother bent over the firepit cooking the evening meal. She smiled up at Yani as they came in.

"Welcome, Child. Did your summer with the Old Knapper go well?"

"Yes, Mother," replied Yani using the polite form of address of the People. "It was a wonderful summer. The Knapper is a kind man and a good father."

She smiled again and returned to the cooking as the girls put the spinning under one of the benches and joined in the preparations for the evening meal. Yani held back and seemed unsure of what to do next. Lamu's mother caught the uncertainty in the girl's face and said, "The Knapper always takes his meals with us when he is in our village. He and my husband have been friends since they were boys. You are just where you should be. The men will be coming to dinner soon, so come and help us make ready."

That decided, Yani joined the group and soon felt as if she were home with her sisters again. It was good to have women around her once more and hear the merry chatter of gossip about the neighbors in the village.

Chapter Two

Later, the men entered the house and settling down to the comfort of the firepit began to eat their evening meal. As they ate they discussed the preparations for the coming hunt and the weather signs for the coming winter. As she waited her turn to eat, Yani listened to the conversation.

"There were more beech nuts this year than usual" offered Knut. "And I noticed as we came though the oak grove just to the north, the acorns were larger than usual."

Lamu's father and brother nodded, "The muskrat I killed last week had the thickest pelt that I have even seen," offered Birg, the brother.

"Yes," agreed Hawn, Lamu's father. "The signs all point to a hard winter. Are you sure you don't want to spend the winter here, Knapper? It will be crowded but we can make room. The fishing has been good and, with the new points, we should have no trouble taking several deer in time to dry."

"Thank you for the offer, but we must move on. But, I would like to trade for a new pair of winter moccasins for Yani before we leave. Who in this village, makes the best ones?" this last was directed at Loki, Lamu's mother.

She knew that the Knapper already knew what her answer would be. They had played the game of words many times. Pretending to be insulted, she replied, "Knapper, you know I make the best moccasins in all to the northern villages. But it will cost you dearly." Her faced frowned but her eyes danced merrily.

"Not too dearly, I hope. I am only a poor traveling craftsman. But, the poor girl needs a good covering for her feet to keep the snow out before we start our journey. Perhaps we can come to an agreement. Bear in mind though, I will not be robbed by a contrary woman."

"Let's see, good moccasins that come to the knees of that long legged crane," she said pointing at Yani's legs causing her to blush and pull them up under her. "That will cost you four knives and three scrapers."

Yani gasped at the ridiculously high demand. All the adults looked at her causing her to quickly lower her head. Her long blonde hair hung down hiding her face, which was red with shame. When the attention shifted back to the bartering, she ventured a glance at the men again. To her surprise, she saw that Birg was watching her intently. As her eyes locked on to his, he smiled at her. Not sure what to make of that since he had appeared to take no notice of her until now, she turned her attention back to the trading.

"Woman, do you want to rob me? But what am I to do. Look at those old moccasins that I remade for her. They will do now but when the snow comes it will be another matter. I guess I am in a difficult position. But I am a generous man, two knives and a scraper."

"Huh," scoffed Loki, "now who is trying to rob who."

And so, the bickering continued as the coals in the fire burned down. Yani held her breath sure that the deal could never be struck. So intent was she on the proceeding, she didn't notice the rest of the family chuckling at the antics of the two old friends. Birg added wood to the fire when it appeared in danger of going out. Finally to Yani's relief, terms were agreed upon with the Knapper offering two knives and two scrapers along with a small pouch of shells added to clinch the deal.

As soon as the women had finished cleaning up after the meal, although it was late, Loki took two pieces of tanned rabbit hide and began constructing the boots. She measured and cut the soles to fit Yani's feet and then cut two pieces for each foot to form the uppers. Using an awl to punch holes and strips of deer hide for lacing, she soon had the rough shape of the boot formed. Long after the girls had snuggled down on the bench for the night, Loki was still working on the boots.

Chapter Three

The next morning, Yani awakened to the morning light peaking though the smoke hole at the top to the roof. As she lay there enjoying the feel of being in a house again, she heard the sound of the others stirring into wakefulness. She dozed, listening to Lamu's and Honi's breathing as it changed from the slow rhythm of deep slumber and into the more rapid breathing that said they were waking up. Soon she heard Loki stirring the coals in the firepit and adding wood so the morning porridge could be cooked.

Yani quietly slipped from the sleeping bench and walked to the firepit. "Would you like for me fetch some water?" asked Yani.

Loki looked up and smiled at the girl. "That would be very helpful. The water basket is there by the door. And when you come back, you must try on your new moccasins. I want to see if they fit properly."

Yani picked up the basket and headed for the lake. The morning was brisk and the reeds at the edge of the lake were lightly coated with frost. The eastern the sky, painted pink and orange by the morning sun, colored the rime on the reeds, making them look unreal. Dipping the basket in the lake, she pulled up a basket full of water and, being careful not to splash the icy water on her legs, hurried back to the house.

She set the water basket by the fire and, huddling as close as she could, rubbed her hands together to warm them. Loki looked up and seeing the shivering girl asked, "Do you have a good fur cloak for this journey or has the old man forgotten something as important as that?"

"I have my sleeping cloak and he made me a beautiful fur cap from the otter pelt he traded for last spring," Yani replied quickly in defense the old man.

"Huh," snorted Loki, "that cloak will never keep you warm. It is good to keep you dry in the warmth of summer, but you need a good fur cloak. There is no telling what kind of weather you will run into on this trip. I will have to talk to the Knapper. You are not leaving this village without a decent cloak."

Not knowing how to respond to this, Yani busied herself by looking though her pack for her fur hat. She wanted to show Loki that the Knapper was taking good care of her needs. Before she could find it, Loki interrupted her search. "Come, Child, try these on." Turning around she saw Loki holding out a pair of beautifully fringed knee high moccasins. Unable to believe that these could be meant for her, she stood gaping in amazement. "Close, your mouth or a fly will fly in," laughed Loki. "Come and try these on."

Going to the bench behind the firepit, Yani sat down and pulled the moccasins on her cold bare feet. "Oh, they feel wonderful!" The fur, which lined the inside, felt silky against her feet and legs.

"Now remember, these are to wear when the weather is cold. Wear your old moccasins as long as you can. The journey ahead of you is a long one, and if you begin wearing them too soon, they may not last the whole journey. It will be two winters before we see you again. I wish the Knapper would see reason and let you stay with us."

"Oh, please, no!" cried Yani before she thought how rude it sounded. Seeing the raised eyebrows on Loki, she quickly continued. "I'm sorry. I didn't mean that I wouldn't be happy to stay with you, but Knut is growing old and he needs me. And," she continued looking at her hands in her lap in embarrassment, "I want to see the mountains that are always white with snow. That is where my mother came from. I may even find some of her family to give them word of her. It has been such a long time since she has been there. And I want to..." and her voice trailed off as she ran out of things to justify her reaction. After a moment she risked a peak at Loki. The woman was looking thoughtfully at the girl.

"I was a wild, adventuresome girl, too. I would have loved to have gone on just such a journey. And you are right, the old man needs a companion on his treks. He has aged much in the last few summers." With that she turned and walked to a pole ladder that led to the loft over the sleeping bench she shared with Hawn. After a few minutes she climbed back down carrying a bundle under her arm. As she walked to the fire, she began to unfold and shake it out. Walking up to Yani she held up a bear skin cloak. Placing it around Yani's thin shoulders, she said, "That looks just right. It is the last gift my mother gave me before I left my village to join Hawn's hearth. I have not used it in years and the winters are rarely cold enough for the girls to need it. I will feel much better knowing you have this to keep you warm."

Tears burned at Yani's eyes. She looked up into Loki's kind face now soft with motherly emotion. Unable to find words to express her thanks, Yani reached up to her neck and pulled one of the shell necklaces over her head. Handing it to Loki, she said, "Please, this is all I have that I can give you. It is my favorite- see the way the inside of the shell catches the light and changes colors."

"It is wonderful! I think I got a fair trade." To Yani's surprise, she saw tears in the woman's eyes also.

Yani folded the bear skin and placed it in the top of her pack. When she returned to the firepit, Loki had put a clay pot of water on the fire to heat. Yani watched as she added acorn meal. Wanting to contribute to the family breakfast, she returned to her pack and, reaching into the pouch of dried berries, brought a large handful for Loki to add to the porridge. Together the woman and the girl watched as the mixture began to bubble and send out a nutty aroma that soon aroused the sleeping family.

Later in the morning, after having made the last few trades for items he thought they would need for the trip, Knut and Yani shouldered their packs and prepared to leave the village. At the edge of the marsh they paused to wave one last goodbye to their friends before leaving the village. Yani had bent to take her old moccasins off to carry across the sunken causeway when suddenly Birg came running from the back of the nearest house. Stopping beside her he thrust a small pouch into her hand. "It is something I found," said Birg.

Looking from the pouch to the boy, Yani could only mutter a quick thank you before Birg turned and ran back to the shelter of the house. Not knowing what to do she looked at the Knapper who only smiled at her and returned to his preparations for crossing the causeway. Tucking the pouch into her pack, she pulled off her moccasins and stood up. She put her foot into the icy water and the cold nearly took her breath away. The old man and girl did not linger once they had started the wade to the main land. Walking as quickly as possible without losing their footing and falling into the deeper water on either side, they made their way to the far shore. The Knapper quickly scooped up a mound of dried leaves and grass and, using the flint and firestone soon had a small fire burning. Yani eagerly held her cold feet near the flame to dry and warm them before slipping them into the old moccasins for the day's trek. Taking up the packs once more and turning to the south, they were soon into the long, striding gait of walkers who had a long way to go.

Chapter Four

Midday found the travelers at the edge of a wide lake. They found a sheltered place near a clump of white barked birch trees and lowering their packs to the ground sat down beside them. Yani took the pouch of dried meat out and handed it to the Knapper. He took a couple strips of the meat and handed the pouch back to her. She also took a couple of strips and they sat in silence watching the wind make patterns on the surface of the lake. Yani shivered when the sun slipped behind a cloud depriving them of what little warmth it had to offer. The wind had a bite to it, reminding the Knapper they had a long journey before reaching the safety of the next village on his circuit.

While they ate Yani slipped her hand into her pack to retrieve the small pouch that Birg had given her. She untied the strings and turning the bag over emptied the contents into her hand. There in her hand lay two transparent golden stones. They reflected the sun's giving off a satiny glow. While she held them, they seemed to give off a warmth which matched their golden color. As she looked more closely at them, she saw that one contained a perfect tiny butterfly.

"Look, Knut," she said holding it up for him to see. "How did he get the butterfly inside the stone? And feel it, it is so warm."

"Birg did not put the butterfly into the stone. He found it that way. I have seen such stones before. Some times with bees or flies but never with a butterfly. I think, Daughter, that you have an admirer," chuckled the Knapper.

To hide her embarrassment at the Knapper's suggestion, Yani looked out over the lake and asked, "Will we travel far today?"

"Yes," answered the Knapper, turning his attention to the young stout trees that lined the lake.

When he had finished his lunch, he took a large hand axe from his pack and, approaching a clump of birch trees, chose a nice, straight

72

young one. Using the blade, he chopped it off just above the ground. Handing it to Yani, he instructed her to use a smaller blade and strip it of its branches. While she worked at cleaning the small tree, he cut another sapling, that he stripped. When the trees had been stripped of their branches, he cut the tops out of each tree making two sturdy walking sticks. Handing the shorter one to Yani, he started off at his steady, shuffling pace along the edge of the lake to the east.

The sun was low in the sky when they came to the end of the lake at last. Here the rolling grasslands gave way to scattered trees. As they continued to walk toward the east the trees became more numerous, until sunset found them in a dense hemlock forest.

As the light faded from the sky, Yani and the Knapper made camp. After gathering the firewood, Yani used her hands to rake up beds of hemlock needles that had collected on the forest floor. The Knapper cleared an area of needles and in the center built a small fire. Yani picked up the water basket and began looking around for a spring or stream. "Knut, where can I get water?" she asked when it appeared that there was none near the campsite.

He picked up a branch from the fire that had caught at one end to use as a torch. With it he led the way down a steep slope at the edge of their camp area. "I should have walked faster this afternoon so we would have been here before dark," he said. As they started down the slope to the stream, Yani could now hear gurgling below. "It is too rocky and damp to camp down near the water," he continued. "We must climb down to get the water and then come back to the camp."

As they descended the slope, the footing got more and more perilous. When the Knapper stepped on a loose rock and almost lost his footing, Yani became concerned for his safety. "Why don't you just hold the torch and let me climb the rest of the way. I think I can see from here," she suggested. She didn't add that she was afraid he would fall.

"That is perhaps a wise idea," he replied, somewhat shaken by his close call.

She carefully climbed the rest of the way down and after dipping the basket in the stream, climbed back to the glow of the Knapper's torch. As they climbed slowly back to the camp together, he rested his hand on her shoulder for support. As they rose out of the gorge, the glow of the campfire was a welcoming sight. After an evening meal of acorn porridge and dried berries, they wrapped in their sleeping cloaks and were soon fast asleep by the fire.

Chapter Five

During the night, Yani had no idea how long after she had gone to sleep, she was awaken by something. She lay very still and listened to see what it was that had disturbed her sleep. She had almost convinced herself she had dreamed it when she heard the rustle again. It was the sound of an animal- a large animal- moving in the forest behind her. She looked over to where the Knapper was sleeping soundly and tried to think of a way she could waken him without alerting the animal. She knew that sometimes animals that were not hunting would just pass by a camp. Only a starving animal would attack a man unless it was provoked or frightened. She was afraid any movement on her part would do just that.

Her eyes roved the campsite looking for something to use as protection. They lighted on the walking stick she had laid down next to her when she started to rake up the hemlock needles to make their beds. Slowly, she slipped her hand from under the sleeping cloak. It closed around the stick just as she heard a branch snap behind her. This time it was very close. Slowly she turned the stick until she could touch the Knapper on the shoulder with is. Gently she nudged him. Instantly, she sensed that he was awake. He had not uttered a sound but she had seen his body tense. Then slowly his face turned toward her. With a slight movement of her hand, she pointed toward the forest behind her. There was a small nod of his head indicating that he understood. His hand too inched out and found his walking stick.

Then Yani's heart froze as she heard the sound of two more animals moving toward their camp. The only animal that moves in groups like this at night is the wolf. Afraid to look, yet needing to know, she slowly turned over until she was able to peer into the dark beyond the light of the campfire. Then she saw them. Three pairs of yellow eyes glowed from the dark forest. As she watched six more eyes joined them.

75

Her fear overcame her wisdom and she whispered, "What should we do, Knut?"

Hearing the naked terror in her voice, he wanted desperately to move to her side but knew that would be the worst thing he could do. "Keep your stick ready. If they attack, swing it and make as much noise as you can. Wolves are not really as vicious as people say," he answered also in a whisper. "Usually they are only curious."

Perhaps encouraged by the voice, one of the wolves slunk forward toward the man and the girl. "Don't move, Yani," the old man whispered. "It is not an attack. Wolves attack as a group."

Terror gripped Yani's throat as the wolf edged nearer to her. Taking a few steps then pausing, it made its slow progress toward the girl until it stood only inches from her. There it sat on its haunches looking down into her frightened eyes. Now too afraid to move, Yani stared back into its yellow eyes. Then to her surprise it lay down and stretched a front paw forward until it gently touched Yani's arm. The girl and the animal lay perfectly still gazing into each other's eyes. When nothing happened the girl began to relax. The huge wolf inched closer to her on its belly and tapped her arm with its paw. It stared into Yani's eyes for what seemed forever then to her amazement, it whined. Turning her head slightly she looked over at the Knapper. Seeing her puzzled look, he could only shrug his shoulders. He had never seen such strange behavior.

Yani looked back at the wolf and on a sudden impulse, she gently reached out her hand toward the wolf's head. His ears lifted and she froze. After staring at each other for a moment, the wolf relaxed again and Yani moved her hand closer to the wolf. Slowly she inched her hand forward until it was resting on the wolf's huge head. She began to stroke the fur like she used to do to the new lambs back in the village. To her surprise, the wolf closed his eyes and seemed to go to sleep. She lay there with her hand on the wolf's head for what seemed like an eternity. Soon she found herself drifting in and out until she slipped into a sound sleep.

Chapter Six

The next thing she knew she was aroused by the bell-like trill of a cedar waxwing. Looking into the branches above her, she spotted it hopping from limb to limb. She had always loved to watch them in the forest by the village. They were so pretty with their rust colored topknot and the black and red tips of their wings. As she watched the sky lighten, she realized her hand was out from under her sleeping cloak. It was very cold and she puzzled over why it would be out in the air. She always slept curled up on her right side and here she was on her back with her hand flung out like that. Why would she....... The wolf! It all came rushing back. But, no, it had to be a dream. It could not have been real, could it? She turned toward her left, half expecting to see the wolf still lying there. The ground beside her was empty. She turned to where the Knapper was and was surprised to see him still so sound asleep. It must have been a nightmare. A wolf would not have come and slept beside her like that.

She dozed a few minutes more on her back before turning over to her more natural position. As she did she felt a sharp poke in her side. Reaching under her, she found the walking stick. Now she was wide awake again. The walking stick had been at the edge of the bed of needles she had raked up. Why was it so close to her now? She sat up and looked around the camp. There was no sign of the wolves, yet......

She got up and began to feed the last of the wood into the fire and bent down to blow new life into it. Then she took the basket, once again climbing down the steep bank to the stream below. When she reached the water's edge, she looked down at the soft mud there. Clearly outlined in the mud were animal tracks. Many tracks that she knew well. Wolves had drank at this stream during the night. She knew that for sure. One of the tracks was showing clearly in the center of the footprint she had left the night before. Had the track been there last night when she filled the basket, her step would have obliterated it. Looking around her fearfully, she filled her basket and climbed back up the bank.

As she came back into camp the Knapper was stirring in his sleep. He opened his eyes as she set the basket down by the fire and looked at her. For a moment neither of them spoke. Then Yani broke the silence.

"Was it a dream?" she asked.

"If so, we both dreamed it," he replied.

In silence they prepared some acorn porridge and after eating and drinking packed their sleeping cloaks and resumed their trek.

Chapter Seven

All day long Yani had the feeling that she was being watched. She would have that creepy feeling that made the hairs stand out on the back of her neck but when she turned around there would be nothing there. The journey was taking them through a thick hemlock forest, so after a while she decided it was just the gloom of the trees that was making her uneasy. Or perhaps, it was the lack of sleep.

When they stopped at noon, she noticed that the Knapper kept glancing into the trees around them as if looking for something, too. When he did it for the fifth time, she asked, "Do you feel something there, too?"

Not taking his eyes off the forest, he replied, "Yes, Child, we have been followed all day. I can not decide if it is a two legged or four legged animal stalking us." Yani looked around her with growing uneasiness. Without a word they shouldered their packs and glancing around started on their journey again.

As the day faded, they emerged from the forest into a wide, marshy meadow. The ground was too damp to be suitable for a campsite but Yani at least hoped that they could either get a glimpse of their follower or perhaps lose it in the open. As they crossed the meadow, they both kept looking back over their shoulders. Although they had a clear view for as far as they could see in either direction, they saw nothing.

Soon the ground began to rise and, become less marshy. Clusters of small trees began to accent the meadow. Knut stopped and scanned the open area they had just crossed. Seeing nothing, he turned toward the woods that was just coming into view on the other side of the meadow. When he started on his way again he headed toward a rather thick cluster of trees. Reaching it, Yani saw that a small brook was trickling out of the trees before it meandered across the meadow adding to the dampness.

When they reached the trees, the Knapper followed the brook into the thicket until he reached an opened area by a clear pool. As she neared it, Yani saw that the pool was being fed by an underground spring. The water formed circular ripples as it bubbled up from the white sandy bottom. As she bent over the spring to drink its cool sweet water, she noticed a brightly colored stone resting on the bottom. In the crystal clear water it appeared to be just below the surface. To her surprise, even though she put her arm in to above her elbow, she could not reach it. Turning to the Knapper with a puzzled look, she saw he was silently laughing.

"It is much deeper than it looks. I have never understood the why of that. The lesson to be learned is never to trust your eyes when the water is clear. Things are not always as them seem."

She nodded, pulling the sleeve of her dress as high on her shoulder as possible, tried again. When she still could not reach it, she looked around the pool until she found some vines. Breaking off several small ones she knotted then in a small net basket just large enough to hold the stone. Then she tied two long strands of vine to this. She placed a stone from the edge of the spring in the net as a weight and lowered her scoop into the water. When she had maneuvered it near the stone she wanted, she dragged it sideways spilling the ballast stone and scooping up the colored stone. The Knapper watched the procedure, pleased with Yani's inventiveness. She took the stone from the net and held it up with a smile for the old man to see. After he had admired it, she put it in the pouch with the stones Birg had given her and began gathering wood for the fire.

Building the fire higher than usual, they cooked their supper of acorn porridge. The stress of the day and lack of sleep from the night before soon overwhelmed them and almost as soon as they were wrapped in their sleeping cloaks, they were sound asleep.

Yani had been so intent on the colored stone and the old man so amused by watching her that they did not notice the eyes watching them from the edge of the thicket. When the girl's breathing took on the slow regular patterns of deep sleep, the eyes raised from their position against the ground to the height of a man's waist. Silently, they moved forward until the wolf appeared in the glow of the fire. He stealthily slid to the side of the girl and dropping to his belly inched forward until his huge muzzle was resting against her back. There he too fell into a peaceful sleep.

Chapter Eight

The next morning Yani woke feeling rested and at ease. She rolled over onto her back and let her arm drop to the ground beside her. *That is strange,* she thought, *the ground is warm here.* She moved her hand a short distance over to one side but the ground was cold. The Knapper woke to find her crawling around the area near her sleeping cloak feeling the ground.

"Yani, what is it? Have you lost something?" he asked.

"This is very strange. When I woke the ground was warm in this one place. Now it is growing cold? What can it mean?" The old man just shook his head as puzzled as the girl.

For the next two days their journey followed much the same pattern as the ones before. The only difference was the lay of the land. They moved out of the marshy meadowland back into a forest that changed from maple and alder to majestic oak. Finally they emerged from the oak forest into a wide river valley. Each morning, Yani had discovered the same warm spot by her side when she woke. Both the old man and the girl puzzled over it as they walked.

When they came to the edge of the river, the Knapper turned south and followed the riverbank until Yani began to see the telltale signs of people and knew they were nearing a village. Her first clue had been a snare she had seen laid on a low game trail through the berry brambles. She noticed the trails that crisscrossed the blackberry brambles indicating that someone had been picking the berries. Soon, she began to hear the voices of children at play and the bleating of sheep.

As soon as she began to smell smoke, she knew they were almost to their destination. Looking toward the sounds, she saw a large cluster of houses on the far side of the river. Fearing that they might have to swim the river, which had to be icy cold this time of year, she followed the Knapper as he made his way along the bank. When they were directly across from the village, they reached a place along the bank that had been worn away by many feet to form a path down to the water's edge. They climbed down to the water, and the Knapper reached up into a tree and grabbed a ram's horn that was hanging from a rope there. Placing it against his lips, he gave it three hard puffs sending a trio of blasts across the river to the village on the other side.

Watching with interest, Yani saw a group of men gather on the opposite bank. The Knapper raised his arm and waved to the group who quickly returned the gesture. Two of them moved away from the group and walked up stream to a narrow beach along the river's edge. Pushing what looked like a log into the water, they climbed into it and picking up poles began to move the log across the river. The current pushed them downstream so that when they reached Yani and the Knapper's side they landed right in front of them. They poled the log so that one end was again the bank. The man in that end climbed out and, holding it steady, motioned for the Knapper and Yani to climb into the hollowed out center of the log. With the Knapper's help, she climbed in, alarmed at first when the log began to rock on the surface of the water. Soon she was settled in the far end of the log boat with her knees bent under her. The Knapper climbed in and settled in behind her. The man who had been holding the boat climbed back in giving them a shove away from the bank as he did so. Turning toward the far side, they began to pole the boat back across. She held tightly to the sides of the boat. She was fearful at first but soon she relaxed and enjoyed the ride across the river.

When they reached the other side, the current had carried them down stream passed the village. Reaching the shallow water near the bank, the men poled the boat back against the current until they reached the group of men waiting for them. Using the poles to hold the boat against the bank, the men helped the Knapper and Yani scramble out.

One of the men grabbed the Knapper's shoulders when he was safely on the bank and embraced him.

"Knut, we had all but given up on seeing you this year. Are the years finally slowing down my wandering brother?" asked the man.

Taking a better look, Yani could see that he had the same reddish colored hair and icy blue eyes. As if sensing her interest, he turned to Yani, asking, "And who is this little bird you have with you? You are too old to have taken a wife and I don't remember hearing that you had a daughter hidden away in one of the villages you winter in."

"I have always told you I was a man of many surprises," laughed the Knapper. "This little bird is Yani. She has agreed to be the daughter I always wanted in exchange for the opportunity to see the Mountains That Are Always White. We both think we got the best end of the deal."

"Come," laughed the brother, "you must be tired and hungry. My wife has a pot of venison stew simmering and she has baked bread today in the village oven. She is an amazing woman. She said you would arrive tonight." Yani followed the men toward the house as they began telling of all that had happened since their last meeting.

Chapter Nine

The village Yani entered was unlike any she had ever seen. The houses were made of sturdy oak logs each sharing a common wall with the next so they formed long rows. All the door openings were on the south side of the dwellings, denying the cold north wind an entrance and catching the warmth of the winter sun, which hung low to the south. Between the rows of houses was a walkway paved with logs that had been hewn flat on the surface. The walk, like the log houses, had been chinked with a mixture of mud and straw. When the men reached the entrance to one of the houses Kurf, the Knapper's brother, pushed the plank door open and the travelers followed him inside.

They entered a small room that ran the length of the house. The doorway was in the middle of this room dividing it into two sections. On the side to the left were large baskets that Yani guessed must hold the grain from the fields she had seen from the river. Hanging from the rafters were net sacks of squash and cabbages. On the right side of the door was a plow and other farming tools. Lingering only long enough to add their packs to the collection in the entrance rooms, the travelers followed Kurf through a deer hide curtain and into the living area.

On one side of the room were two large sleeping shelves, one above the other. Yani was surprised to see that the beds were wide enough to sleep four or five people without crowding. To the left of the door was the firepit. The walls were lined with benches providing seating as well as work areas. The roof sloped steeply up and at the top was an opening to allow the smoke from the fire to escape. Hanging from a rope attached to one of the rafters that supported the roof joists was a clay pot. The pot was filled with oil into which a wick of twisted vegetable fibers had been inserted. The wick burned with a bright flame providing light to augment the glow of the fire.

As they entered, Kurf's wife looked up from the stew she was stirring and smiled. "You are here at last, Brother. My husband has been fretting for days. He has nearly worn a groove walking back and forth to the river."

"Now, Woman," Kurf said, "what is this foolishness. I've hardly thought about this old fool."

Knut laughed and hugged her. "It is good to see you, too, Sister. Has the year gone well?"

"As well as can be expected, living with this contrary old man." Then noticing Yani standing shyly at the door she asked, raising an eyebrow at her brother-in-law, "And what have we here?"

Pulling the girl forward Knut introduced her. "This is Yani. She is traveling with me now." Turning to girl he added, "Yani, this is Muira. And the two pups you see hiding in the upper bed are my nephews, Durk and Holt."

Yani looked up in time to catch two small heads disappear into the shadows at the back of the top bed. Then a hand was pulling her to the fire as Muira guided her to a place on the bench. To her surprise as soon as the men had been served their bowls of stew, Muira fill two more bowls handing one to Yani and sitting down on the bench beside her with a bowl of her own. She had then given Yani a large piece of something that was soft and warm and smelled absolutely delicious. It had a dark rough texture and as she watched the others, they dipped it into their stew allowing it to soak up some of the juices before taking a bite of it. Yani guessed that this must be the bread that Kurf had mentioned to Knut when they arrived. Following their lead, she dipped her slice into the stew and took a bite. It was the best thing she had ever tasted. When she had eaten the last of the bread, she used her fingers to scoop up the large pieces of the stew. There were pieces of meat, cabbage and orange colored chunks. When Muira noticed her studying them, she whispered to her, "They are carrots. They grow as roots and when you dig them and bury them in a bed of straw in a pit, they will keep almost all winter. There are also onions and cabbage in it."

Yani gave her a grateful but tired smile. As she was finishing the bowl of stew, Muira handed her another slice of the bread. Fearing that she would appear greedy, she hesitated. "Take it, Child," the Knapper said from across the fire. "You will need all the fat you can store for our journey. While we are here you must eat your fill for there will be times that we will not be so fortunate."

When she had finished a second bowl of the venison stew and had helped Muira clean the dishes, she curled up in a corner of the bench to listen to the talk. Soon the warmth of the fire, her full belly and the rhythm of the voices were too much for her and her eyes began to droop. She had not realized she had dozed until she jerked awake at the touch of Knut's hand on her shoulder. "Come, Child, climb into the top bed and go to sleep. You have had a long day."

Obediently, she climb the ladder where she found the two boys snuggled together at one end of the bed, sound asleep. Knut handed her up her sleeping cloak that he had fetched from the storage rooms. When he was sure that she was asleep. Kurf turned to Knut and asked, "So, Brother, tell me how you came to have this bright little bird with you."

Knut shifted uneasily on the bench, searching for the proper way to tell his brother how he came to have Yani. He decided that the simplest way was to begin the story with his first glimpse of her dancing with the butterflies. The fire was down to glowing coals when he had finished. "And so that is the story. She has brought joy into my life and I find her a constant source of wonder. For instance, on the trail one night the strangest thing happened. We were camped at the deep gorge one day's walk from the Village in the Marsh. In the night Yani awakened me. In the woods around us, we could see the yellow eyes of wolves. There were at least six of them. After what seemed like days of waiting to see if they would attack, one of the wolves left the pack and

88

came to Yani's side. To our surprise, it laid its muzzle on her arm, closed its eyes, and went to sleep. Finally exhaustion over took the girl's fear and she too slept. In the morning the wolf was gone.

"At first I was not sure but what I had dreamed it. When the girl spoke of it too, I knew it had to have happened. Have you ever heard such strange behavior from a wolf?" asked the Knapper when he had finished his tale.

"I wonder," pondered his brother. The brothers sat watching the dying glow of the coals and finally Kurf spoke again, "It was last winter before the terrible blizzard struck. Surely you remember it, the wind blew the snow so hard that I could not see the back of the next row of houses. Anyway a traveler had stopped at the village and asked to be ferried across the river. He created quite a stir in the village because he was traveling with a wolf. It was very gentle and even the children got over their fear of it. He told us he had found it as a pup and had raised it to be a companion on the hunt.

"When he left the village, we warned him that it would be best to winter with us and then move on but he was anxious to reach the village of his father that he said was beyond the Village in the Marsh. He said he had to go all the way to the Sea then follow its shore for ten more days to reach the village. The day after he left the blizzard struck."

"Yes, I see where your mind is headed. If he were caught by the blizzard and didn't know to make a shelter and stop, he would have likely gotten lost in the snow and frozen to death. Perhaps this wolf is his wolf. It was certainly gentle."

After contemplating this for a while, the Knapper spoke again. "That would also explain another mystery from the trail. The next day we both had the feeling that we were being followed. And each morning Yani woke to find a warm spot by her. I think the wolf was joining our fire each night and sleeping by the girl."

Kurf nodded in agreement. Then slapping his thighs he turned to his wife who was dozing on the bench and said, "Woman, it is time to go to bed."

Muira added a few more sticks to the fire and raked some of the hot ashes around it, banking it for the night. The three adults moved to the lower sleeping shelf. Arranging their sleeping cloaks so their feet were to the warmth of the fire, they settled into the layer of reeds that softened the board planks and were soon asleep, too.

Chapter Ten

Yani awakened to the sound of the family waking up. Enjoying the luxury of a roof over her head and a warm bed, she lay there for a while listening. Finally her conscience over came her and she roll to the edge of the loft bed and climbed down to the hearth area. Muira had added wood to the fire and was stirring the meal into the clay pot she used for cooking. Hearing the girl descending the ladder, she looked up and smiled. "Good morning, Yani, did you sleep well."

Returning the smile, Yani replied, "Yes, very." She watched the preparation of the breakfast and when Muira sat back from the fire onto the bench, she asked, "What am I to call you? I do not know the correct address of your people."

Muira thought for a minute before replying. "I think you should call me, Aunt Muira. Knut tells me he has finally found in you the daughter he has always wanted. Yes, I think Aunt Muira will do."

Nodding at the correctness of it, Yani asked, "Then should I call your husband, Uncle Kurf?"

"Knut will love that! I am not sure about Kurf, but, yes, you should address him as Uncle. He may roar at first but his roar is mostly hot air. He will come to love it, too."

Hearing this Yani decided to try to avoid addressing Kurf directly. She did not want to see the effect of calling him Uncle Kurf.

Soon the men joined them at the fire, and Muira dished each of them a steaming bowl of porridge. The morning had added light to that of the oil lamp and of the firepit. Yani was able to see that the bowls they were eating from were also made of clay. Her family had one such bowl that had been traded for shortly after she had been born. The traveler they had gotten it from had explained how they were made but after weeks of searching for a source of clay the village had given up.

They decided wooden bowls were better any way. They did not break as easily and were lighter to carry on a journey.

When Yani and the adults were nearly finished eating, the boys came scampering down from the loft bed. Huddling together in the corner of one of the benches, they openly stared at Yani. She smiled at them hoping to win them over. To her surprise, the older of the two boys stuck his tongue out at her and made a face. Before she could stop herself, she burst into laughter at the imp. She quickly squelched it though, fearful that the parents would have seen and punish the boy. Glancing their way, she saw that they had indeed witnessed the whole thing. Their faces were looking at the boy sternly but their eyes contradicted the stern look.

Kurf spoke to his son. "Durk, apology to your new cousin. That is no way to welcome her. Now tell Yani you are sorry."

Hanging his head in shame, he mumbled, "I am sorry, New Cousin."

Yani worked hard to keep the laughter from her voice as she replied, "You are forgiven, Cousin Durk."

The parents had hardly returned their attention to their conversation when Durk saw his chance and catching Yani's attention again stuck his tongue out at her. This time Yani was able to smother her laughter. She slid across the bench until she was next to the boy and, being careful to keep her back to the adults, whispered in a voice just barely audible, "I am going to tickle you until you can't breathe."

This had been her favorite revenge on her younger sisters when they had proved to be pests. She found it was the only form of revenge that adults would accept. With her threat made, she settled back on the bench to listen to the adults, leaving the boys to watch her for signs that the attack was coming.

When the adults had finished their breakfast, the men left the house to make the rounds of friends and relatives. Yani and Muira

92

settled themselves by the fire to spin and get better acquainted. As Muira picked up the spindle, Yani began teasing and carding the wool from the basket Muira had pulled from under the bench. The morning passed pleasantly as the woman and the girl reminisced about their pasts and speculated on the future.

Chapter Eleven

In the afternoon, Yani left the house to explore the area around the village. It had been such a long time since she had walked without a pack on her back that it felt like she was floating on air. As she walked into the open, Yani's eyes searched the surrounding countryside. The forest was much the same as near her village but she noticed quite a few more beech trees. Thinking that there might be a few beechnuts left on the ground, she returned to the house and got her water basket from her pack in the entry rooms. She wandered back toward the forest enjoying the late fall sunshine.

As she approached one large old tree she saw that the ground was littered with nuts. *The squirrels here must be slow or there are just so many they haven't had time to carry all of them off,* she thought. She was so intent on gathering the nuts that she didn't hear the snapping of the twig in the forest behind her. She busied herself picking up the largest of the nuts and discarding the small and empty ones. As she worked she reflected on what the men in Lamu's village had said about the number of nuts indicating a cold, hard winter.

Plunk! The pinecone came out of nowhere and caught her square in the back of the head. Jumping to her feet and darting toward the sound of the giggles, she got to their hiding place just in time to see two small backs disappear behind a tree a short distance away. Smiling to herself she decided to play along with the boys. Returning to her basket, she picked it up and moved off in the other direction. As soon as she was sure she was out of sight, she gathered several pinecones and lay her ambush. She didn't have long to wait before the muffled giggles and breaking of twigs indicated their approach. She had a pine cone in her hand and a small pile at her feet when they slipped into view around a tree. *Their stalking techniques have a long way to go,* she thought. Suddenly, she began pelting them with pinecones. Squealing, they ran back into the forest. Yani listened for a moment or two to see if she could detect the direction they had taken. Hearing nothing she picked up her basket and as quiet as possible moved off further into the forest. Every thirty or forty steps, she would stop and listen. Finally, when she heard nothing after several stops, she decided the boys had given up and returned to her search for nuts.

She was humming to herself and planning how she would surprise Muira with all the nuts she had collected when she heard the snap of a twig again. She looked around for the pinecones she had dropped on the ground when she stopped here to gather nuts. Seeing them off to one side, she crawled that direction trying not to let the boys know that she was aware they were there. As she moved toward the pinecones, she heard more movement in the brush behind her. Judging that they were close enough to begin their attack, she snatched up the pinecones and jumped up to face the boys.

What she saw made her freeze in her tracks. For there, at the edge of the clearing, stood the wolf. For an eternity the girl and wolf stared at each other. Yani knew it would do no good to run since the wolf could out pace her in a few steps. She looked around for a tree that she might climb but the only trees in the vicinity were mature beech trees. Their lowest branches were higher than the height of several men. As they faced each other the wolf dropped to his haunches and to Yani's surprise wagged his tail. Slowly, she knelt down and placed the pinecones on the ground. She held out her empty hand to the wolf. He whined softly but made no attempt to approach her. Still fearful of the huge beast and his mouthful of sharp teeth, she hesitated to go to him. The wolf started to rise and Yani froze. It took one tentative step toward her.

Suddenly, a screech and whoop broke the silent and Yani turned toward the sound of crashing branches. Before she could gather herself to ward off the attack, the air was full of pinecones. Looking back to where the wolf had been, she found that he was gone. Quickly, scooping up some pinecones for ammunition, she ducked behind a tree just as the boys ran into the clearing. Now it was her turn and the disappointment of having the almost magical moment with the wolf interrupted added zeal to her attack. She soon had them in retreat down the trail toward home. She returned for her basket, which was now almost full. She stood in the clearing searching the surrounding underbrush for any sign of the wolf. Seeing none, she turned back toward the village.

That evening as the adults visited around the fire, Yani roasted the beechnuts she had gather in the forest. She knew she should tell them of seeing the wolf but for some reason she was reluctant to do so.

The boys were much quieter than usual. They watched Yani work expecting her at any moment to tell their parents of the pinecone assault. Their past experience with girls her age led them to believe all girls were whiny tattle tails. They were constantly getting into trouble for their antics, usually because of sneak attacks on the older girls in the village. But there she sat, calmly roasting and cracking nuts.

Yani felt the boys' eyes on her as she worked. Smiling to herself, she decided to let them suffer a bit before reassuring them. After all the trouble her little sisters had gotten her into by their tattling, she had no intention of reporting the little culprits. When she had a bowl almost full of roasted nuts, she took a handful and joining the boys on the bench began to place them in her mouth one at a time chewing slowly and softly smacking her lips. Finally, she glanced their way. Shifting on the bench so that the adults could not see, she ran her tongue over her lips and silently mouthed "Hummmm." Then she popped another nut into her mouth and slowly chewed and swallowed.

Torn between wanting to tell on Yani to make her share the nuts and fear that if they did she would tell on them, the two boys squirmed uncomfortably on the bench. When Yani decided she had made them suffer long enough, she smiled innocently at them and said, " Oh, I'm sorry, do you like beechnuts? Here have some. These seem to have a distinct pine taste to them for some reason."

Handing the rest of the nuts to the boys, she returned to her place by the fire to finish roasting the nuts. When the last of them were roasted and cracked, she asked Muira if she could borrow her grinding stone. Soon she had the bowl of roasted nuts ground into meal to use for their morning porridge.

The travelers spent the next four days resting in the village. Yani spent several hours each day walking in the woods and gathering nuts for Muira to use. She had hoped to see the wolf again but he had not reappeared. On the evening of the fourth day, the Knapper announced to his family that they would be leaving in the morning at first light. The days had been pleasant enough for Yani, but she too was anxious to be on their way.

Before the stars had faded from the sky, Yani and the Knapper had packed their carrying baskets. Muira had cooked an extra large pot of porridge for breakfast and insisted on Yani eating a second bowl full. When they had their packs shouldered and were ready to leave, the older of the boys inched up to her and whispered, "Yani, I am sorry we threw the pinecones at you." He stood by her looking at the ground.

She reached out and ruffled his sandy hair. "That's alright. If you remember, I won the battle. Maybe the next time I visit your aim will have improved. It would be nice to have some fair competition."

He turned an indigent face up to her and started to come back with an angry retort until he saw the look of mischief on her face. "Oh, we just let you get in a few shots because, well, after all, you are our guest and Mother always taught us to be polite."

"Why, of course," she replied in mock seriousness. "You always show the utmost respect for your guests. I must remember when I return to this village that the polite manner to greet people is like this." She stuck her tongue out at Holt and made a face.

This was too much for the boys and dissolving into a fit of giggles, they wrapped their arms around her waist and hugged her. "We will miss you, Cousin Yani," Durk mumbled with him face buried in her side.

"And I will miss you, too.

Chapter Twelve

When the sun had risen high enough to burn off the hoarfrost that had coated the trees, Yani and the Knapper were far from the village. It didn't take long for their muscles to warm to the pace of the trail. Keeping the sun at their left, they headed almost due south. Soon the land began to rise and the plain gave way to rolling hills. Here it became more difficult to keep a constant southern coarse and Yani noticed the Knapper frequently checked the sky. As the hills became higher they started following the contour of the land thus going around, rather than over them. At noon the hills were becoming high enough that they had started following streams where they made natural passes. They stopped to eat where the branch they had been following emptied into a larger creek. Sitting on the boulders that littered the convergence of the two streams, Yani stretched. The sun had become warm enough by midmorning that they had rolled their sleeping cloaks and returned them to the packs. Basking in the sun after they had eaten, Yani asked, "Will it be far to the next village?"

"It is perhaps three days' walk," replied the Knapper. "I hope this pleasant weather will hold until we reach there. Traveling in rain and snow is not enjoyable."

Yani nodded in agreement. They sat in silence for a short time more, enjoying the warmth of the sun. Then the Knapper rose, shouldered his pack and Yani followed his lead.

The next two days, they traveled without event. They had fallen into the habit of speaking little saving their breath for the walk. They were content to let their own thoughts occupy them. On the afternoon of the third day, the Knapper broke the silence saying, "Our next village is not far now. We only have to cross this ridge of hills and drop down into the valley beyond. Tonight we sleep in a house again."

Yani had guessed that they were nearing a village because for quite a while they had been on a well-worn trail. As they walked she speculated on what this new village would be like. So far each village they had visited had been different.

Suddenly the Knapper came to an abrupt stop in front of her. Since she had been day dreaming, she almost bumped into his pack. Peering around the old man, she saw what had made him come to such an abrupt stop. In the trail in front of them was a huge brown bear. It stood swaying from side to side, shaking its head. The Knapper whispered to Yani, "Slowly move back. Perhaps if we back down the trail, he will go his way."

Yani started to back away from the Knapper. As she moved back, he began to back off, too. They had only gone a few steps when the bear reared on his hind legs and began to growl. As soon as she could, Yani turned and hurried down the path the way they had come. She had gone about a hundred steps when she heard the Knapper cry out. Turning back, she saw that he had stumbled over a root as he was backing away and the bear was now on all fours running toward him. Yani screamed and ran forward hoping to distract the bear until the Knapper could regain his footing. She raised her walking stick prepared to swing at the bear if he continued to charge. Suddenly, she caught a blur of movement out of the corner of her eye. There was vicious snarling as a streak of gray darted out of the trees straight for the bear. As she helped the Knapper to his feet the snarling and growling mixed with the bellowing of the bear. When he was on his feet, Yani turned to see what had attacked the bear. There on the trail facing down the angry bear was the wolf. She knew that a wolf was no match for a full-grown bear, so she turned pleading eyes to the Knapper.

Swinging the staff, Knut advanced on the angry bear. Yani gathered up some stones from the trail and, taking aim, began to pelt the bear. Taking one last swipe at the snarling wolf with its lethal claws, the bear turned and retreated from his attackers.

Gasping for breath Yani and the Knapper stood on the trail facing the wolf. For an eternity they stared at each other then Yani took a step towards the wolf. Holding out her hand to him she spoke softly. "So, my friend, we meet again. The last time I was attacked you ran away. This time you knew I truly needed your help so you rescued me, didn't you?"

The wolf stood his ground and as the girl spoke his head cocked to one side as if weighing the girls words. When she had finished speaking, the wolf whined and took a step forward. Kneeling, she whistled softly hoping to encourage him. The Knapper, fearing for the girl, tensed and took a firmer grip on the walking stick. Seeing the slight movement, the wolf spun round and bounded off into the forest. Still shaken by the close encounter with two of the most feared animals in the forest, the Knapper rested his hand on Yani's shoulder. Taking a deep breath, he said, "Come, Child, let's get to this village before dark sets in. I don't want to meet either of our friends in the open again tonight."

Chapter Thirteen

They moved rapidly over the last ridge and arrived in the village just before the sun dipped below the hills to the west. Their arrival created a stir of excitement that swept through the village. To Yani's disappointment this village was very much like her own. The houses were circular with high thatched roofs. The arrangement was a little different since the village ran along the edge of a stream but that was about the only difference. At first glance, there seemed to be no pattern to their placement. But, as she walked through the village, she saw that they were arranged in a fan shape. The largest house was at the center of the fan and the other houses formed two semi-circular row extending out from the Large House. As they approached this dwelling, the raw hide door flap was thrown back and a tall dark haired man walked out. When he saw the Knapper he raised his hand in welcome.

"Knapper, so you come at last!" he cried. "Come, sit by the fire, eat, and tell me of your journeys."

Yani slipped into the house behind the Knapper and hugging the wall sat as quietly as she could, hoping she would not be noticed. For some reason she did not feel as at ease in this village as she had in the others they had visited. She took off her pack and resting her head against it, she surveyed the interior. Although the exterior looked much like the houses in her village, the interior was much different. The Knapper, their host and several other men were seated on logs around an open fire that was built in the center of the dirt floor. Looking around the walls for the sleeping benches, Yani saw that there were none. She peered up into the gloom above the men and saw that there was a loft that circled the house. The smoke from the fire had blackened the roof above the loft before exiting though the smoke hole in the peak of the roof adding to the gloomy atmosphere of the place. Yani hoped that they didn't linger long here. The idea of sleeping in that smoke filled loft did not appeal to her. Her attention was pulled back to the men's conversation when she heard the Knapper mention the bear. It was all she could do to keep herself from crying out to him, begging him not to mention the wolf. Her intuition told her these unfriendly men would not understand. A wolf this near a village could send every hunter in the village into the woods intent on bringing back a wolf pelt to prove his skill as a hunter and provide a warm winter cloak. To her relief, the Knapper left out the part about the wolf's attack. He led the men to believe that they had frightened the bear off with their walking sticks and Yani's stones. Soon she found she was dozing as the Knapper visited with their host.

Sometime later Yani felt a hand on her shoulder. Looking up with sleepy eyes, she saw the Knapper smiling down at her. Offering a hand, he pulled her to her feet pointing her toward the ladder that led to the sleeping loft. The aftereffect of the bear attack had so drained Yani, she was hardly aware of the smoky air in the loft and quickly drifted into a sound sleep.

The next morning as the Knapper made what few trades there were to be made in this poor village, Yani explored the stream that ran passed it. When she saw the flashes of the speckled bodies of trout in the cool, clear water, she looked around for the weirs that the men of her village carried each summer to the stream that flowed out of the mountains a day's journey from the village. It was always a time of celebration when the men returned with the fresh trout packed in baskets filled with wet grass. This year she would have been permitted to make the trip. It was a long hard trip and only the older children were allowed to go with the men. This village had a trout stream at the very edge of their village and no weirs had been set. She was truly puzzled. Wandering to the forest side of the village, she looked for the sheepfold. She listened as she walked, knowing the bleating would give away the location, but when she got to the other side of the village, she saw no sign of the fold. Turning back to the village, she looked with new interest at the people. It dawned on her that they were not wearing woven clothes but only tanned skins. Other things caught her attention now too. They didn't have any tilled fields around the edge of the village and there was no well.

Returning to the edge of the stream, she sat down and began to skip flat rocks across its surface. What children she saw were just sitting around the houses or idly drawing in the dirt with sticks. They lacked the energy of Holt and Durk in the Knapper's village and her sisters. *Where were the ruddy cheeks that children are supposed to have in the wintertime,* she thought

Shortly before the sun had reached its zenith, the Knapper joined her by the stream. "I have done all the trading that I can here. If we start now we can reach a good camping site on the other side of that ridge before nightfall. We will have to move quickly and eat our noonday meal as we walk, do you...."

But Yani did not wait for him to finish. She scrambled to her feet and they started toward the Large House to retrieve the packs.

Chapter Fourteen

The day had been a hard one, beginning with a steep climb out of the valley but the need to be gone from this depressing village had helped them on their way. When they reached a rock outcropping at the top, Yani looked back one last time before they started down the other side. She told herself that she must ask the Knapper why this village was so poor when they lived in such a promising spot. But that could wait. Now she needed all her breath to move as quickly as possible over this ridge and away from the village.

When they came to the campsite, it turned out to be a shallow cave that cut back into a sandstone cliff. There was a circle of stones that someone had left, forming a fire pit. The floor of the cave was covered with the sand that had eroded from the roof and walls of the cave by the freezing and thawing of many winters. Putting her pack in the shelter, Yani searched the area for wood they could use for the fire. When she had come back with an armload, the Knapper said, "Yani, I think you will need to get another armload. The weather is going to turn cold tonight. Before we have our supper over, it will probably be raining and by morning there will be snow."

"How...," she started to asked but then remembered the storm at the sea. The Knapper had said his crippled foot was the best predictor of weather there was. She turned from the shelter and returned dragging several limbs as big around as her leg. Even if they could not break them by stepping on them, they could put one end in the fire and they could push the limb in as it burned. Seeing her load, the Knapper smiled.

Soon they had the fire burning and water heating for the evening meal. Because of the coming cold, the Knapper added a few pieces of the dried meat to the acorn meal porridge. As they were eating, rain began to patter on the leaves around the cave. They took their sleeping cloaks from the pack and spread them on the ground one on top of the other near the back of the cave. Then Yani took the fur cloak that Loki had given her from her pack and laying down together on the double thickness of cloaks, they covered up with the fur.

They had just settled in their beds with their feet to the fire when they heard a twig snap near the mouth of the cave. The Knapper reached for his walking stick then paused. To their amazement, the wolf trotted into the glow of the fire straight to Yani's side. He stood there looking into her eyes for a moment then circled three times and dropped down on the edge of the sleeping cloak beside her. She turned to the Knapper who could only shake his head in wonder. He chuckled, lay back down and was soon sound asleep. Yani turned on her right side toward the wolf and reaching out rested her hand on his soft fur. Soon all three were sleeping peacefully as the rain began to fall in earnest.

Yani awakened to a totally silent world. Before she opened her eyes, she knew it had snowed. Only a snow filled forest is so quiet. As she lay there, a wet tongue licked her face. Startled, she opened her eyes to see the huge muzzle of the wolf above her. He licked her again, then ran his nose under her hand until she understood that he wanted her to pet his head. She scratched his ears and smoothed the soft fur back along his neck. Inching closer to the girl, he laid his head on her chest and dozed off again contently. Watching the snowfall outside the cave Yani wondered at the situation she found herself in. She could hardly believe that she had a full-grown wolf sleeping with his head across her chest. And, not only was she not afraid but she felt much safer for his presence.

Soon the Knapper woke and added more wood to the fire. Yani got up and taking her winter moccasins from the pack pulled them on before going to fetch the water. When she returned the Knapper was attempting to win the wolf over with a piece of dried meat. He was having limited success and it became very clear from the welcome she got that Wolf was Yani's.

When they continued their journey south a third pair of tracks was added to that of the man and the girl. Any hunter seeing the tracks in the snow would conclude that the two humans were being stalked by a lone wolf and therefore in mortal danger. But the hunter could not have been farther from the truth. The wolf had become a part of the family that was moving through the winter landscape to the Mountains That Are Always White.

Part 3
The Steppes

Chapter One

"Wolf! Come!" Yani called as the animal bounded ahead to the edge of the snow filled meadow. They had been traveling together for many days now and the wolf had learned to respond to her commands. Normally she would have allowed him to roam ahead in search of game to provide a meal for his appetite, which matched his size. But, the Knapper had warned her that they would be nearing a village by nightfall and she was afraid that some hunter would mistake Wolf's friendliness for aggression.

"Wolf!" she called again this time allowing her impatience to enter her voice. He stopped and looked back at the girl as if debating whether to obey or continue on the trail of the rabbit's scent. Looking one last time in the direction in which the tempting smell had gone, he turned and loped back to the man and the girl. As he neared he could sense her displeasure with him and he approached them with his head hung low and his tail between his legs. Meekly, he fell in beside them setting his pace to match that of the girl. When she did not give him his usual pat on the head when he joined her, he nudged her with his nose. Still she took no notice of him so he nudged again, this time accented with a whine.

The pitiful look was too much for Yani and she dropped to her knees, looking him in the face, she ruffled his ears and stroked his head. "Wolf! You are so silly. I am not mad at you but you must stay close today. Do you understand me?"

The Knapper chuckled at the girl. He found it amusing to think that she thought the animal could understand her words. He believed that it was just the language of the body that animals understood.

But as the day progressed, the wolf never strayed from Yani's side. As the sunset, they made camp near the ford of a large stream. It had been a good season. The Knapper had traded nearly all of his blades for goods, which could in turn be traded for food when they reached the southern village at the base of the mountains. The winter had been snowy but without the bitterly cold temperatures that made travel so dangerous. They had not had to hold up in villages for days on end as the Knapper had often been forced to do in the past which meant they were nearing the Mountains That Are Always White much earlier in the season than usual. This would be the last village before the seven-day trek across the high wind swept Steppes that separated the northern valleys from the southern mountains.

They had the usual supper of acorn meal before rolling up in their sleeping cloaks for the night. Wolf had stayed close to the camp all that evening. Yani wondered if it was the result of the reprimand that she had given him earlier in the day or if he had just been alerted to the proximity of people by their scent. He paced uneasily just inside the circle of the firelight as they prepared the meal and made ready for sleep.

Chapter Two

When Yani had settled for the night with Wolf in his usual place at her side, she began to get the unsettling feeling of being watched. She peered into the darkness around the campfire but could see nothing. Wolf seemed to sense something, too. From time to time the hair on the back of his neck bristled and his ears kept flattening against his head as he peered into the dark outside the ring of the campfire's light. The Knapper seemed unaware of anything unusual, so Yani decided it must be just some scavenging animal. Settling more comfortably she soon was dozing. She had only just dropped into a sound sleep when Wolf began to growl softly. She reached out to quiet him when a branch snapped nearby bringing both of the travelers wide awake.

Instinctively, they both reached for their walking sticks as Wolf rose to his feet and moved menacingly toward the sound. He had taken several steps toward the source of the sound when a frighten voice called out from the darkness. "Don't let your wolf kill me! I only want to share your fire."

Yani and the Knapper were both on their feet by now, walking sticks held at ready. "Wolf! Stay!" commanded Yani quietly.

"Come into the firelight. The wolf will not harm you if you do not try to harm us," said the Knapper.

"I'm coming in." There was a rustling of leaves as a small boy walked into the circle of light. "Are you sure the wolf won't hurt me?" he asked hesitantly.

"Wolf! Come!" said Yani softly and Wolf walked back to her side after a last disdainful look at the boy. As if deciding that this small human posed no danger to his humans, he dropped down beside Yani's sleeping cloak and stretched out closing his eyes.

The boy moved into the ring of light formed by the campfire, staying as far away from Wolf as possible and stood there uncertainly.

111

"So, Boy, who are you and what are you doing in the woods this late at night," demanded the Knapper.

"I am called Sepp. My village it across the stream and over the ridge." He looked down at his feet, hesitant to continue.

"And, so, Sepp, what are you doing so far from the village this time of night?" prodded Knut.

"I….," began Sepp.

"Yes."

"I, ah, I ran away from home because my mother said I had to fetch the water for dinner or I could not eat!" looking up at the Knapper who was a man and therefore would understand, he continued with more confidence. "Fetching water is a woman's job. I am seven summers so I am almost a man. I should not have to fetch water."

"And do you have sisters to fetch the water?" asked the Knapper.

"I have a sister," mumbled the boy, "but she is only three summers old."

"And you think she is old and strong enough to fetch the water? Or did you think your mother should be the one to carry the water for the family?"

"But the big boys laugh at me when I fetch water and call me a girl!" blurted Sepp with tears in his eyes.

"So you decided to run away and live by yourself in the forest, is that it?" asked the Knapper.

The boy nodded then continued, "But it got dark and I heard animals hunting. I tried to find my way home but I got lost. I saw the light from your fire and thought it was the village looking for me. I started to come to your fire when I saw the wolf."

He looked at Wolf still not sure he could trust him.

"Have you eaten?" asked the Knapper.

Sepp shook his head and a hopeful look crossed his face.

"I think that if you fetch some water from the stream, Yani might cook you some acorn mush," said the Knapper with a serious look on his face. Yani had been watching the exchange from her side of the fire.

"But, she....," began Sepp then he stopped at the thought of offending his host and being sent back into the dark. His stomach rumbled at the thought of food, so he sheepishly picked up the water basket and headed for the stream. As soon as the boy's back was turned the Knapper looked at Yani and smiled broadly.

Yani giggled softly as she rummaged through her pack looking for the pouch of acorn meal. She could just imagine Holt or Durk doing the same thing. *Boys are such silly creatures*, she thought

When they had fed the hungry boy, the Knapper asked, "Are you planning to return to your village in the morning or continue to live in the woods?"

After thinking it over for a few moments, Sepp replied, "I think I have worried my mother long enough. I will return to the village when you go there tomorrow."

"That seems a wise choice," said the Knapper, "but what are you going to do about the carrying of water?"

Scratching his head, Sepp considered that for a moment. Finally, he replied, "I like to eat."

This brought a fit of laughter from the Knapper. Yani giggled also, a little too much for Sepp's comfort. "Well, if I don't carry the water, my mother can't cook and the whole family will be hungry," he declared brashly. Continuing in a hushed voice, he mumbled, "And my father will probably beat me if I don't. He will probably beat me anyway for running off."

Yani felt sorry for the miserable boy who had had a chance to think over the consequences of his actions. He had been humiliated by the big boys and fled. Now he realized that there were worse things than

113

being called names. She remembered her own father and how he was quick to strike her if she did not obey as quickly as he thought she should. Reaching out to stroke Wolf who had stirred in his sleep an idea stuck her.

Speaking to the boy for the first time, she asked, "Sepp, do you think that if you enter the village beside a full grown wolf, the boys might think twice about calling you a girl?"

He looked at her with a look of terror on his face at the thought of being close to the wolf. Then he looked at the peaceful animal sleeping at her side and thought it over. *The wolf is the most feared animal next to the bear. If I come into the village with a wolf all the boys would have to say I am brave. Almost a man. "*But will the wolf let me get close to it?" he asked, still not sure of this beast.

"There is one way to find out," smiled Yani, beckoning with her finger.

Looking at the Knapper to check his reaction to this plan, Knut nodded at the boy and motioned toward Yani with a jerk of his head.

He slowly rose to his feet and moved toward the wolf and the girl. Hearing the boy's approach, Wolf opened his eyes and raised his head. Freezing in his tracks at the movement of the animal, Sepp looked from the man to the girl. "It's all right," said Yani. Stroking Wolf's head she whispered, "Wolf, this is Sepp. He wants to be your friend." Turning back to the trembling boy, she beckoned again.

He crossed the last bit of ground separating him from Wolf's massive jaws and sharp teeth and stopped. Wolf looked up at him and then reached out a paw, tapping the boy's foot. Jumping back, Sepp gasped. Yani laughed, "He likes you. That is his way of asking you to pet him."

"He likes me," whispered Sepp. "But is it for his supper that he likes me?"

Mustering his courage, he reached out and touched Wolf's head. When the animal didn't move, Sepp moved in closer and petted his neck and back.

"Here," said Yani, "I will make room on my sleeping cloak for you to sit."

He sat down between Yani and Wolf and continued to stroke the wolf. "His fur is so soft," he whispered half to Yani and half to himself. He had just started to relax when Wolf turned his head and licked him across the face with his big gray tongue. Rolling backward and scrambling behind Yani, he cried out in fear.

Laughing, Yani giggled, "Wolf, likes you. He just gave you a kiss."

"Are you sure he wasn't tasting me?"

"No, Silly," laughed Yani, "That is the way he kisses."

After a while Sepp began to relax. Wolf yawned and closed his eyes. Laughing softly, Yani said, "I think Wolf is the wisest one among us. There is room on my cloak if you would like to sleep here."

Sepp gave Wolf one last pat before curling up beside Yani under the bearskin and dropping off to sleep.

Chapter Three

So the next day Sepp entered the village with his hand resting on the back of a full-grown Wolf. Although his feat of courage impressed the other boys, it did nothing to impress his angry father and fearful mother.

As Sepp turned to face his parents, Yani watched sympathetically. She hoped his punishment would not be too severe. As the boy entered his house with his head hung low, the Knapper approached his father. Greeting the travelers, he said, "Thank you for returning my wayward son to his village. It has been a difficult night for his mother who was certain he had been eaten by wolves." Then looking at Wolf he continued, "But it appears that the wolf has returned him instead."

Chuckling Knut explained the boy's absence, "It seems the village boys have been giving your son a very hard time, as we know boys will do. When he joined our campfire, he was a very repentant young man. Nothing helps a boy think clearly like an empty belly and a dark cold night lost in the woods."

With a smile, Sepp's father agreed, "Yes, that is true. I remember similar thought provoking experiences when I was his age. Don't worry I will only beat him lightly. Just enough to know that this is not acceptable behavior. I am sure he told you he expected to be severely beaten when he returned."

"Yes, I do recall him speculating on that."

"It is strange how that boy can convert a firm swat on the bottom with my hand into a beating. Now my father, he knew how to give a good beating..."

And the Knapper and Sepp's father broke into laughter.

"I am glad to see you again, Knapper. Will you allow us to repay your kindness by sharing our firepit tonight."

"We would be honored. This is Yani and her friend, Wolf. He looks fierce but is as gentle as a lamb. That is unless someone or something threatens his girl. Then he becomes a terror. You need not fear for your family while he is near. Why, on the trail one day he attacked a full grown bear that was rushing us...."

As the men entered the house the Knapper continued with his tale of Wolf's courage and loyalty. Yani followed along behind and as she entered Sepp met her with the water basket in hand. He looked up sheepishly and mumbled, "If Mother is to cook for us she needs water."

"If you call him, I think Wolf would like to go with you. I am sure he is thirsty from the trail."

Smiling his gratitude, he called softly. Looking to Yani for her permission, Wolf paused only a moment before turning to follow beside the boy. As she turned back to the firepit she caught the look of gratitude in Sepp's mother's eyes. Joining her there she said, "I am Yani."

"Thank you, Yani. I am Sari." Yani removed her pack and set it in a corner, as Sari returned to her chores. Soon Yani had joined her, falling easily into the natural rhythm of the hearth.

Later when Knut and Doff, Sepp's father, returned to the house, Sari and Yani had supper ready. Yani was sitting by the fire playing with Rea, the three-year-old sister and Sepp was sitting beside Wolf stroking his fur. Jumping up as his father came into the house, he walked to him and said, "I am sorry that I ran away and worried Mother. I guess you should beat me now and get it over with." Turning around he bent over presenting his bottom to his father. The gruff voice his father used belied the twinkle in his eye and the twitch of a grin at the corner of his mouth. "Yes, Son, I fear I must beat you. That way you will remember to think before you act."

And with that he swatted his son once on the bottom. As Sepp stood up Yani saw tears in his eyes but knew they came more from

117

humiliation than pain. She couldn't help but think of the difference between this gentle punishment and the angry beatings her father administered to his children and even sometimes to his wife. Sepp returned to his place beside Wolf as the men settled themselves by the fire for the evening meal.

Chapter Four

When morning broke the travelers resumed their journey. By midafternoon the trees and rolling hills had given way to a broad grassy plain. As far as Yani could see in either direction was dry grass waving in the breeze. At first, the trail led them along a stream that drained off the plain and into the valley they had been following since leaving the village. Gradually the stream dwindled to tiny rivulets until miles of monotonous prairie swallowed it all together. As the day progressed a warm wind came up from the west. By noon they had shed their cloaks and Yani was thinking of changing from her winter boots to her old summer moccasins.

As they rested and shared some jerky for their noon meal, Yani basked in the unexpected warmth. "This is lovely!" she mused as she lay on the grass in the sunshine. "I never dreamed spring would come so early and so warm. Is it usual for the land near the Mountains That Are Always White?"

Knut looked out over the sea of grass toward the south. He shook his head and replied, "This is a false spring and I am afraid it is not a good sign. Often warm snaps like this are followed by blizzards. I think it would be wise for us to continue as quickly as possible."

Yani opened her eyes to see the Knapper shouldering his pack to make ready to leave. Puzzled that he could think that this spring-like weather could be a bad omen she, nonetheless, stood and began to make ready to go, too.

"But how can this warm sunshine possible mean there is a blizzard coming. It doesn't make sense."

"I hope I am wrong. It is not good to be caught on the Steppes in a blizzard. There is no place to find shelter and the wind and snow can make you lose your way and become hopelessly lost. Many travelers have frozen to death in just such weather." With that he started off at his steady shuffling pace toward the south.

As they walked Yani became almost hypnotized by the monotony of the waving grass. She wondered how Knut could know his way when it all looked exactly the same. After walking the better part of the afternoon and seeing nothing that she could use as a landmark, she asked, "Knut, how do you know your way across this plain. It all looks the same to me."

"There are markers if you look closely. But if you stray from a true heading you would lose them and quickly be lost. If the sky is clear as today it is easier to keep in the right direction but if the sky is overcast then it is important it use the markers. See if you can find them."

As they walked Yani looked at the horizon hoping to see some change in the land to give her a clue as to what Knut was using to reckon with. It was almost dark when she finally puzzled out the secret. As her tired head drooped, she began watching the ground. They had been walking all afternoon without a break, with Knut setting a much more rapid pace than usual. She sensed his urgency to get them across the prairie as soon as possible and made sure to match his pace. When she first spotted the rock she thought it looked out of place but it was just a flat rock in the sea of grass. When they got to it Knut seemed to veer slightly to the east. The rock had been pointed on that side she had noticed. After that she started watching the ground more intently and soon she noticed another rock. This time it was almost perfectly round. Knut continued in the direction he had been going. After they had passed several more with Knut making adjustments when the rocks had an asymmetric shape she ventured a guess. "It is the rocks, isn't it?"

"Very good, Little One, remember them well. There may be a time when you will need to know how to use them to get you across the prairie. The Ancient Ones placed them here long years ago and they are

120

scattered all across the plain. If you know their key, you can find your way easily. If not, is it is very easy to get lost and wander for days. There is little water here and it is important to know how to get to the next water hole quickly. The round rocks are distance markers. Every third rock will have a direction marker. You must go in the exact direction of the sharp edge of the rock. We are almost to one of the markers that will direct us to the east. You can't see it from here but there is a shallow dip in the prairie over there," he said pointing off to their left. "In the hollow is a spring that breaks the surface there and a few low stunted trees grow because of its moisture. That is where we will camp tonight. We must drink our fill and more because tomorrow night we will make a dry camp. This is the most dangerous stretch of the prairie since there is no hope of finding even a little shelter until we have made it to the next spring. If a blizzard were to catch us before crossing the dry camp we would be in a very bad fix."

As the Knapper predicted they came to a marker that indicated a turn toward the east and as the sun was riding the western horizon they came to a shallow bowl in the vast waving sea of grass.

Following the Knapper's lead Yani drank many times at the spring as they made camp. The night was mild and she used only her deer hide sleeping cloak when she made her bed. As they prepared for the night, Wolf seemed restless pacing back and forth before the fire. Several times he whined and came to her for comfort. She patted his head and gently said, "Wolf, go to sleep. We must rest for tomorrow."

Chapter Five

As they broke camp in the morning, the warm breeze was still at their right. Almost as soon as they were awake the Knapper handed Yani a couple pieces of jerky and taking one for himself told her that they would eat on the move today. Wolf also seemed anxious to be on the move. Rather than ranging ahead as he usually did, he trotted just in front of them often stopping to look back as if to hurry them onward. Late in the morning, the wind began to change direction and to build in strength. Yani noticed it was not as warm as it had been when they had broken camp that morning. When the sun was at its highest rather than stopping to rest and eat, Knut asked, "Do you think you can keep going? I don't like the feel of this wind. I would like to get as much distance in today as possible. We can't make it to the next sheltered camp by night fall but if we keep pushing on we may be able to make it by midmorning tomorrow."

Yani nodded and they continued at the same rapid pace that they had been keeping all day. They passed what Yani could see was the dry camp shortly afterwards but the Knapper hardly paused there. They walked all through the afternoon and continued walking until it became too dark for Knut to see the markers. When he finally called a halt for the day, he quickly made camp. Using the packs to form a wind block, they rolled up in their sleeping cloaks and covering themselves with the bear skin cloak were soon sound asleep. Instead of hunting as was his custom when they made camp, Wolf remained in camp, snuggling close to the sleeping girl.

The next morning broke with a violent red sky. The wind was now howling from the northeast and on the skyline was a thin line of heavy black clouds. Not pausing to eat, again they shouldered their packs and began the race against the storm. Seeing the sky, Yani needed no urging to move out quickly.

They had only just warmed to their walking pace when the wind began to turn bitter cold. Yani was glad she had thought to tie the bearskin around her as a cloak before they had left camp and had pulled the otter skin cap from her pack. The Knapper had also wrapped in his cloak rather than rolling it and packing it. The wind howled around them pushing them toward the southwest and making it hard to stay on course. By midmorning, the sky had become an ominous black and the first snowflakes began to dance around them. Wolf closed the distance between them as the wind increased and by the time the snow started in earnest, he was walking pressed against Yani's legs.

Soon the snow was flying in all directions around them. She lost sight of the Knapper for a few moments causing her to panic. When it cleared again enough to see, she ran to catch up to him and grabbed on to the lacings on his pack. When he felt her tug on his pack, he looked back at her frightened face. Realizing what must have happened, he took a cord from her pack and after looping it though his pack, he made a loop that he slipped over her wrist and at the other end another one that he slipped around Wolf's neck. Reassured that he would not lose them in the snow, he continued to plow ahead. They walked for what seemed like days, blinded by the whirling white. Yani was sure that they must have lost their way in this blinding whiteness when the Knapper stumbled in front of her. Rushing to his side, she helped him to his feet and took his arm. They had only walked a few more steps when she felt what had caused the Knapper to stumble. The land was sloping slightly downward. After staggering from fatigue to the bottom of the bowl that would give them as much shelter as was to be had on this never-ending prairie, they located a few stunted trees. Using the trees and their packs as shelter, they prepared to weather the storm. After brushing away what snow they could, Knut placed Yani's deer hide cloak on the ground and using the bear skin and Knut's sleeping cloak as cover the three of them huddle together to share what warmth was left in their bodies.

Knut had placed the packs so that he could reach into the top of his and doing so pulled out the food pouches. He handed Yani a handful of the whale blubber berry mixture that she had taken to the hiding tree with her back at their summer camp by the sea. Seeing it made her long for the sunny beach of their summer home.

"This will help give you warmth. The people who make this live where the winters are always like this. We must eat as much as we can to help us stay warm. And until the snow covers us and forms a shelter sealing in our body's heat, we must not sleep. Sleep is the greatest danger in the cold."

When they had finished the contents of the pouch, Yani held her hands out for Wolf to lick. He soon had all the traces of the whale fat licked off them. The Knapper wrapped his thin arms around Yani and pulled her close against him. And so with Wolf cuddled close on one side and the Knapper on the other Yani's violent shivering soon began to subside. As they sat there listening to the wind, Yani asked, "Tell me about the Mountains That Are Always White."

Clearing his throat, the Knapper began, "Well, they are tall and jagged. Much taller than any you have seen on this journey. They seem to rise up straight from this vast plain. When this storm clears and we resume our trek, we will see them soon. Perhaps tomorrow evening if the sky clears enough." So the old man comforted the girl with tales of the mountains that neither ever expected to reach until both slipped into an exhausted sleep.

Chapter Six

Yani awoke to a world of silence. At first she could not remember where she was. Her legs and arms cried out to be stretched as if she had been in the same position for days. She tried to remember where she was. She tried to open her eyes but found they were mattered shut. Then she remembered the blizzard and making the shelter. Knut and Wolf should be here too. She had to think. When she had dozed off to Knut's tales of the South Land, Wolf had been curled against her left side and Knut had been behind her to her right. There was warmth radiating from her left but to her right was nothing. Now she was desperate to fight her way back to consciousness. She had to force her eyes open but she needed her hands to wipe the sleep from them. She began by flexing her fingers. They began to sting as if being pricked by thousands of thorns as the circulation returned. Soon she was able to move her hands and, finally, to raise one hand to her face. She rubbed cautiously at one eye and then the other until she was able to force them open. Their shelter was filled with an eerie half-light. She turned her head slowly coaxing her neck muscles to come to life again. Her movement had aroused Wolf who had risen on to his haunches exposing her left side. She had expected the air to be bitter cold but to her surprise it was only slightly chilled. She turned so that she could see Knut's face behind her. It was gray and still. Softly she called his name but got no response. She reached up and touched his face, frightened by its chill.

She was desperate to make her body respond now. Flexing her toes and feet, she was relieved to find that they responded more easily then had her hands. *Wolf must have covered them with his body keeping them warm,* she thought. Carefully, so as not to disturb their shelter, she turned onto her knees and sat facing Knut. Fear gripped her heart as she thought of being alone on this vast plain with no markers to show her the way. Then she was overcome by a terrible sadness. *What would her life be like without this man who had become such a loving father to her?* Quickly, she pushed the thought from her mind and leaned her head against Knut's chest. There had to be a heartbeat. She couldn't lose him like this. Was it her imagination or did she feel a slight warmth? She slipped her hand inside his fur vest and placed it over his heart. Through his woolen tunic she felt a weak pulse. She knew the only hope was to move Knut into the middle of the shelter between herself and Wolf using the warmth of their bodies to bring life back to him. She eased herself around him until she was between the old man and the edge of the bearskin. Sliding her arms under his legs and around his back she lifted him and pushed toward the spot that she had just left. She was shocked at how light his body was. It was almost like lifting one of her little sisters. Quickly she pushed that thought from her mind in her urgency to warm him before it was too late.

Wolf seemed to sense what was expected of him because as soon as she had the old man shifted to the center of the shelter, he curled around the old man resting his head on Knut's lap. Yani slid her arm behind Knut and eased her shoulder against his back. She wrapped the other arm around his chest and then lay her head against his shoulder. Tears stung her eyes as she whispered, "Please don't die, Knut. I need you." She reached up to the old man's cold face with her free hand and softly stoked his cheek. It was so icy cold. She held her hand against first one cheek and then the other trying to warm them. As she looked at the face that had become so dear to her, she whispered. "I love you, Father."

She snuggled against the old man bringing as much warmth to his body as was possible. Soon the silence of the shelter and the exhaustion from the dash across the plains overwhelmed her and Yani drifted into sleep again.

Chapter Seven

When Yani later opened her eyes, it is was to total darkness.
What had disturbed her sleep? She listened and could hear breathing.
There was Wolf's steady sleeping growl. Then she felt a gentle rise and
fall of Knut's chest. She slid her head down until her ear was resting on
his chest. There was his heartbeat. Still weak but stronger than before.
She reached up and rested her hand on his cheek. It was not as cold.
Reassured, she drifted off into sleep again.

It was a savage hunger gnawing at her stomach that woke Yani
the next time. She opened her eyes to find the shelter illuminated by the
same eerie light as the first time she had awakened. She stretched and
sat up. When she looked at Knut, she saw that his eyes were opened.

"So, Little One, we are all three alive." He smiled at her. "But
now we must dig our way out of our nest. The air is becoming stale and
it is time to move on before we get caught in another storm here on the
open Steppes."

Yani raised up on her knees and started to dig through the pack
behind her. Sheepishly, she looked at Knut and asked, "But first, may I
eat, please?"

Chuckling Knut nodded, "That is a wise idea. We both need
some nourishment and then we will see if we can get a fire started to
melt some snow. We need water but you must remember Yani, never
eat snow. It will chill your body and you may freeze. Always melt it to
water first."

Yani had found a pouch of whale fat and after scooping out a
handful, she handed it to Knut. To her surprise, he placed a dollop on
the ground for Wolf before eating himself. Wolf gratefully lapped up
the nourishing mix then licked his chops with his great gray tongue.

As soon as they had finished their meal, Knut reached up and
pushed on the top of the bearskin near the packs. To Yani's surprised it
127

did not give. "You may need to push, too," said Knut. "There is probably a lot of snow on top of us."

Adding her strength to his they managed to force it upwards until they had made a hole at the top of the shelter. As soon as they had broken through the snow, the warmth of their shelter was replaced by a frigid cold. Yani shivered as the icy air hit her body. She started to reach for the bear skin cloak but stopped fearing the snow of the shelter would collapse burying their sleeping cloaks.

Knut had carefully moved her pack to the other side of the snow cave and was clearing the snow from behind it to create a doorway. When he had finished, Yani was able to stand up. She was met with a dazzling whiteness that nearly blinded her. She slowly began to turn taking in the miles of pristine snow when she was greeted by the sight of the distant snowcapped peaks of the Mountains That Are Always White. As she stood there with her mouth agape, she reached out and touched Knut's arm.

"Look!" she breathed in awe.

Chapter Eight

Turning, he followed the direction in which she was looking and when he, too, saw the mountains rising out of the snowy expanse, he smiled at her.

"They are wondrous, aren't they. If the sky stays clear they will be our guides for the next days. In this snow the going will be slow but we should be able to reach the campsite at the edge of the Steppes in five days."

"Five days! But the mountains seem so close. Surely, the snow will not slow us down that much."

The Knapper chuckled, "Even without the snow it would take us three more days to cross the Steppes. Like the depth of clear water, distance on the high prairie is deceptive. I hope we can make it in five days. Going will be hard for we will have to break a trail. Come, we must see if we can find the tops of some of the bushes near the spring to start a fire."

Pulling her sleeping cloak from the ground and wrapping it around her, Yani followed the Knapper through the snow to where the ground was lowest. Wolf bounded after them frolicking in the snow as he went. Yani was the first to locate the top of a branch sticking up from the snow. She began tugging on it until a small twig broke off in her hands.

"We will never have a fire at this rate," she said. "There has got to be a better way. "

She kicked at the snow around where she had been digging and to her surprise is seemed to sink into the ground. She kicked again and more fell away. Then she heard a quiet gurgling. She had found the spring that bubbled up out of the ground. Coming from so deep within the earth, its temperature was always the same; one that was warm enough to melt away the snow from below. She peered into the miniature cavern it made and saw how the trickle of spring water flowed away into the darkness.

"Knut!' she cried. "Look! I don't think we will need to build a fire to get water. See the spring is running."

Wolf had smelled the water as soon as Yani broke the surface and had pushed his way to the edge of the stream and was drinking greedily. Yani, realizing now how thirsty she was, began clearing a wider area. When she could reach the flowing water, she stooped down to drink. The water felt warm on her hands although she knew that if this were summer time it would seem cold. After she had satisfied her thirst, she moved back to let Knut drink. Yani noticed he had trouble standing again he had finished and that disturbed her.

"Are you alright, Father?" she asked, concern showing on her face.

Smiling, he turned to her, "That is the second time you have called me, Father." Gently touching her cheek, he continued, "Yes, I'm alright, it is just that my old joints do not bend as easily as yours. I will be fine as soon as we begin moving." Looking at the position of the sun he said, "If we start right way, we should get some distance behind us. It is still morning, although not early. We will have to make a snow shelter when we stop for the night but if the sky remains clear the stars will provide enough light to see to do that."

Returning to the shelter, he pulled the sleeping cloaks loose from the snow and rolled them. They were frozen too stiff to provide much warmth but tied to the packs the sun would thaw them. Before he tied his to his pack, he took a blade from his pouch and cut a narrow strip from one end. Cutting this in two pieces, he cut two slits in the center of each about three fingers width apart. Yani watch this strange behavior but did not comment. When he had finished, he walked to her and positioning the slits over Yani's eyes tied the strip around her head.

Looking out over the Steppes, Yani realized now how painfully bright the sun had been.

As the Knapper tied the other strip around his head, he explained, "The sun shining on this snow would soon blind us. Although it is only temporary, it is very painful and we can't risk losing the time waiting for our vision to return. This will allow us to see but still block much of the sun's blinding rays."

He removed several strips of jerky from the pack and handed two to Yani. Before starting to chew on his piece, he whistled to Wolf tossing a piece of jerky his way. Then they shouldered their packs and with Knut breaking a trail through the snow started across the sea of white toward the glistening mountains to the south.

Chapter Nine

At first the going was difficult because the snow was nearly knee deep. Each step forward required the Knapper to raise his knees high and then push ahead into the snow. Yani saw that he was tiring so calling to him to stop, she moved ahead to take over. After a few steps, she called to Wolf who had been bounding through the snow in all directions. "Come, Wolf! Here!" Looking at her from the top of a drift, he barked playfully and barreled down at her throwing snow it all directions. He came to a stop just before plowing into her. Expecting her to laugh at his antics as she usually did he looked up expectantly. But the seriousness of their situation kept her from enjoying his play. "Wolf," she said stooping down and putting her arms around his neck. "You must help us. Walk here in front of me and break the trail." The wolf looked at the girl questioningly and watched as she moved off into the snow. She motioned for him to follow and then pointed ahead of her. As if understanding at last Wolf plunged off into the snow ahead of the travelers.

By midday they were all exhausted by their efforts. Even Wolf's strength seemed to be waning. When they came to an area that had been sweep of some of the snow by the howling wind, the Knapper called a halt. Extracting the whale blubber mixture from his pack, he split the last of the pouch into three helpings, handing one to Yani before placing one on the ground for Wolf. They ate in silence too exhausted to speak. Yani gazed off at the mountains, which seemed no nearer than when she had first seen them despite their efforts. Reading her thoughts, the Knapper said, "We have come a good way this morning. Look back along our trail, not at the mountains. That is a better gauge of our journey."

She turned and looked back the way they had come and she felt better for seeing their trail disappearing over the horizon. It was a comfort to know that they had covered so much ground.

As soon as they had finished their meal, the Knapper unrolled his cloak from where it had been tied on the top of his pack. Yani followed his lead with the bearskin and although still cold, it had at least soften enough to allow her to drape it over her shoulders.

"When the sun begins to set the wind will pick up. We will need to have as much of our body's heat from this day's walk trapped inside our cloaks as possible," said the Knapper. With that he shouldered his pack and started off behind Wolf through the snow. Here the going was not as hard since much of the snow had been blown away and they were able to make better time.

When the sun hung low in the West turning the mountain tops a rosy pink, Knut's prediction came all too true. The wind, at first a gentle breeze, steadily increased in intensity until it howled around the travelers. It came from the Northeast and although that helped to push them along their way, it also boded ill since the Northeast wind often brought snow.

As the last rays of the sun faded from the sky, they were in an area with deep snow again. Using a high drift as a windbreak, Knut and Yani scooped out a shelter on its leeward side. Piling the snow in a ring around the other side, they soon had a small shelter to ward off the wind. After eating a handful of dried meat and berries, they huddled together to face the night.

Knut insisted on Yani being in the middle but she only agreed if he would change with her during the night. As before when they were settled as comfortably as possible, the old man began to tell of the summers in the mountains. Yani soon drifted off but before she fell completely to sleep, she told herself she must wake after a short time to make sure Knut did not freeze.

133

Chapter Ten

Sometime later, she awoke with a start. Wolf was standing at her side, his ears alert to something outside their shelter. She turned to the old man to see him sleeping soundly. As she shook him awake, she feared that she had slept too long. But at her touch, his eyes opened at once. He had a dazed expression at first but when she helped him move to the warmth of the center, he went without protest. As soon as they were settled, Wolf again raised his head. Then she heard what had disturbed her sleep, the unmistakable howling of a wolf. Wolf whined but made no move to leave the shelter. Knowing Wolf would alert them to danger, they soon dropped back into an exhausted sleep.

Yani woke from a troubled sleep as the stars began to fade from the sky. As the first streaks of dawn colored the eastern horizon changing it from black to purple to indigo, she stirred. She had pulled her feet up under her in her sleep so they were not as cold as her hands. She longed to be on the move again and have the exertion of the trail warm her body. She did not know if they could hold out for four more days like the last one had been. She turned to Knut and was relieved to see him breathing steadily. She touched his cheek and he came awake immediately.

"Yes, Daughter, I am still with you," he smiled. And with that he stretched his legs and prepared to stand. Using Yani to help him, he managed to get to his feet. He wrapped his cloak around his shoulders before taking some food from the pack. As they ate, they slipped the snow blinders over their eyes. Finishing the last bit of the jerky, they lifted their packs adjusting the carrying straps on their foreheads above the snow blinders. The wind bit at them as soon as they had risen above the shelter of the drift. Yani hoped it would die down again when the sun rose higher as it had the day before.

They started off in silence toward the distant mountains. Unlike the previous day, Wolf needed no coaxing to take the lead but plunge off across the plain as if he had been trained from a pup to break a trail through the snow.

As the sun rose higher, the wind began to die down much to Yani's relief. By midmorning, they had reached another windswept area. With little wind and only ankle deep snow, they were able to move forward at a steady pace. Yani tried to keep from looking at the mountains as she walked, since they did not seem to get any closer as the day stretched on. When they stopped at noon to rest and eat, her eyes were drawn to them and to her surprise, they seemed to be higher. As she gazed at them, the Knapper said, "We have been fortunate to have so many windswept places. I think we may only have two more nights before we reach a village and the last will be in a sheltering cave that has plenty of fire wood." The thought of a fire, even in a cave, was such a welcoming thought that Yani was ready to resume her journey at once.

The sun rode low in the west when the wind again picked up but this time without the intensity of the day before. When darkness over took them, they had come to one of the sheltered camping sights on the plain. They were able to slake their thirst at the spring that bubbled out of the ground, melting the snow surrounding it. Although there was not much wood, they did find a few sticks that they used to build a tiny fire. The Knapper dug deeply into his pack and found the small clay pot he had traded for at one of the villages they had visited and gave it to Yani to fill with water. She placed it in the fire and as they fed twigs into the flame, the water warmed until steam began to rise from the pot. The Knapper stirred in some acorn meal and dried meat and soon they had a warm meal. The hot food gave them the strength to survive another night on the open plain.

Settling for the night, the Knapper did not protest when Yani insisted that he take the middle. They huddled together but unlike the previous nights the Knapper told no tales to lull Yani to sleep. As she dozed with her head against his chest, she heard a troubling sound. The Knapper's chest rattled when he breathed, the first warnings of the coughing sickness that took so many old people to the Other Side. Yani knew that if they did not reach shelter the next night, it could well be too late for the Knapper.

Chapter Eleven

Morning dawned sunny and still. The wind from the Northeast that had greeted them the previous days was missing. In its place was a gentle westerly breeze. Yani slid from under the bearskin and tucked it back around the old man. He stirred slightly then settled back into sleep. Gathering wood for a fire, Yani considered their plight. She had only two options. Should she make a camp here and hope the milder weather held giving the old man a chance to rest or press on to the end of the Steppes and the safety of the cave. When she had enough wood for a good fire, she broke the smallest of the twigs and stirring the coals from the fire of the night, she gently blew on them until she had coaxed a flame. Carefully, so as not to smoother the flame she added wood until she had a lively blaze going.

The Knapper awoke some time later to find Yani stirring a warm pot of acorn porridge. He gratefully took the food from the girl. After he had eaten, they prepared to leave the camp for the last leg of their journey over the Steppes. Yani whistled for Wolf as she picked up her pack but he was nowhere in sight. Knowing it had been days since he had eaten anything except a few scraps, she assumed he was hunting. When he had made a kill and eaten his fill he would return.

At first the Knapper walked at a steady pace, slower than he usually did but none the less a good walking pace. But, by midmorning Yani noticed that he was beginning to tire. He stumbled over every small irregularity in the path. Without a word, she moved up beside him and taking his arm placed it over her shoulder. Smiling weakly, he allowed her to carry some of his weight.

As the morning wore on, Yani carried more and more of the Knapper's weight. By noon his breathing was becoming shallow and raspy. Sensing that he was near the end of his strength she said, "Can we stop for a while? I need to rest a bit and I'm hungry."

Without protest the old man lowered his pack and dropped to the ground. When he lowered his head to his chest, Yani realized that he had fallen asleep. He seemed comfortable enough resting against his pack as he was. She knew he needed to rest but the need to press on weighed heavy on her. She scanned the horizon wondering where Wolf had gotten to and for the first time that morning an edge of concern crept into her mind. Remembering the night they had heard the wolves howling, she feared he had gone to join the pack. Taking a piece of jerky from her pack, she chewed on it. The seriousness of their situation weighed heavy on her young shoulders.

"Father," she touched Knut's arm to awaken him. He was still sleeping soundly but the sun had moved across the sky as far as she dare let it. "Can you walk some more?" she asked gently. "The wind is beginning to shift again and I think we may be in for another storm."

She had decided what she must do. She knew her strength would not allow her to support Knut and both of the packs so she had decided to leave his pack here on the prairie. She would return for it once she had Knut safely to shelter. If they made shelter before nightfall, she was sure traveling alone she could return for it and be back in a half day's time. And if they were farther from shelter than that, it wouldn't matter. Knut would not need the pack if they had to spend another night in the open.

She helped him to his feet and as he reached down for his pack, she took his hand. "I can't support you and both packs. We must leave it for now. I will return for it tomorrow."

He looked into her eyes for a moment and then nodded. She lifted her pack, slipping the carrying strap around her forehead and settled it between her shoulders. She wrapped her arm around his waist and as he draped his arm over her thin shoulders prepared to make the final leg of their journey across the Steppes. As she walked, her eyes roved the endless white hoping to catch a glimpse of Wolf bounding after a hare in his search for food. But, all she saw was endless drifts stretching off to the horizon.

Chapter Twelve

Late in the afternoon, she began to sense a change in the land. Here and there were low shrubs. When she looked toward the south, she could make out a faint line of black between the snow and the base of the mountains. When they reached a small stream trickling beneath its coat of ice, she knew they were nearing the end of their ordeal.

Knut had remained silent as they walked. Only the sound of his labored breathing broke the stillness. He seemed to be concentrating on putting one foot in front of the other. "Stop," he wheezed. Yani stopped and looked up at him in alarm but he was searching the horizon as if looking for a landmark. Then his eyes seemed to find what he was seeking and smiled. Lifting his hand he pointed to a dark object in the distance. "There," he whispered. "That is the marker. Behind it is the trail to the cave. It is not far now. We will make it."

The sun had left the sky and a full moon was creeping over the horizon as they reached the pile of rocks as high as a man's head that served as the marker. Grateful for the moon's light, they continued their slow and tortuous walk toward the safety of the sheltering cave. As they left the Steppes, Yani pushed her worries for Wolf from her mind. He would either return or he would not. She would miss him but if he had chosen to return to his own kind, she would understand. But even as she thought this, tears filled her eyes threatening to over flow and freeze on her cheeks. When the sun had dropped low enough to no longer cause a glare, she had removed the leather strap that protected her eyes. Now they needed all the light they could get to pick their way across the snow-covered landscape.

She had no trouble finding the trail where it started a short distance from the marker. Soon they were seeing bushes and then trees scattered across the terrain. The land itself was becoming more and more uneven and Yani could see a forest looming ahead of her. The mountains which had seemed so close when they were on the high plains now seemed distant with the trees to give prospective. The trail led them into a gully made by a small stream flowing along its bottom. As they followed the stream, the moon cast shadows in the darkness. The creatures of the night began their stealthy activities. An owl hooted from an oak tree that stood like a sentinel in the eerie stillness. A fox watched them pass, then as if disdainful of the two legged animals that had entered his nocturnal domain, turned and sauntered off into the night.

As the night wore on their pace slowed and Yani feared that the Knapper's strength would give out before they reached the cave. Abruptly, the Knapper stopped. He looked around as if awakened from sleep walking. Wordlessly, he pointed to a faint path that led off to the right toward a shadowy blackness in the cliff face high up the side of the gully. Yani breathed a sigh of relief. *We have made it to shelter but have we come in time for me to ward off the coughing sickness?* she thought.

Helping the Knapper up the bank and into the cave took more strength than she had expected but finally they reached the welcoming shelter. She spread her sleeping cloak on a pile of leaves that the wind had blown into the back of the cave before easing him on to it. The leaves would provide some extra insulation from the cold of the ground. She removed the bearskin from her pack and covered him then turn to the task of making a fire. Remembering the firestone and flint, she knelt by the Knapper's side and gently removed the pouch from round his neck. But he was not aware of any of this since he had drifted into a fitful sleep as soon as he lay down.

Returning to the mouth of the cave, Yani quickly collected enough firewood to get the fire started. She knew that was the first concern. Then as the fire took the chill from the cave, she could look for more wood. She was hampered in her housekeeping efforts by the

141

darkness of the cave. Unlike the other cave shelters they had used on their journey, this one was more than just a hollowed out place in the cliff. It had a narrow opening and only where the moon shone its light into the mouth, could she see. Using her hand to locate the fire pit, she soon had a collection of leaves and twigs to get her fire started. Over these she built a twig pyramid as she had seen Knut do so many times before. Holding the stones in the way she had seen him do, she stuck them sharply against each other. A spark jumped out but did not land in the tinder to start the blaze. She smiled a grim smile thinking how easy Knut always made it look. She struck again and then again. Finally on the seventh try the spark cooperated and landed in the dry leaves. Quickly, she began to blow gently at the tiny glow created by the spark. The tiny orange dot spread along the edge of the leaf outlining it in red and orange before eating its way toward the center. Nudging the twigs and leaves against the glow one at a time, Yani gradually coaxed a small flame and her pyramid caught and began to blaze. She continued to add larger twigs until she had a lively blaze. To this she added large pieces of wood which she knew would continue to burn for some time. When the fire was safely started, she again left the cave in search of enough firewood to keep the fire going through the night.

Chapter Thirteen

Her search for fallen limbs that were recent enough dead fall to provide a hot steady fire over a long time lead her further from the mouth of the cave than she had intended to go. She had been able though to collect a full armload of wood. She turned to return to the cave when she realized that she was being watched. A pair of amber eyes glowed from the darkness that separated her from the entrance of the cave. She froze in her tracks. The eyes began to move in her direction. She knew the worst thing she could do, would be to run since that would only encourage the animal to attack. A strange muffled whined slipped from the animal's throat. The animal began to move toward her faster as if preparing to lunge in attack. Dropping her load of wood, she grabbed up a sturdy limb. In the moonlight, a startled Wolf skidded to a stop. Looking at her as if to ask why she held that stick like that when he had brought her a present, he dropped the hare he had been carrying at her feet.

"Oh, Wolf," she breathed as she dropped beside the huge animal. "Wolf" and she buried her face in the fur of his neck and began to cry. All the fear and tension welled out of her in that moment of relief. Wolf turned his huge head and lovingly licked her on the face and neck as she sobbed away her fears- for the Knapper, for her future and for Wolf.

Finally, she regained control and as Yani gathered up the firewood, Wolf reclaimed his catch and they started back to the cave together. She saw as soon as she entered that the fire had done its work making the cave warmer. Knowing the Knapper would need the nourishment of fresh game when he awoke, she took a blade from his pouch and moving to the mouth of the cave gutted and skinned the rabbit. The warmth from the abdominal cavity told her it was a fresh kill. When she had it dressed, she cut a long stick from a shrub growing at the mouth of the cave to skewer it on. She drove one end of the green branch into the ground near the fireplace then bent the branch so she could do the same on the other side of the fire which had by this time burned down to a mass of glowing coals. These would burn slowly all night. When dawn came she would awake to find a tasty hare roasted for breakfast. A very tired Yani crawled under the bearskin beside the Knapper and with Wolf warm against her other side immediately fell asleep.

Chapter Fourteen

It was not yet dawn when Wolf's low growling awaken her. She reached out to touch him and felt the bristle of the hair at the back of his neck. At her touch, he rose to his feet and started toward the entrance to the cave. Yani slid from under the bearskin and clutching the walking stick followed behind him. Staying in the shadows, she peered into the woods around the mouth of the cave. The moon had set and the faint pink glow of first dawn was the only light. She looked down at Wolf to see which direction he was looking and following his lead, peered intently into the gully that led to the cave. At first she could see nothing but then she saw what had disturbed Wolf. Something large and hairy was moving up the trail toward the cave. Slipping deeper into the shadows, she waited to see where it was headed. The movement wasn't quite right for a bear but its form was all wrong to be a man. As it climbed, the path turned to the right and she saw that there was a large hump protruding from the "thing's" back. As it labored up the last bank before coming level with the cave, the weak morning light gave her a look at their visitor. Just as he reached the top, he stopped and looked directly at her. She slunk further back now sure that this was not an animal that Wolf might frighten away but a man.

"Knapper! Hello!" he called much to Yani's surprise. "Are you there? I am coming in. Have that girl of yours hold her Wolf. I am too tired for a fight."

Yani called softly to Wolf, still unsure of how to handle this situation. He obviously knew the Knapper and also knew of her and Wolf. But was he a friend or a foe. The scare with the Seapeople had made her less trusting of strangers. But he continued walking straight toward the cave as if he expected a welcome, so placing her hand on Wolf's neck, she ordered him to stay and moved out of the shadow to meet this stranger.

When she stepped into the light the stranger stopped and looked at her. "So, the Knapper has sent you to greet me. Where is your pet wolf?"

"He is near. The Knapper is in the cave. Who are you?" she asked suspiciously, still clutching her walking stick.

The stranger chuckled, "A friend who has come to find out why the Knapper would have left his pack on the prairie." And with that he swung Knut's pack from the top of his own and onto the ground. "A double pack is a heavy load but the distance was short and the way level. From the tracks I would say that the Knapper is in need of help."

"We were caught in a storm and I am afraid he is developing the coughing sickness. I was going back for his pack today as soon as I found some angelica or perhaps some sunflower roots to make tea for him. I hope the dead stalks might show though the snow to help me find some."

"Well, the pack is here. The roots are another problem. As hard as the ground is frozen, you would need to build a fire over the plant to thaw the ground before digging them."

"I had not thought of that," whispered Yani, picking up the Knapper's pack and leading the way back toward the fire.

"I smell a hare roasting," said the stranger.

"Wolf caught it for me last night," replied Yani. On hearing his name, Wolf moved forward with a low growl.

On seeing the wolf, the stranger stopped. "Wolf, be good," commanded Yani. "This man is a friend."

Wolf quieted down but made no effort to greet the stranger. From the sound of coughing coming from the cave, Yani knew that the Knapper was awake. As they entered Knut broke into a smile at the sight of the stranger.

"So, Deet, you are not smart enough to find a warm hearth to winter at either," said the Knapper in a weak voice.

"And you can thank the gods that I did not or this skinny girl of yours would have had a long journey back to get the pack I found in the middle of the prairie," replied Deet. "Since I lugged this load all the way here, do you think you could spare a leg off that hare you have on the fire."

Noticing it for the first time, Knut looked questioningly at Yani, "So, Daughter, you are a hunter now too?"

Laughing nervously, she replied, "No, it was Wolf. He brought a fresh kill to me as I was collecting firewood last night. It was still warm when he dropped it at my feet so I cleaned it and put it to roast for our breakfast."

"See what good traveling companions I have now," said the Knapper with obvious pride.

Chapter Fifteen

Yani moved to the fire and carefully removed the stick that the meat had been roasting on. The juices dripped into the fire causing it to flame up briefly. The added light was enough to illuminate the old man's face and what she saw frightened her. His cheeks were too rosy in his pale face. She knew that if she were to touch his forehead, it would be hot with fever. She held the hare out to Deet who carefully pulled off a leg and began to gnaw at the meat. She then went to the Knapper and tore the other haunch off handing it to him. He began to tear shreds of meat off with his teeth and slowly chew. Only then did she pull one of the front legs from the hare for her breakfast. She was pleased to see that the Knapper was able to consume most of the haunch before whistling softly to Wolf who eagerly took the offered bone. She and Deet finished pulling the meat from the rest of the bones then gave them to Wolf to finish up.

Looking over at the Knapper, they saw that he had curled back up in the bearskin and was sleeping fitfully. Motioning Yani to follow him, Deet led the way toward the path to the stream. In the moist sheltered gully, she knew they would have the best chance of locating the roots they needed to relieve the old man's congestion and cough. As she followed behind Deet, she wracked her brain trying to think what the old women of her village used for fever. So intent was she on the problem that she did not notice the branch hanging down over the trail until the twigs trailing down from it whipped her face. Reaching out to push them away her eyes focused on the exact thing she had been looking for- the tree was a poplar and the slender twigs were all heavy with winter buds. *Of course,* she thought, *strong tea made from poplar buds is what I need to break his fever. But this can wait until we have found the roots.*

For most of the morning, Yani and Deet searched the edges of the stream looking for the dried flower stalks that might indicate a growth of angelica or sunflower. Twice they had found promising looking stalks but when they dug through the snow, the dried leaves told them that it was not the plant they sought. They had worked their way along the stream, one on each bank, and had almost reached the edge of the Steppes when Yani spotted a large cluster of stalks protruding through the snow. Kneeling at the edge of the stalks, she began to scoop the snow away. Not for the first time that morning she vowed that she would learn all she could about medicine plants at the next village where they stopped and over the summer collect and dry all that she would need in the future. When she finally broke through to the withered vegetation below, she saw the heart shaped leaf of the sunflower and even found a brown flower head that had fallen from the stalk.

"Deet, here!" she called. "I have found some sunflowers." She eagerly used her cold hands to shovel the snow from the area around the plant she had found. When Deet reached her, she had uncovered several plants.

He dropped to the ground beside her and using his skinning blade began to chip at the rock hard earth. After several tries he gave up.

"It is too solidly frozen. We will have to build a fire."

Yani moved quickly to collect enough dried wood to build a good-sized fire. She was concerned that they had been away from the Knapper for so long but also knew the roots were necessary to ward off the coughing sickness that she feared. As Deet used his firestone to start the fire, she looked for a poplar tree to begin collecting buds. If she collected here while they were thawing the ground to get at the roots, she would still have the ones near the cave for later.

By the time the fire had died to ashes, she had a pouch full of plump winter buds. Deet brushed the hot ashes away with a stick and using his skinning blade again tried to dig the roots out of the earth. This time the ground gave more easily and soon he had several roots pried loose from the ground. Yani placed them in a different pouch than the buds as Deet wiped his mud covered hands in the snow to clean them.

Before they reached the cave, they began to hear the ragged coughs of the Knapper. As they entered the Knapper greeted them with a weak smile from his place on the sleeping cloaks. Yani took the water basket and returned to the creek for water to make the tea and cough syrup that the Knapper would need. As she retraced her steps to the cave, she decided she would begin with the poplar buds. She had only to crush them slightly before steeping them in hot water to make a tea. She would need to wash the roots then rub off the thin bark before crushing them and allowing them to simmer to remove the healing juices. The poplar bud tea could be working on Knut's fever while she made the cough medicine. She wished she had some honey to add to sooth his throat too but she knew that the chance of finding a bee tree in the winter was not likely. As soon as she reached the fire, she put the clay pot filled with water in the fire to heat. Using a large flat rock as a base and a smaller one for a hammer, she gently crushed the buds and added them to the water. Soon she had a layer of crushed buds in the bottom of the pot and the pungent smell of the steeping tea filled the cave. Picking up the other pouch, Yani returned to the stream to wash the sunflower roots. Kneeling in the snow, she broke the thin ice that had formed over the opening she had made early when she had come to get the water. The icy water numbed her fingers as she scrubbed the dirt from the roots. As soon as she had them clean, she hurried back to the cave and gratefully held her cold red hands to the fire. As the warmth returned to her fingers, she saw that Deet had poured some of the tea into the Knapper's eating bowl. The old man was sipping the warm liquid. As the steam rose off the hot tea, he inhaled deeply sending its aromatic warmth to his lungs.

She knelt by the rock she had used to crush the buds and began to rub the roots across its rough surface. As she rubbed she slowly turned them until she had all the protective skin worn off revealing a clean fibrous root about the diameter of her finger. She laid this to one side and began to clean another. As she worked Deet came over to the fire and handed her another pot that he had taken from his pack.

"This will make the heating of the water easier than if you have to put rocks into the basket. With two pots you can keep a fresh supply of tea and still make the sunflower root medicine," he said.

Yani smiled her thanks and the look in Deet's face told her that he shared her concern for the old man. She looked over at Knut and saw that he had finished his tea. He had pulled the bearskin around his shoulders and was dozing where he sat by the fire's warmth. She filled the pot with water from the basket and placed it in the fire. The water would be heating as she finished preparing the roots. After the roots had boiled for a time she would allow them to simmer until dusk, producing a thick syrup. She hoped that the winter roots still had enough of the healing goodness to help the Knapper. She had never known the women of her village to gather the roots in the winter. It was during the summer and early autumn that plants were collected and dried. As she rubbed the roots back and forth over the stone, she tried to block out the fear that her efforts would be too little and too late.

When she had finished cleaning the roots, she placed three of them on the platform rock. The others she returned to the pouch to be used later. She began to pound them, one at a time, with firm even blows. She had to be sure to bruise the tissue enough to release the healing juices when she placed them in the water but not so much as to force the juices from the roots during the pounding process thus losing them.

As she finished with each root she added it to the pot of warm water. Finally she was done with the preparation and now she had only to wait. Wolf paced nervously from the firepit to the mouth of the cave until Yani could stand it no longer. "Go on!" she cried. "You can go run." He looked at her as if to ask "Aren't you coming too?" then giving a short bark turned and bounded toward the entrance of the cave. As he disappeared round the bend in the passageway, Yani called, "And you can bring us another hare for supper too. Or better yet a deer." She turned back to her work chuckling.

Chapter Sixteen

She checked the pots, stirring the contents of the one containing the roots and moving the tea back a bit so that it would stay warm but not boil away. She added a few more sticks to the fire to keep the heat constant around the pots. As she worked with the fire, she yawned. The lack of sleep and exertion of the days on the Steppes began to tell. She took some jerky from a pouch in her pack and, after handing the pouch to Deet, began to eat. As soon as she had finished the meat, she walked over to where Knut was sleeping and curled up beside him. She dropped off to sleep immediately.

The pungent smell of herbs mixed with that of roasting meat woke her from her sleep. She lay there for a few moments enjoying the warmth of her bed before opening her eyes and stretching. The Knapper was sleeping soundly beside her and when she looked over toward the fire, she saw Deet stirring the coals under a deer haunch on a spit over the fire. Sitting up she asked, "Did you go hunting while I was asleep?"

Chuckling, he replied, "I didn't have to. Your friend over there took you at your word."

Yani looked to where Deet was pointing and there at the entrance of the cave lay Wolf chewing contently on the lower part of the leg that Deet was cooking. When Wolf saw that she was looking his way, he stood up and whined as if to say, "Aren't I wonderful?"

Yani shook her head as she walked to his side. "Good boy, Wolf. You are so wonderful." She rubbed his huge head and scratched behind his ears.

Yani returned to the fire and checked the contents of the pots. She saw that the pot with the tea was almost empty. Looking at Deet she asked, "Has he drank more or did it boil away?"

"No, he had two more bowls while you slept. His breathing is ragged at times but the tea seems to be helping the fever. You will need

153

to make some more soon. He only sleeps a short time before he begins to cough again. It will take longer for the cough medicine to take effect."

Yani checked the water basket. It had enough water to refill the pot for the tea. When she had done that she took the pouch containing the poplar buds and crushed a handful, placing them in the pot. She then took the basket and went to the stream to fetch more water. Her breathe made clouds of steam, as she left the warmth of the cave. She hurried down the bank toward the stream, the cold nipping at her thin body. When she reached the stream, she saw that the ice had again sealed off the water and she picked up a rock to break an opening. This time it took several tries to crack the clear covering of ice. She filled the bucket then turned back toward the path up the bank. The wind bit at her as she hurried back to the protective warmth of the cave. The first snowflakes began to fall as she reached the entrance.

The next day, they awoke to the sound of the wind howling outside the entrance to the cave. When Yani went in search of more firewood, she quickly returned to the fire empty handed.

"It is snowing too hard," she told Deet. "I am afraid if I go out to look I will get lost in the snow."

Deet looked at the dwindling pile of wood and nodded, "I will go. Wolf, come."

Looking at Yani for approval, Wolf rose to follow the man.

While they were gone, Yani busied herself preparing more of the sunflower root for Knut. She checked the pouch of poplar buds and was relieved to see that there were still plenty of them. As she pounded the tough root on the table stone, Knut rose and moved over beside her at the fire.

"Are you feeling better, Father?" she asked as he joined her there.

"I think so," he replied. "I wish we had made it to the village before this storm struck though. It will make the traveling difficult."

"We can always stay here until the snow melts. We have enough food, there is water and when it stops snowing I can easily find enough wood," she suggested. "At least we are not still on the Steppes." The last she added in a whisper.

Hearing the fear in her voice, the old man replied, "Yes, Daughter, for that we can be thankful."

Yani moved to the fire and took the pot of tea from its place at the edge of the flame pouring some of the hot liquid into the Knapper's eating bowl. Handing it to him, she said, "Try to drink some more of this, it will make you strong and help your sickness."

"Thank you, Daughter."

Chapter Seventeen

The Knapper had gone back to the sleeping cloaks long before Deet and Wolf finally returned with more wood. As they staggered in, snow covered and exhausted, Yani was startled to see Wolf dragging a large supply of wood behind him. Seeing her expression, Deet's gaze followed hers, "I will explain..." he began but found he didn't have the breath.

"Later," said Yani as she began to untie the thongs that held two long poles to Wolf's shoulders. On these poles, Deet had piled as much firewood as he could find before lashing it down. As soon as Yani released Wolf, he dropped down by the fire, exhausted. Taking the pot of hot tea from the fire, she poured a bowl for Deet. "Here," she said, "This will warm you. I will get some snow to melt then cook some acorn porridge to go with the deer meat left from last night." Picking up the water basket she moved to the entrance of the cave.

When she returned, Deet had finished the bowl of tea and had fallen into a sound sleep where he sat by the fire. Getting his sleeping cloak from the back of the cave, she draped it over his shoulders to help keep him warm. She set the basket next to the hearth to melt, added more wood to the fire then wrapping in her sleeping cloak curled up beside Wolf by the fire also. Soon all of the travelers were sleeping soundly while the storm raged outside their shelter.

Knut's coughing awakened Yani. Dragging herself back to the reality of the storm locked cave from her dream of a warm summer day by the sea, she hurried to his side. Kneeling by him she placed her ear against his chest. It still rattled some but not like it had when they had first arrived at the cave. Sensing her presence, the old man opened his eyes and smiled at her.

"Would you like some more tea?" she asked.

"That would be fine, Yani, but what I would really like is something to eat. Do you have any more of that venison from last night?"

Going to the fire she took the haunch of roasted deer meat from the hide she had wrapped it in the night before and pulled off several pieces. Taking these to the Knapper she returned to the fire and poured the last of the tea into his bowl. After she had taken this to the old man, she added water to the pot and set it to boil while she searched the packs for some acorn meal to make a hot porridge for their supper.

Chapter Eighteen

Later that evening, when they had all had a good filling meal, the Knapper joined them by the fire. As they huddle together around its warmth, Deet suddenly asked, "Knapper, are you strong enough to tell a tale?"

Chuckling, the old man replied, "When the day comes that I am too weak to tell a tale, you will know I have traveled to the Otherside."

"Then can we hear The Old Woman and the Bear?" asked a hopeful Deet.

"Now why did I know that was the one you would ask for?" chuckled the Knapper. "He always asks for that one," he said in a false whisper to Yani.

Clearing his voice and taking a sip of the hot tea, he began. "In the days before the People built houses but always lived in caves, an Old Woman discovered that her family had become too large to live comfortably in their cave. What with her daughters having babies and her sons bringing home new wives. So she called them all together around the fire. When they had all assembled she began, 'This cave is much too small for all of us. Some of us must move on.'

" 'But Mother,' began the oldest son, 'this is my home. I was born here and as the oldest son I should be allowed to stay. Make her move,' he said pointing to the youngest daughter.

" 'But, Mother,' began the youngest daughter, 'I am your baby. I should stay. She is fat and lazy, make her move,' and she pointed at the oldest daughter.

"And so each child demanded their right to stay while suggesting another brother or sister should be the one to move on. Soon they were all squabbling and quarreling over who should move and who should stay. Hating all loud noises and commotion, she called for them to be quiet. But, being selfish, willful children, they ignored her. After

158

she had called many times and they still ignored her, she cried, 'May the Great Bear of the Sky take you all.' Picking up her sleeping cloak, eating bowl and a few other essential items, she left the cave in disgust.

"As she wandered looking for a new cave to live in she became angrier and angrier with her ungrateful family. 'They should be looking for a new cave, not me,' she muttered as she walked. As the sun was setting in the West, she saw the mouth of a very fine cave up ahead. Looking around she saw that it was just perfect. There was a fine spring bubbling out of the ground beside the entrance to the cave. A few steps below it was a babbling brook that flashed with the silver bellies of trout as they jumped after flies. Looking at the trees she saw within a short walk nut trees, persimmons and elm to make elm bark tea. Elm bark tea was her very favorite tea. So she had found it- the perfect cave. Shuffling up the path to the cave, she chuckled with her joy at having found such a perfect place.

"She dropped her belongings inside the cave and gathering up some firewood near the mouth, she soon had a fire blazing in the firepit she had built. She filled her cooking pot with water from the spring and began to make her evening meal. As she sat on her sleeping cloak and watched the cheerful flickering of the fire, a huge bear came lumbering up the trail.

" 'Old Woman,' he roared when he saw her, 'what do you think you are doing smoking up my cave with your cooking fire?'

"Seeing this Great Bear so near, she knew she had to think quickly. She replied, 'Your cave! But surely a Great Bear like yourself would have a much larger, finer cave than this?'

"Looking around the bear asked, 'What do you mean a finer cave?'

"'Well, see for yourself, this is such a tiny cave it is only fit for a tired old woman. Now a Great Bear, like yourself, would need a much larger cave. One that is large enough that all the animals of the forest could come and hear the wise words of the Great Bear and obey them.'

"Now this Great Bear was also a very vain bear. Looking around he noticed that his cave was indeed rather small. Trying to imagine all the animals of the forest crowding in here to listen to his wise words was difficult. 'Hum, perhaps you are right. But where would I find such a cave?' asked the bear.

"'Why I saw just such a cave earlier today on my search for a humble place for an old woman such as myself to live. If you follow my scent back the way I came, I am sure you will find it,' answered the Old Woman, smiling to herself.

"And so the Great Bear followed the Old Woman's scent until just as night fell he found a magnificent cave. One that was big enough for the Great Bear that he was. And when he got inside he found a feast there waiting on him, a feast made up of many tasty ungrateful children. And the Old Woman lived happily in her small cave by the babbling brook."

"And so, Little Yani, you must remember to always be grateful and respectful of your elders or the Great Bear of the Sky may sneak into your cave at night and gobble you up!" said Deet and with a menacing growl grabbed Yani sweeping her high into the air. As she let out a startled squeal, Wolf lunged at Deet snapping at his leg in warning. Deet quickly set her back on the sleeping cloak as Yani called to Wolf to stop.

"Wolf, it's alright. He was only playing!"

"Easy, Friend," said Deet in a calming voice. "I will not hurt your girl."

But Wolf remained watchful as Knut continued, "Well, Deet, I don't think Yani has to worry about the Great Bear. To begin with she would never be the ungrateful whelp that you were the first time I told you that story and even if she was, she has a defender that would gladly take on the Great Bear to protect her."

"I can see that," replied Deet rubbing his calf.

"Did he bite you?" asked Yani. "Let me look to see if the skin is broken. An animal bite can fester and make you sick if it isn't cleaned."

She knelt by Deet and pulling up the leg of his trousers looked over his calf carefully. "No, he did no real damage. But I am afraid it will be bruised tomorrow."

"Don't worry, Yani, Wolf was only reminding me to mind my manners. Come here. Wolf, let's make up," said Deet with a soft whistle.

With a playful bound Wolf was at Deet's side ready to have his ears scratched. Laughing Deet roughed the fur on the back of his head and soon they were rolling on the floor of the cave like two young pups.

"I guess all is forgiven," said Knut with a smile.

While Deet and Wolf continued to play, Knut wrapped up in his sleeping cloak and curled up by the fire. Yani yawned, and after a few moments, she too prepared for the night. After a while the man and dog tired and they, too, joined their sleeping companions.

The travelers spent three days holed up in the cave while the last snowstorm of winter raged outside. During the forced rest Knut regained some of his former strength. On the fourth day, bright sunlight streaming in the entrance of the cave woke them. By mid morning the air had taken on a promise of warmth and so they prepared to resume their trek to the Mountains That Are Always White

Part 4
The South

Chapter One

"This one!" said Yani with a smile as she pointed to the small pile of dried leaves on the edge of the deer skin robe.

"How do you know?" asked the old woman sitting opposite Yani.

"The smell. It is like the feel of snow- all tingly and cold."

"That is a good description," laughed the old woman. "Catnip is like the other mints. They are all tingly.

"Now what would you use for a burn?"

Yani considered for a few moments then pointed to a long, oval shaped leaf. "That one! Slippery root."

"Good! And what would you do with it?"

"You could tear the fresh leaves into small pieces and pour enough hot water over them to just cover them. Let them set until the water cools. When they are cool put them on the burn. Or if it is winter, use the dried leaves to make a very strong tea. After you have steeped it, mix it with honey and animal fat. That makes an ointment to apply to the burn. Am I right?" asked Yani, looking hopefully at the old woman.

"Yani, you are quite right," she agreed enthusiastically. "You are also the best student that I have ever had."

Yani beamed at the praise from the old woman. As they continued their question and answer lesson, Knut and Wolf emerged from the forest behind Yani to join them in the warm spring sunshine. He watched with obvious pride as Yani correctly identified the proper herb for each of the ailments that the old woman named.

"Well, Gyla, what do you think of my smart daughter?" ask Knut.

Turning to smile up at Knut and hug Wolf, she looked back to see the response of her teacher as Wolf dropped down on the ground at her side.

163

The old woman answered, "I think she will make a fine medicine woman. As soon as the plants start to reappear, she will begin to learn in earnest. Most of my dried herbs are gone and the most important lesson is how to find the correct plants. There are many that can easily be confused with harmful plants. I'm afraid you will not see much of Yani in a few weeks. I'm going to steal her away from you."

"No," replied the Knapper, "I cannot let you steal my Yani, but I will let you borrow her for a few months. Just until it is time for us to start our journey back to the sea. I need Yani on that journey," he said and a knowing look passed between the old man and the old woman.

"Yes," she replied in a hushed voice, "I can see that. I will take care to teach Yani all she will need to know for both of your journeys to come."

Something in the tone of their voice drew Yani's attention away from the herbs she had been studying. She was about to ask what they had been saying but something in the look on their faces told her to hold her peace.

Seeing her troubled expression, Knut reached out and patted her reassuringly on the shoulder. As he did so he realized how tight the woolen dress was across her shoulders. Looking at her, he suddenly became aware of how much she had grown since he had bought her that long year ago. Shaking his head and chuckling, he said, "Gyla, my old friend, I think before you take my Yani wandering through the meadows and hills in search of roots and leaves for your brews, I had better do some trading to get her a new dress. She is about to break out of this one like the butterflies she love break out of their cocoons."

"I was wondering if you were going to notice that or if I was going to have to point it out to you," she scolded. "Why don't you go see that new wife of Han? She is the one he brought back from his trip over the Mountains five summers ago. You remember, with the dark skin and eyes?" Knut nodded as he recalled the strangely beautiful

164

woman that Han had brought back from his last trip south. "She makes the most remarkable cloth. Each summer she grows a patch of flowers, they are as blue as the sky, and then in the fall after the flowers drop off, she cuts the stems and hangs them to dry. When they are dry, she takes them to the pond at the other end of the meadow and soaks them until they turn positively rotten. The stench is awful. When they are putrid, she pulls them out and rinses off the outer flesh of the plant and dries them. When they are dry she bends .."

"Enough!" cried Knut. "I don't want a lesson in making cloth. I will take your word for it that the fabric she makes is wonderful. And if you are finished with your lesson, Yani and I will take the best of the blades that I have left and see what we can do." With that he slowly pulled himself to his feet using the walking stick for support. Yani jumped quickly to her feet and helped him stand. Each time she helped him up she became more aware of how thin he had become.

"May I go now, Gyla?" ask Yani before turning to follow Knut who had started to shuffle off toward the other end of the village with Wolf at his side.

"Of course, Child," replied the old woman with a smile.

Chapter Two

Later that afternoon when they arrived at the house of Han and his dark eyed wife, they found her sitting before her loom. She hummed softly to herself as she moved the shuttle across the length of warp threads stretched tight by stones that hung at the bottom. Yani watch in fascination as the nimble fingers seemed to fly between the thread moving the smooth wooden shuttle full of yarn through the maze of threads until it reached the other side. There she made a quick loop around the last warp thread before starting it back the way it had come. When she turned slightly to begin the shuttle's return trip through the maze, she noticed her visitors. Smiling an acknowledgment of their presence, she continued her weaving until she had reach the other side of the warp. There she unwound a length of the yarn from the shuttle and placed it on the broad beam that formed the base of the loom.

"Good day," she said in a soft, silky voice. "I welcome you to my husband's house. He is not home at the moment but if you care to wait I will be honored to bring you some tea." Yani was fascinated by the sound of her voice. The rhythm of her words reminded her of the soothing sound of the sea. There was a song like quality to the ebb and flow of them as she gently greeted her guests.

"Thank you, for your welcome. My daughter and I would be most grateful for a bowl of tea but it is you we have come to see, not your husband," answered Knut formally.

"Oh," this lovely dark eyed woman replied. "I do not often have guests, especially not strangers to the village. But you are most welcome. Please be at ease while I prepare tea for you."

"May I help you?" asked Yani, reluctant to let this remarkable woman out of her sight.

"That would be most welcome," replied Han's wife as she led the way into the house.

As the two women disappeared through the doorway to prepare the tea, the Knapper lower himself to a log opposite the door. As he listened to their voices, the thought struck Knut that Yani had indeed grown into a young woman on the journey to the South. She was now eleven summers old. In a year or two the young men would be seeking her out hoping to win her for their wife. Watching her help to make the tea at the fire pit through the open door, he knew she was going to make someone a fine wife. Smiling he recalled Birg's gift of amber before they left the Village in the Marsh last fall. *He had had the look of a young pup in love for the first time,* mused Knut. *He would make a fine husband for Yani.*

What am I thinking? Here I am speculating on a husband for her when she is still a girl. There is plenty of time. Or is there? He knew this trip north would be his last. He hoped to make it to their home by the sea and there he would stay until he made the trip to the Other Side. *Yani could easily make her way to the Village in the Marsh when that time came. It was only a long day's walk. And with Wolf to protect her, she has little to fear. They would have to dry extra fish and berries to get them through the winter if they were to stay at the sea. They would also have to improve their shelter. The winter winds come off of the sea, damp and cold. If they made a framework of wood and then wove mats they could cover them with pitch to keep out the moist sea air and.......*

"Father!" Starting, he looked up to see Yani smiling down as she extended a bowl of streaming tea to him.

Returning her smile, slightly embarrassed, he accepted the tea. "Thank you, Daughter. I am afraid my mind was miles away and I didn't hear you."

As Yani sat down by the Knapper, their hostess joined them there in the late afternoon sun. "I am sorry that I forgot my manners. I am called Hava. And you are Yani, the girl who tamed the wolf and the Knapper who travels the forests. I have heard many tales of you. The

167

most recent how this beautiful girl of sunshine lead you off the Steppes in the midst of a raging blizzard and cured the coughing sickness saving your life," said Hava in her melodic voice.

"Oh, no!" cried Yani, "it was not like that at all. The snow had stopped and I could not have made it without my father showing the way. And he did not have the coughing sickness yet. I just kept him warm and gave him tea. It was really nothing. "

"I take it Deet has been entertaining you with his tales again," chuckled Knut. "He tells a better tale than the facts would have it."

"So I suspected," smiled Hava. "But you said you had come to see me. How can I be of help to you?"

"As you can see, Yani is in need of a new dress and I am told that you make the most wonderful cloth in the village. I had hoped to trade some blades for cloth enough to make a new dress for her. As you can see, she is nearly splitting the seams on this one."

"Yes, I have some fabric that would be suitable for a dress for Yani, the Wolf-Tamer. I will go and fetch it for you to see." Hava placed her bowl on the ground by her loom and entered the house. In a few moments she returned and lay a soft golden and cream cloth on Yani's lap.

"It's beautiful," whispered Yani. "It is like sunshine! But it is much too fine for a dress for me. I need a strong fabric that can stand the days on the trail."

"Don't be deceived by the look of it. This is a much stronger fabric than the woolen dress you are wearing. See the creamy threads that go this way," said Hava pointing to the threads that ran the length to the cloth. "That is from the flax plants that I grow. It is much stronger and softer than wool. And the yellow is wool that I dyed using chamomile and yarrow flowers. This will make a fine dress for a girl of sunshine who can tame a wolf."

"This is the last of my blades. Look and see if they are sufficient to buy this wonderful cloth," said Knut hesitantly.

As Hava looked politely at the blades spread before her, Yani gazed at the wonderful cloth. *It is the same warm gold as the stones that Birg gave me,* she thought. *Of course, the stones! The one with the butterfly I can't part with but the other would be an adequate trade.* Reaching to her neck she pulled on the raw hide thong drawing the small pouch in which she kept the stones from her dress and removed one of the glowing golden stones.

"Would this be an acceptable trade?" asked Yani hopefully. "It was given to me by a friend before I started this journey. He gave me two but I can't part with the other one. But perhaps one will be enough?"

Hava reached out and took the stone from Yani. "It is lovely. I have seen such a stone only once. In my homeland the wife of the chief of the ten tribes came to our village and she wore such a stone from a chain around her neck. It is more than enough for the cloth. For this I will also sew the dress for you. Is that acceptable."

The smile on Yani's face answered for her.

Chapter Three

"Knut!" Yani called as she ran to catch up with him, Wolf trotting at her side. "Look! Isn't it beautiful?"

Watching her approach, he marveled at how pretty she looked in the new golden dress that Hava had just finished making. As she spun to let him see it, he nodded in agreement. "Yes, Yani, it is indeed beautiful. A beautiful dress for a beautiful young woman." The last he whispered to himself.

"Look what else Hava made for me? See now I can wear my butterfly stone," she cried holding up the amber. "She took some of the threads made from her flax and knotted them so that they hold the stone."

"I am sure it will please Birg that you are wearing his gift," teased the Knapper.

Blushing, Yani quickly changed the subject. "Gyla is waiting to teach me more about healing herbs, I must go."

Knut watched her run through the meadow toward where Gyla was sitting in the sun waiting. Looking down he saw that Wolf had stayed at his side. Roughing the fur on his neck, Knut asked, "Wolf, how would you like to go for a walk with an old man. It looks like our girl has left us men to fend for ourselves this afternoon." Wolf answered with a gentle whine. The two travelers started down the path toward the stream, Wolf slowing his pace to match the shuffling gait of the old man.

The briskly flowing stream that bordered the village brought with it flints that the Knapper used to make his blades. This was his southern source of raw materials for his trade. With Wolf playfully splashing in the stream, Knut began to follow it working his way along the water's edge. Several times he found a likely looking rock and used his foot to nudge it into a cleared area where it could be spotted easily on his return. He had not gone far when he began to tire. Finding a flat rock in the sun, he sat down to rest. It worried him that he had not regained his strength. If he did not begin to grow strong, he feared he would not be able to make the trek north again.

He watched Wolf's antics until his breathing became less labored then whistling for Wolf, he turned to retrace his steps to the village. As he walked back along the stream bed, he collected the flints that he had found on his upstream journey. Soon the weight of the rocks and the exertion of the walk forced him to rest again. By the time they reached the village again, he was too exhausted to begin the process of chipping off the flakes for the blades he would need for the winter's trade.

When Yani returned to the small house that the Knapper used when he was here on his bi-annual visits, she found him sleeping soundly on his bench. She gently touched his forehead to see if he was feverish again and was relieved to find his forehead cool. Covering him she picked up the pouch of rocks from the floor where he had left them. As she did so she wondered if she could learn to make the flakes for him that he would need to shape into blades. She had watched him for hours during their summer by the sea. She knew what a good flint looked like, perhaps she could learn the flaking process, too. Covering him against the chill of the coming evening, she slipped out of the house and headed towards the stream that she knew was the source of his flint

With Wolf at her side, she followed the stream until the sounds of the village had faded away, then to be sure she would not be discovered, kept walking for a while longer. When she was sure she was far enough not to be detected, she began looking for a usable flint. Soon she had found one that satisfied her. She looked around for a flat rock to use for a platform and then a rounded hammer stone of the multicolored rock that the Knapper used. When she had all the necessary tools assembled, she sat on the ground by the table rock and placed the flint

171

firmly in the middle. As she raised the hammer stone to make the first strike, she whispered a prayer to the God of the Hunt asking his forgiveness for entering the realm of men. She made a solid hit chipping off a large section of one end of the flint. As she looked at the results of her first hit she knew that the God of the Hunt had blessed her work since the flint now had a prefect flat end to use as the base. Setting the flint upright on the base she again whispered a pray, this time a pray of thanks. She struck the flint again causing a thin weak flake to fall off. Examining it, she knew it was not a usable flake. Taking aim again she struck once more. This time the flake was better but still not the perfect flake that Knut produced. *But,* smiled Yani to herself, *Knut has been doing it for many more years than I have. This is only my first try.*

Wolf soon lost interest and wandered off into the woods in search of game. Yani was so intent on her task that she did not notice him go. Nor did she notice the hunter as he watched from the edge of the forest.

Chapter Four

When the sun began to slip below the western rim of the mountains, a very tired Yani made her way along the stream bed back to camp. She had processed four flints during the course of the evening and from those had only managed to produce five usable flakes. She felt she should have been discouraged but instead was excited. She knew that with practice, she would be able to make flakes that were as good as the Knapper's.

As she entered the house, the Knapper was sitting by the fire inspecting one of the flints he had gathered that afternoon. He looked up as she came in and asked, "Where have you been, Daughter? I have been worried."

"I am sorry, Father," she replied shamefaced to have caused him concern. "I came back from Gyla's and you were sleeping so I went for a walk up the stream towards the mountains. My mind was wandering and I forgot the time."

"And did you have a pleasant walk? I too walked that way today but my walk was more of an ordeal than a pleasure."

"Yes, it was a very interesting walk," replied Yani. Changing the subject she said, "You must be hungry. I will make us some supper."

While she prepared their evening meal, the Knapper began chipping flakes off the flint he had been examining. When he stopped to inspect his work, Yani asked, "When you first started to learn to be a knapper, how long did it take to produce a good flake?"

Chuckling, he answered, "It seemed like forever but if I remember correctly it was only several weeks. I had a nice pile of flint chips around our house before the old Knapper pronounced my work acceptable." Remembering the long ago day, he looked up at Yani. The look on her face told him she wanted to ask more.

"Why do you ask, Daughter?"

Hesitating she replied, "Would it be possible for a girl to learn to be a knapper?"

His penetrating gaze made her uncomfortable. Since coming to live with the Knapper, she had never kept anything from him. She felt she should tell him the whole story but feared his reaction. As he looked at her, he noticed small splinters of flint clinging to her dress. Smiling he said, "How successful were you?"

Blushing, she pulled the flakes she had made from her pouch and handed them to him. He examined each one with care then looked up at her, a mixture of surprise and pride on his face. "These are very good! I could not produce such flakes until I had been working at it for a full summer. This is your first try?"

Yani nodded her reply.

"Tell me," demanded the Knapper.

"I saw how tired you were when I came home. As I was moving your pouch to its place by the fire, the idea struck me that perhaps I could learn to make the flakes and ease your work some. So I went up the stream far from the village and tried it. I was afraid at first since I knew the God of the Hunt cursed women who tried to do men things. I asked his forgiveness before I made the first hit. He must have approved because it was almost a perfect hit. Of course from then on it was harder but I knew I had to learn how to do it on my own. After many tries and four flints I was able to produce these. Are they useable?"

"They are more than useable, Yani. They are very good. But you were right to be secretive about this. I am not too sure if the village elders would take kindly to a girl making hunting tools. For now this will be our secret. When it is possible, I will teach you all I know. And don't be too concerned about the God of the Hunt. I think he is more concerned with a successful hunt than who makes the tools."

Just as Yani was finishing cooking supper, Deet's head appeared in the doorway of their house. "Do I smell acorn porridge with rabbit in it?" he asked.

"Deet, come in and join us. I have never known Yani not to cook enough to feed one more," called the Knapper.

"I was hunting in the forest today and have several plump squirrels. I thought maybe I could persuade Yani to put these over the fire," he said as he held the dressed squirrels out to the girl.

"Thank you, Deet, "she said. "They will go well with the porridge." Taking them she threaded the spit of hickory wood though them and place its ends in the two forked uprights at each side of the fire pit. As they settled by the fire to wait for the squirrels to cook, Yani said, "Deet, you never told me how you got Wolf to pull the fire wood back to the cave. I have often wondered how you thought to do that."

"And I, too," added the Knapper.

"Actually it was more Wolf's idea than mine," laughed Deet. "As I was stumbling back though the forest with this big arm load of wood I kept dropping the long branch, I was pulling. Finally, when I had dropped it for the third time, Wolf took it in his mouth and began dragging it behind him. I was walking backward watching him when I tripped over another branch about the same size. As I sat there in the snow with my backside freezing, I came up with this brilliant idea. If I tied the branches on either side of Wolf, he could also carry a load and we could have enough wood that I wouldn't have to go out and freeze the rest of me to go with my frozen backside."

"Do you think if I had straps of raw hide that his head would fit through and attached them to two long pole he might be taught to pull a load for me?" asked Yani.

"Are you thinking of a load about as heavy as the Knapper's pack?" asked Deet, grinning at her. "For you, Yani, I think he would pull Knut's pack with him attached to it. Wouldn't you, Boy?" Deet said as he patted Wolf's head.

"Would you like me to make straps to fit him?" asked Deet. "If it works I may have to try to tame a wolf, too."

"That would be wonderful. I would love to try it," replied Yani.

When they had finished the last of the squirrel and had licked the porridge bowls clean, Deet looked over at Yani. He cleared his throat and using the sing song voice of a storyteller launched into a tale.

"Once in the days before the People, when animals had not yet learned their roles on Earth, there was a beautiful yellow butterfly. Now this butterfly was not only beautiful but she was also very clever. She knew how to find flowers when other butterflies could not. She could fly higher than any of the other butterflies and do many other things that ordinary butterflies could not do.

"One day while she was flitting from flower to flower she noticed a honey bee visiting the same flowers from which she was gathering nectar. In the morning, the bee was at the purple morning glories going into one then buzzing away only to return a short time later to stop at another.

"After watching this puzzling behavior for a most of the day, the butterfly asked the bee, 'Why do you keep coming and going from the flowers? Wouldn't it be better if you were to stay at the flowers until you had drunk your fill of nectar?'

" 'You silly, butterfly,' he replied, 'all you do is look pretty and drink nectar. Of course that is as it should be. But we bees have a different purpose. We make honey from the nectar. The honey then can be used as food.'

" 'Oh, how wonderful,' cried the butterfly, 'please, show me how to make honey, too!'

" 'You make honey!' laughed the bee. 'That shows how silly you butterflies are. Only bees make honey. That is as the Creator wished it.

176

No, you must look pretty and drink nectar. Making honey is a bee's job.'"

When Deet paused in his story to shift into a more conformable position, Yani squirmed uneasily. She did not like the direction this story was taking.

"As the bee flew away toward his hive, the butterfly followed. She was determined to learn to make honey, too. For days she watched in hiding until she learned all the secrets of how to make honey. Then flying far from the hive, she collected nectar from the flowers and finding a hollow tree hid there and taught herself to make honey.

"Now a wise Raven also lived in that hollow tree. When he saw that the butterfly had learned to make honey, he trembled with fear for her. He knew that the bees would become jealous if they knew that not only could a mere butterfly make honey but her honey was by far sweeter then the honey they made. He feared that if they discovered this they would come and kill her with their spear-like stingers.

"The Raven knew he had to warn this beautiful yellow butterfly of the danger she was in, so coming to her at night, he whispered his warnings to her in her sleep.

" 'Butterfly, you must go far away from the bees before you try to make honey,' he whispered. 'Go to the sea where the wind will blow the bees away and there it will be safe for you to make your honey. Do not make honey here where the bees will see. You are too beautiful and clever to be killed by bees.'

"The next day the butterfly woke with the memory of the Raven's words in her ear. Leaving her hollow tree, she flew far way until she came to the sea. There she made her honey and lived a long and safe life."

As he finished the story, Deet added another piece of wood to the fire. The three friends sat in silence for a while thinking of the message in the story.

Finally, Yani looked over the flames at Deet and said softly, "Thank you Raven, I will be more careful in the future and not make honey until we return to the sea."

Smiling at her, he added, "I think you would be safe here but in other villages you may not. I know that Gyla, Hava and I would all speak for you before the elders but some of the young men would be very jealous since they all try to make blades and have little luck. If you continue to learn here in the house, it would be safer." Turning to Knut he continued, "How long has this butterfly been a knapper?"

Knut broke into a rumbling laugh before he answered. "Let me see, I came home to my nap when the sun was about half way between its higher point and setting. She taught herself sometime after that!"

"I think then, my old friend, that this butterfly is going to make honey much sweeter that the old moth that she has watched so closely."

Yani stood in the door of the house and watched the rain. It seemed to be falling in sheets, blocking the mountains from view. Returning to the firepit, she added a few twigs to keep the small fire going thus providing light for them to see by. "Will this rain ever quit?" she asked Knut. "It has been days since I have seen the sun."

"Patience, Yani," replied the Knapper. "We need the rain. It has been dry for too long. Didn't you notice how brown the grass had become?"

"Yes, I know, we need it. But couldn't it come in smaller batches with some sunshine in between?" she lamented.

"Come I will show you how to work one of your flakes into a knife. That will take you mind off the weather and it is unlikely we will have visitors on a day like this. Wolf will warn us if anyone is coming."

Yani sat down beside the Knapper and watched while he finished putting the edge on the spearhead he had been working. "When you finish the blades, you must hold the deer antler point just so. See how the end meets the flint at an angle? Then you must not be timid

178

when you use the hammer stone. At first you will split some of the flakes. I still do from time to time but usually they are flakes that have weak spots in them. Better to split them while working them than to have them split while they are being used."

So as the rain beat on the roof of the house, bringing moisture to the land, Yani continued her instruction as a knapper.

Chapter Five

"Stand still, Wolf!" commanded Yani. "This is going to be a fun game. Let me slip this over your head."

"I am not sure you have him convinced," laughed the Knapper as he watch Yani trying to slip the harness that Deet had made for Wolf over the reluctant animal's head. "Keep talking to him though. The sound of your voice is reassuring, if not convincing."

"I hope I got the fit right. I couldn't think of any way to make it adjustable. I probably should have tried to fit it as I went," said Deet.

"There, Wolf, see that wasn't so bad. Now for the poles," continued Yani in her calming voice. She lifted first one pole and then the other, tying the ends of the strap around the stubs of limbs that Deet had left at one end of each pole. Wolf gave Yani a questioning look, as if to asked, "OK, now what do we do? This doesn't seem like a fun game to me."

When she had the poles lashed in place, she walked away from Wolf and turned back to him. In a cajoling voice, she called to him, "Here Wolf. Come!"

Hesitantly, he took one step towards her but as soon as he felt the drag of the poles, he stopped. He looked around to see what was causing the drag then shook his head in an effort to free himself from the harness. When that was unsuccessful, he began to chew at the leather straps. "No! Wolf! Stop that!" called Yani. Obediently Wolf stopped his chewing and looked at her. Again, she called to him urging him to come forward.

By this time several of the villagers had gathered to watch the spectacle. Among the watchers was Hava. After several futile attempts at making Wolf move forward with the poles attached, Yani walked to his side and took hold of the harness. Gently, she pulled forward while encouraging him to move. He took several steps but, to the amusement of the watchers, as soon as Yani let go, he stopped. As Yani pleaded with Wolf to come to her, Hava slipped away from the crowd. The harder Yani tried to get Wolf to come to her the more the group, made up mostly of men, laughed. Yani was almost to the point to admitting defeat when Hava returned. Quietly walking to Yani's side, she held out her hand. Yani looked down and saw that she was holding several scraps of meat. "I think this may be your answer," said Hava in her melodic voice.

"Of course," smiled Yani. "Wolf is a male. They will do anything for food."

As the two women giggled, Yani let Wolf smell the food in her hand. Walking several paces away, she extended her hand toward Wolf and called softly. This time he took several steps forward before stopping to shake his head trying to dislodge the poles. Again Yani called and this time Wolf closed the distance between them without stopping. Kneeling beside him, she patted him and handed him one of the scraps of meat. "Good Wolf," she crooned all the while. "Such a good boy! Now let's try again."

Yani again backed away several paces and stopped. This time when she held out her hand and called he came directly to her before stopping. Once more she praised him and gave him a scrap of the meat. As the crowd lost interest and dwindled away, Yani continued to work with Wolf. By the end of the afternoon he was following her wherever she went without the reward of meat scraps.

Chapter Six

That evening when Deet joined them for supper, he brought with him several rabbit pelts that he had stretched to dry. As he laid them by the fire, he asked Yani, "Do you think you could work these into some moccasins for me? There should be enough to get new moccasins for you too and perhaps a vest for the Knapper. His vest is about to fall apart. It seems to me that is the vest he wore the first time he came to my village when I was a small boy."

"It is not quite that old," retorted Knut. Then looking down at the vest that had more bare areas than fur covered ones, he continued, "But I can see that I do need a new one."

"Let me have the pelts and I will get started right away. From the looks of you, a new vest would be in order, too."

"I was thinking I may go into the mountains in search of a bear. There is nothing like a bear skin to make a warm vest," mused Deet.

"But not now. Supper is ready."

As they ate, Yani and Deet discussed the success she had had with Wolf and the trailing pack. Not sure what steps to take next Yani asked Deet's advice.

"I think you should continue to harness him for a while each day. When he is used to the trailing pack following, him start adding weight to it. He needs to be comfortable with pulling weight before you start the journey north."

Deet and Yani ate in silence for a few moments then Deet added, "You will not be able to travel as quickly, I think. Also, I am not sure if it will travel well in deep snow. Even with me pulling too it was difficult to get the wood back to the cave that day of the snowstorm. Knut, have you considered the possibility that you will have to spend more time on your move north?"

The old man pondered this as he chewed on a squirrel leg. Finally he said, "Yes, that has been on my mind. I think that we may have to spend the worst part of the winter in one of the villages on the way. The question is which village."

"I know which village I do not want to spend the winter in," declared Yani, startling the men by the strength of her statement.

"And which one is that?" asked Deet.

"The village by the stream full of trout that had no weirs out and the children were hungry and listless. You remember, Knut, it was the village we went to just after Wolf saved us from the bear."

"Oh, yes, that village. I promise you, Yani, we will not be staying in that village. After this last visit I have decided to avoid it all together," replied Knut.

"I wanted to ask you about it but the way was so hard the day we left that I needed my breath just to climb. Then as we traveled my mind was so taken by Wolf and his nightly visits that I forgot. But now we have time. What was wrong with the people in that village? They all seemed so strange. They even looked different." Yani paused to consider then continued, "No, that is not right. They did not look different, they all looked alike."

"And," said Knut, "that is the problem. It is a very strange village, but it has not always been that way. The Old Knapper told me that in the days of his grandfather's grandfather, the people were much like those of any village. They caught the fish and planted grain and hunted the forests. That all changed when a new shaman was born into the village. This was said to be a very powerful shaman since all the time that his mother carried him a great ball of light with a long sliver tail could be seen in the sky. As her time neared it faded until the night that he was born it disappeared from the sky never to be seen again.

"As he grew to manhood it became clear that he was not a natural man but one that had no interest in women. This had always

183

been a sign of super natural power. The old shaman began to test him when he was thirteen summers, all of which he passed. As he grew and matured his power became more and more evident. He saw visions and heard voices. The messages he was said to receive from the gods demanded that people of his village follow a new life style or the village would be punished by a terrible storm. It would come in the form of a serpent cloud that would tear the trees from the ground by their roots and carry off houses and children.

"The people thought that the shaman surely was reading the signs wrong since what he was demanding of the village was unnatural. He said the spirits had told him that the people of the village should isolate themselves from the other villages of the People. They should take wives only from their own families. The marriage codes of the People had always required that a man take his wife from a clan different from his and now this shaman was demanding they ignore a law that had been followed as long as there had been People.

"For many moons the shaman continued to preach this message until one afternoon he told them that they had two days left to change their ways or the serpent cloud would come to punish them. The village was uneasy but no one was ready to accept his new ideas. The morning of the second day dawned to an unnatural stillness. The air was heavy and sultry with little wind. As the day progressed, it became hotter and more humid until late in the day the sky turned a peculiar yellow. The village was distressed when one of the young men returned with a new bride ahead of an angry black bank of clouds. When the shaman saw the new couple, he called to the heavens to send the serpent cloud.

"As the couple entered the village, the story goes, a long thin cloud snaked down from the sky and when it touched the tops of the forest, huge oaks and cedars splintered like twigs. The people watched in horrid fascination as it curved and slithered its way toward the village. Soon, the mysterious cloud was ripping houses apart. When it

184

reached the young couple, where they stood frozen with fear, it sucked them up into the air and they were never seen again.

"From that day on, the people of that village married only within their families. The serpent cloud has never returned and the shaman has long ago gone to the Other Side but the people continue to follow his commands. Each generation has begun to look more and more alike, to have less energy and, it would seem, less intelligence. I have also noticed more children with crippled legs and strange speech patterns.

"And that, Yani, is the story of the village by the trout stream where the people do not fish," concluded the Knapper.

The three friends sat in silence for a while thinking over the tragic plight of the village when Yani whispered, "Is there nothing that can be done to save the children?"

"Perhaps if a new shaman came who could convince the people to go back to the old ways but short of that, no," replied the Knapper.

"The village will probably die out before that could happen since the daughters of the other tribes would not marry a man from that village now, even if they changed," added Deet. "And you can be sure that I would not marry one of their woman."

"I was not sure you were interested in marrying any woman," teased the Knapper. "Not that any woman would have you with your wandering ways."

"You never know," replied Deet, "I may find a woman like Yani who would be glad to travel with me. You don't have an older sister do you, Yani?" he asked.

"No," she answered, "only younger ones, but I don't think they would like to travel even if they were older."

"Then I guess I will just have to wait for you to grow up so I can steal you way from this ugly old man." Standing and stretching, Deet started toward the door. "Good night, friends, I need to get an early start if I am to get a bear in time for the pelt to cure so Yani can make me a

185

vest this summer," he called over his shoulder as he ducked out the door.

Yani sat by the fire in silence for a long time after he left.

The Knapper watch until he finally broke the quiet by asking, "Why the serious face? Are you worried that he will try to steal you away."

Giggling at the idea Yani answered, "That's not it. What I was thinking was that I don't think you're ugly at all."

This time it was the Knapper who laughed.

Chapter Seven

As spring blossomed into summer, Yani added to her knowledge of plants. With Wolf by her side, she roamed the meadows and forests at the foot of the Mountains That Are Always White. On her treks she collected plants to dry for use in the winter and from time to time chose a flint nodule to make into blades at the fireside in the evenings. Some days she allowed Wolf to roam free but on others she harnessed him to the poles that she hoped would carry the packs when they began their travels north at the end of the summer.

While Yani rapidly gained knowledge and skills, the Knapper was slowly gaining his strength. Gyla prepared teas to augment the meals that Yani prepared. Each day Knut would walk farther from the village as he searched for flint nodules.

One evening as their meal sizzled over the fire, the Knapper said to Yani, "Do you think Wolf is ready to carry a pack for a half day's walk?"

After some deliberation, Yani replied, "Yes, I think he will. I have not added much of a load to his poles yet. Sometimes if I have a big load of plants to dry I will tie them to the poles but they are never heavy. But we can try. Where do you want to go?"

"I thought we could try to do some trading to prepare for the trip north. We both have some blades to barter, although I think it better that you don't mention that some of them are yours. And since the village your mother came from is only a half-day's walk that might be a good place to start. I think my legs will carry me there if you think you would like to go."

The smile that lit up Yani's face was answer enough to tell the Knapper that tomorrow they would be traveling again.

"Hold still Wolf!" cried Yani in exasperation as Wolf walked away from her. "It is not going to kill you to carry this pack. If you don't let me tie this down we will never get on the trail!"

"Can I help?" asked the Knapper as he emerged from the house with both their walking sticks. Joining Yani he leaned them against her pack and knelt to hold Wolf's head.

"Wolf, old boy, we men must help each other." As he patted Wolf's head he slipped a small scrap of the rabbit they had for supper the night before from his pocket and held it under Wolf's nose. As Wolf licked at the meat, Yani secured the pack in place on the poles.

"At last!" she sighed as she got to her feet. Handing Knut his walking stick, she settled her pack in place and, stick in hand, they started on their way.

By midmorning it was clear that they were not going to make Yani's mother's village in a half-day's walk. The Knapper was not able to keep up his normal walking pace. When they reached a rapidly flowing stream, Yani suggested they take a rest. As Wolf lapped at the water, Yani helped the Knapper to a flat rock in the sun.

"I can see that I am not as strong as I had thought," said the Knapper. "This may not have been such a good idea after all."

"We are in no hurry," replied Yani. "I brought our sleeping robes so, if we must, we can always stop for the night and finish the journey tomorrow."

After drinking, Wolf dropped down on the ground. Although strong, he was not used to pulling a heavy pack yet. While they rested, Yani explored the stream bed. She had only gone a short distance when a flash of movement caught her eye. Peering into the pool formed by a curve in the stream, she saw the outline of a large trout. Although the clear water looked shallow, she remembered her lesson from the day she had tried to pick up the colored stone from the bottom of the pool on their journey here. Tucking the hem of her dress into the belt at her

188

waist and taking off her moccasins, she slid one foot into the water feeling for the bottom. She was pleased to find it was not quite knee deep. She eased her way to the side of the pool where the fish lay. As she moved forward, she circled so that she was approaching the fish from behind. Bending over she dipped both of her hands into the water until they were in up to her elbows. Slowly, she approached the trout. The icy water numbed her feet and hands as she continued inching forward, her movement barely perceptible. Inch by inch she moved closer to the sleeping fish until her fingers were almost touching its smooth belly. With a sudden lunge, she grasped the fish and tossed it onto the bank where it landed on the rocky shore and flopped around frantically. Scrambling out of the water to where the fish struggled to get back into the water, Yani picked up a rock and quickly ended the fish's struggles with a sharp blow to its head. Picking up the fish by the gills, she carried it back to where the Knapper watched.

"That is a fine fat trout you've caught," said the Knapper. "It will make us a nice lunch."

Yani laid the fish on a flat rock then took her knife from her pouch. Expertly she slit the fish's belly and removed the entrails, tossing them to Wolf. Then she used the blade to scrap the scales from the fish. When she had the fish cleaned, she broke a hanging tendril from a nearby willow tree and threaded it through the gills before tying it around the top of her carrying basket. She squatted at the edge of the stream and washed her hands then joined the Knapper in the sun. She laid back on the rock letting the sun warm her cold hands and feet.

"Tell me about my mother's village," she asked the Knapper.

"Let me see what I can remember," he began. "It has been many years since I have been there. It is not one I usually visit any more. The last few years the men who needed blades have come to me over the summer to do their bartering. But if I remember it is much like our village. The people are friendly and most of the villager are related to you in one way or another."

"That will be strange," said Yani. "In my village I had only two cousins. My father had only one brother and his wife died after the second child was born. My uncle took a second wife but they never had a child."

"I think I am rested now. If we don't get on the trail, we will never get there."

Yani picked up her pack and whistled to Wolf. This time he followed willingly as they waded the stream and continued along the trail through the woods on the opposite side.

Chapter Eight

The sun was just past its zenith when the travelers again stopped for a rest. While Knut rested Yani gathered some firewood to build a fire to roast the fish over. As soon as she had the kindling laid and a pyramid of twigs over it, Knut handed her the flint and firestone.

"You are going to have to get used to making your own fire someday," smiled Knut. "Perhaps you should carry them in your bag from now on."

"But, you will be here to make the fire for a long time yet," protested Yani.

"For a time yet, but I am not sure that it will be a long time." Knut smiled at her and reached out with a finger stroking her cheek. Yani smiled back at the old man for a moment, then turned to the task of making the fire. As the fish cooked, the Knapper took his sleeping cloak from Yani's basket and stretched out on the grass in the sun. Soon he was sleeping peacefully. Yani went over to Wolf and removed the harness from him to let him have some freedom before they resumed their journey. He shook himself and gave Yani a wet kiss before wandering off into the woods, exploring the interesting scents that littered the forest floor. As he nosed his way into a thicket, Yani called. "Now don't go too far or be gone too long, we still have a long way to go."

When the fish was done, Yani called to the Knapper. "Father, it is ready."

The old man sat up yawned and stretched. Smiling at Yani, he said, "I feel much better now. And that fish smells delicious."

As he started to rise, Yani called, "Stay there, Father, I will bring it to you." When she was settled on the robe beside the Knapper, she propped the stick between her knees and pulled off a steamy, flaky piece of fish and handed it to the Knapper. Then she pulled off a piece for herself and popped it into her mouth.

"Nothing tastes better than fresh caught trout," mused the Knapper, reaching for another bit.

Soon there was nothing left of the fish but the head and bones. Yani got up and tossed the stick into the brush at the edge of the clearing. She whistled for Wolf and picked up the sleeping robe. She had just packed it back in her basket when Wolf came bounding out of the woods. He trotted to her side for a pat and then walk obediently to the pole and waited to be harnessed.

As Yani slipped the straps over his head she crooned, "Wolf, you are such a good boy. I'm so proud of you."

Turning to the Knapper, she asked, "Are you ready, Father?"

"I think I will do fine now. If I remember correctly it is not much further. We should be there long before sunset."

Chapter Nine

The sun was tinting the snow on the mountain tops pink when they at last entered the village. Although the villagers had heard of the Wolf that traveled with the Knapper and his daughter, they still created quite a stir when they entered the village. Hearing the commotion, the chieftain came out of his house to greet the visitors.

"Knapper, it has been many years since you have been to our village. You are most welcome. But I must say that I am surprised to see you. I had heard that you were not well since you were trapped in the blizzard on the steppes."

"You heard correctly. But I am better now. I still do not move as fast as I once did but then that is a normal problem as we get older."

"How true," chuckled the chieftain. "But if you have been ill why make the trip to our village when you know the young men would bring their goods to you to trade?"

"I have come to bring my traveling companion and new daughter to meet the people of her mother. This is Yani, daughter of Suti and Gret."

Shyly, Yani stepped forward to greet the chieftain. "I bring greeting from my mother to her family."

Looking at the girl, the chieftain said, "Yes, I can see a likeness in her to Suti. Welcome Yani, I am, Tenk, the brother of your mother. Come both of you. You must be tired and hungry after your journey. My wife is one of the best cooks in the village. Yani, we have much to talk about. It has been years since I have heard from my sister."

As the Knapper followed Tenk into the house, Yani removed the harness from Wolf. He shook himself and circled three times before dropping to the ground. She patted him, then turned her attention to the Knapper's pack. When she had it untied from the poles, she leaned hers against the side of the house and carried the Knapper's pack inside. As she entered she heard the Knapper saying to Tenk, "And so that is how Yani came to be traveling with me."

"What was the man thinking to sell his daughter for a few blades? And how is it that Suti allowed it? I am not saying that you are not a good man, Knapper, but she is only a child. If she were a woman then it would be natural."

"Uncle," interrupted Yani softly, "my mother could not have stopped it when my father had made his decision. Had she tried he would have beaten her. I am not unhappy with the bargain."

Tenk started to make an angry reply but thought better of it. The girl looked well and happy. Instead he said, "Come, Yani, sit here and tell me of my sister and her family."

Settling herself on the bench near the Knapper, Yani began, "When last I saw my mother she was well. I have two younger sisters but no brothers. That is a disappointment to my father. Perhaps that is why he is cross with my mother so often. The village is a prosperous one. We have a well and a growing flock of sheep."

While the Knapper dozed, Yani told her uncle of life in her village, answering his questions about his sister.

The fire had burned low and the rest of the family and the Knapper long since curled up on the bench to sleep when Tenk was finally satisfied with the news of his sister. Yani stretched and yawned. "Where am I to sleep, Uncle?" she asked.

"What am I thinking to have kept you talking for so long! You must be exhausted. Do you have a sleeping robe or should I wake Meta to get you one."

"It's alright. I have my own in my pack. I will fetch it now."

"Then I think you should be able to find room with the girls to sleep. I will bid you good night," he said. Standing he put his arm around Yani's shoulder and continued, "It is good that you have come. Tomorrow you will meet others of your family."

Chapter Ten

Yani awakened to the sounds of the household stirring as the first birds of morning began to sing. She lay on the bench beside the youngest of Tenk's three daughters wondering if her mother had been frightened as she left this village for the long journey to her husband's village to the north. Her mother had never talked of the trip or how she had met her father. She would ask Tenk if the opportunity arose.

Finally she stretched and being careful not to waken the sleeping children slipped from the bench to join Meta at the firepit.

"Good morning, Aunt," said Yani. "Is there something I can do to help you with breakfast?"

"Good morning, Yani. Did my husband keep you up all night talking?" asked Meta with a smile.

"Well, not quite all night," replied Yani. "It was good to talk of home. There is so much that I had not thought of for so long."

"Yes," mused Meta, "that is the way when we first go to another village to begin our life as a woman." Then giving the girl a thoughtful look, continued, "But you were hardly a woman. Was it difficult?"

Yani was silent for a moment, looking down at the fire before answering. "At first I was terrified. I had never been far from the village before and I did not know how the Knapper would be. But soon I found him a kind and gentle father. It has been good. I have seen more than I ever dreamed. Much more than most girls do in a lifetime. It is good."

"That will make your mother happy when she can learn of it. I know it seemed that she had abandoned you but believe me Yani, it hurt her terribly to do it. No mother wants to give up her child."

"I understand that now," replied Yani.

A comfortable silence settled between the two women as they watched the fire and considered the plight of women. After a while the sleeping family began to stir and Meta roused herself from her thoughts

195

to prepare the family's breakfast. "Yani, would you please go to the stream and get the water. The basket is there by the door."

Picking up the pitch-coated basket, Yani smiled her answer. As she emerged from the house, Wolf greeted her as he came from under the bench by the door. Patting him as he fell in beside her, they walked side by side to the stream. Wolf noisily lapped at the water as Yani filled the basket. Straightening and stretching, she breathed the crisp morning air. Even in the middle of summer the air here had the smell of snow in it. Returning to the house, she marveled at the beauty of the snow covered mountains outlined against the rosy morning sky. She wondered how her mother could have stood to leave this beautiful village.

When the family had finished breakfast, Tenk announced to the Knapper, "You can set up on the bench by the door with your blades. I will let the men of the village know that if they wish to trade, they should come to you."

"I should object to your offer but I realize after the difficulty I had on the trail yesterday that I will have to start changing my ways if I am to continue with my trade. Your suggestion is a wise one," replied the Knapper.

When Yani had the Knapper settle in front of the house, Tenk said to her, "Well, Yani are you ready to met your family?"

" Yes, please," smiled Yani.

As they walked off to make the rounds of the family, the first of Knut's customers joined him on the bench in the sun.

Chapter Eleven

"Thank you for your kindness, Uncle," said Yani as she was placing the last of the bartered goods in the pack. "I am so glad I got to know my mother's people. When I see her on the journey north she will be overjoyed to hear the news."

Following her out to where Wolf waited to be harnessed for the trip, Tenk asked, "Are you sure that the Knapper can make the trip to the North Sea. I am told it is a long and difficult trip. He can't have many summer's left."

Gazing off at the mountains, Yani thought for a time before she replied. "I think it is his wish to spend his last days at the sea shore. It is a beautiful restful place."

"But what will you do when he has passed to the Other Side?" her uncle asked.

"I will live at the shore," answered Yani, confidently.

"But how can you do that? You are just a woman and scarcely that."

"I will know what to do when the time comes," replied Yani. "Perhaps I will become a knapper."

"A knapper!" cried her uncle. "Is that possible! Can a woman learn to make blades?"

"What would you think if a woman were a knapper, Uncle?" asked Yani, guardedly.

"I don't think..." began Tenk. Then he stopped and looked closely at his niece. "Would the God of the Hunt permit such a thing?" he asked. "I wonder?"

Yani stooped by the Knapper's pack and removed one of the knife blades she had made. Handing it to her uncle, she said, "Here is a gift for your kindness."

Looking closely at the blade, he saw that is was very well made. He examined it carefully as Yani placed the harness over Wolf's head and attached the poles to it. As she stood up to get Knut's pack, she saw that Tenk had taken his old knife from his pouch and was comparing it to the blade that Yani had given him. Looking up at the girl, he said, "The technique is the same but there is a subtle difference between the two. As if they were made by different knappers."

Smiling at him, Yani softly said, "Use my gift in good health, Uncle."

A knowing looked passed between the two before the rest of the family began to gather to bid the travelers goodbye.

Chapter Twelve

It was a very weary old man that finally entered Gyla's village in the late afternoon. Feeling a need to build his endurance for the coming journey, he had insisted on fewer rest stops on their way back. Yani was concerned but knew he was right. When they reached their house, he went without protest to his sleeping bench and let Yani help him lie down. By the time she had removed the harness from Wolf and brought in the packs, the Knapper was sleeping soundly.

Yani unpacked the Knapper's sleeping cloak and gently covered him. Then she turned to the tasks of unpacking and preparing supper. As she was gathering firewood, she met Deet returning from his day of hunting.

"So, you are back," he said when he saw Yani. "How did Wolf do?"

"Wolf did just fine, but Father had a very difficult time. He tired so quickly it was nearly dusk when we got to my mother's village," replied Yani.

Deet frowned at that bit of news. "That's not good. Do you think you can talk him out of going North?" he asked.

"No," replied Yani. "I think he wants to go back and make the journey to the Other Side there."

They walked in silence for a few paces then Yani turned to Deet and asked, "Do you think Wolf could carry Father if it were necessary?"

"Perhaps," responded Deet. "Maybe not right now since he is just becoming used to the harness but in time as he builds muscles."

"And as Father becomes less. Oh, Deet, he is so thin."

The man reached out and placed a comforting hand on Yani's shoulder. Both knew that there was nothing either of them could do to ward off the future.

Yani was up early the next morning. After preparing some breakfast that she left at the edge of the fire so it would stay warm, she took a knife and started up the valley. She had had a restless night sparked by concern for the old Knapper. Toward morning she had come up with an idea and was anxious to put it into action. With Wolf at her side, she headed for a tangle of grapevines she had seen in her foraging for plants.

When at last she reached the tangle of vines, she took the knife from her pouch. Selecting a vine that was still young enough to be flexible but mature enough to be strong, she cut its base and wound it into a coil. Using the end to tie it off, she laid it on the ground and cut another. When she had a dozen coils of vine, she slipped them over her arm and whistling for Wolf, started back down the valley toward the village.

The Knapper was sitting in the sun eating his breakfast as Yani entered the village. He looked at her load with interest as she joined him. "You have been busy this morning," he said. "But we don't really need more baskets and those vines are too big to weave well anyway."

Smiling, she teased, "For the basket I have in mind, they will be just perfect."

Sitting down on the ground near him, she took the knife and began to strip the bark from the vines. The Knapper watched her with interest but decided she would tell him of her plan when she was ready.

Soon she had all the vines smooth and clean. Taking the poles that attached to Wolf's harness, she propped them against the side of the house not quite the length of her arm apart. Picking up one of the coils of vine she split the narrower end and using the two halves tied it securely to one of the poles. Being careful not to the move the poles, she began to wind the vine back and forth between them. When she ran out of the coil she was using, she laid the end along one of the poles and picked up another. Splitting the end of this one, she tied it to the pole

200

over the end of the last one thus securing them both. Soon she had a mesh of vine almost as long as she was tall laced between the poles. Using this as a warp she wove more vines over and under these vines until she had a strong woven basket between the poles. She called Wolf and when he obediently walked over to the poles, she slipped the harness over his head. This time when she attached the poles there was a sturdy sling between the poles to support any load she chose to place on it.

She went into the house and soon returned with several empty baskets that she tied to the grapevine mesh. Turning to the Knapper, she asked, "What do you think of my new idea?"

"I think that is a very useful plan. But what are you going to put in all those baskets today?"

"I haven't decided yet. I may just fill them with rocks!" laughed Yani as she started off toward the meadow. The Knapper's laughter followed her as she left the village.

When she was sure she was out of view of the village, she stopped and knelt by Wolf. Taking his head in her hands she said, "Wolf, you must learn to pull a much heavier load. There may be a time when you will have to carry Father on our journey North. Today we start building your strength."

Leading him to the stream, Yani gather up several large stones and placed them in one of the baskets. "Now we can go see what plants we can gather today."

As the summer passed and signs of early autumn showed in the forest at the foot of the mountains, Yani and the Knapper began to make plans for their journey. Yani had made the pelts that Deet provided into new moccasins and vests for the men and a vest for herself. Deet had indeed killed a bear that Yani had fashioned into a handsome vest using the claws as decoration. The village had had a feast of the meat the night after he had returned staggering under the weight of the heavy load.

They had dried meat and fresh acorn meal packed away. Yani had used the scraps of the hides to make many small pouches, which held the herbs she had collected and dried under Gyla's supervision. As she rolled the bear skin that Loki had given her what seemed like years ago now, Hava entered the house.

"I have come to say my goodbyes," said Hava.

Looking up from her packing, Yani smiled. "You are most welcome but we don't leave until tomorrow."

"Yes," replied Hava, "but I am not fond of goodbyes. This is better. I also brought you this." She held out a small pouch.

Taking it, Yani said, "Thank you, Hava, but you have given me so much already."

"Open it and look inside," she said. As Yani opened the pouch, Hava continued to explain. "Those are flax seeds. The plant I make my cloth from. They will not grow enough plants to make cloth the first year but if you collect the seed at the end of the season, you will soon have enough plants to make your own cloth. You must remember to plant them very close together. You want the plants to grow tall with few branches. You watched me harvest the plants and ret them. The spinning is much like spinning wool but you must keep your fingers wet. It is easier to work with then."

"Thank you, Hava," said a tearful Yani.

"I shall miss you, Yani Who Walks with the Wolf. Go in peace," said Hava. She placed her hand on Yani's head and quietly sang a few words in her language. Smiling, she turned and left the house.

As dawn broke over the mountains, the people of the village all gathered to bid goodbye to the travelers. Many knew that this would be the last time they would see the Knapper. Yani had Wolf harnessed and the Knapper's pack tied securely to the carrying platform on the poles.

As she was settling her pack in place on her back, Deet rounded the end of the house carrying his pack.

Looking somewhat sheepish, he said, "I decided since I would be going that way in a few weeks anyway, I might as well leave a little early and have company on the trail. At least until we get across the Steppes."

"Your company will be most welcome," replied the Knapper. Yani could only smile her thanks.

So amid tearful goodbyes, their journey north began.

Part 5
Return to the Sea

Chapter One

The early morning sun made long shadows as the travelers stepped from the shelter of the autumn forest to the edge of the Steppes. They had spent the first night on the trail in the cave where the travelers had first met. That morning as they left the village they had quickly fallen into an easy pace, one Knut could keep without too much effort. Nonetheless, by late afternoon he had become exhausted requiring frequent rests. As soon as he had eaten a bit of jerky, he had wrapped in his sleeping robe and gone to sleep. As the night sounds had whispered though the forest, they had all curled up in their sleeping robes around the fire. They had slept soundly despite the ache of muscles unaccustomed to the demands of the trail.

Now they were beginning their journey in earnest. Standing by the rock stele that marked the beginning of the Steppes, Yani looked out over the vast plain and a shiver ran through her lean body. They had survived the Steppes last spring. Would they be so fortunate this time? She turned full circle and surveyed the landscape. Looking back the way they had come, she noted the color in the trees. The reds and golds of the maples, the browns of the oak and the bright yellow aspen, all reminded her that winter could not be far away. The colors were breath taking as they played against the background of the mountains blazing white in the morning sun. The fresh snowfall of the night before caused them to glisten.

Sighing she turned back to the plain. "I guess we should go," she said somewhat wistfully.

"As always the wise Yani is right," joked Deet. "We should get started if we are going to make it to the first campsite by evening."

The Knapper only stood up resignedly and picked up his walking stick. Wolf, who had been waiting patiently in his harness looked from one human to the other, waiting to follow where they would lead.

Yani started north from the stele in the direction of the first marker when to her surprise, Deet called, "Where are you going?"

Turning she saw that the men had begun walking parallel to the edge of the forest along the margin of the Steppe. "But that is not the way north?" she protested hurrying to catch up.

"No, but the markers we must follow north are further into the setting sun. If we were to follow the southern markers we would soon be lost. Think how they worked."

Joining the men, Yani thought of the stones that marked the way across the plain. On the way south they had made a turn at each marker but she remembered the markers had pointed the direction to the next one, not the previous one. She now saw that following the markers back would be impossible. Looking out over the wide featureless plain she was thankful not to be traveling alone. She still had much to learn about this wandering life.

Their shadows were only half as long when they at last turned toward the plain to begin their journey north. The warmth of the sun and the exercise soon had Yani sweating. She fell easily into the slow pace they were keeping but the grim determined look on Knut's face caused her concern. She knew this would be a very difficult trek for him. She also had come to realize it would be his last. She just hoped that he would be able to make it to their shelter by the sea before his time to pass over to the Other Side arrived.

By midmorning Knut's strength was beginning to flag. When he stumbled, Yani wordlessly walked to his side and placed her arm around his waist. Looking down, the old man draped his arm over her strong shoulders and smiled weakly.

"We can stop for a rest, if you would like," Yani said.

"No, Daughter," the old man wheezed. "I still have the strength to go a little further. I am glad for your help and concern but we must keep going. There will be time to rest later."

"Do you think the whale fish will come again this year?" ask Yani. "I can still remember the day I saw it. How I ran to you all excited! Did I ever tell you that when I first saw it I thought it was the boat people come back? Well, I did. I was so frightened that I started to run straight to the hiding tree. But then I stopped and looked again and it was no longer there. That is when I saw that it was a fish." As they walked Yani kept up a gentle chatter of memories, but whether it was to distract the Knapper from the rigors of the journey or to keep herself from worrying about the Knapper, even she was not entirely sure.

The midday sun found them near a rocky windswept knoll. Looking out over the endless waving grass, Yani felt very small. When she looked back the way they had come she could just barely see the line of trees that marked the beginning of the forest. Knowing that they had made such progress the first morning gave her a feeling of satisfaction that dispelled some of the dread of what lay ahead.

As they rested, they ate a frugal meal of jerked deer meat and dried berries. They drank sparingly from the water gourds since they knew it would be many miles before the next water hole. As they ate Deet searched the sky for any signs of approaching weather. The Knapper drifted into an uneasy sleep. Seeing how peaceful he looked, the two young people were hesitant to interrupt his rest.

"Do you think he will make it?" Yani asked in a whisper.

Deet considered for a moment before responding. "I think he will make it. He has a need to be in his home before he crosses over. It will not be an easy journey for him and we may have to stop often to rest but, yes, he will make it."

"Will the weather hold?"

"You are a girl of many questions today, Yani," chuckled the man. "That I can't tell you. The sky would indicate that we have at least today and tomorrow clear but after that, I can't say. I know the ways of the old man better than I know the ways of the weather on this

207

lonesome plain. But now, we must be moving. I hate to wake him but it is time," said Deet stretching and standing.

"A moment more," said Yani as Deet was reaching out to touch the old man's shoulder. "I must call Wolf and put the harness back on. Let him sleep while I do that."

Nodding at the wisdom of this, Deet sat back down on the rock he had occupied while Yani walked off in the direction that Wolf had gone to hunt. When she had gone far enough not awaken Knut, she gave her shrill whistle that was Wolf's signal to return.

Chapter Two

Days later as the sun was setting in the west, the travelers finally sighted the line of trees that marked the end of the Steppes. Looking back over the waving grass, Yani thought how it resembled the waves of the sea. She couldn't help but wish that the watery waves were the ones she was seeing now instead of the dull green-brown that lay before her.

"We didn't make it off the Steppes today but tomorrow night we will camp beneath the shelter of trees with a real fire. If luck is with us, I may raise a rabbit or a deer tomorrow and then we will have fresh meat, too," said Deet as they made camp for the night.

"I will miss the stars," mused Yani. "I will not see them so clearly until we are home again."

"Ah, home," sighed the old man as he dropped to the ground by Yani. "It will be good to be there. But it is still a very long way."

"We will make it though, Father, don't worry," said Yani as she pulled the sleeping robe from the trailing pack. "Now you must rest."

Deet knelt by them and began to clear an area in which to build a small fire. As he worked Yani shook the drinking gourds. Finally she sighed, "If we had more water I would have made us some acorn porridge for supper but …." Her voice trailed off telling the others what they already knew. Their water was nearly gone. This had been a constant worry as the weather had been unseasonably warm increasing their need for moisture. Now that the end was in sight they could relax on that point but they still lacked enough for cooking.

"Tomorrow night will be soon enough, Daughter," said the old man.

"Acorn stew and fresh rabbit! My mouth is watering already," put in Deet. "But now we must sleep. Tomorrow is another day."

"Now that you have seen us safely across the Steppes, I imagine you will be going your way soon," said Knut.

"Well, now," began Deet. "Actually, I was thinking that I might just go along with you all the way to the sea. I have a yearning to see that whale fish that Yani has told me so much about. That is, if it is agreeable with the two of you." Deet suppressed a chuckle when he saw the look of relief on Yani's face.

"Why, Deet, I didn't know you were such a student of nature. Or, is it my pleasant company that is the attraction," said Knut looking over at Yani as he did.

"Well, if I'm not welcome," began the young man as he stood. "I can always.."

"No, Deet, your company is most welcome," cried Yani a little too quickly. Blushing she continued, "The whale fish is a marvelous thing to see and having a hunter for fresh meat will help to keep our strength up during the cold days and...."

"Of course, you are welcome, Deet. Your company will make the journey much more pleasant. But what you said earlier is right. Now we must rest. Tomorrow is another long day of walking." With that the old man rolled in his sleeping cloak and was soon asleep.

Chapter Three

The next afternoon, they left the Steppes for the shelter of the forest. Soon after that the trail wound by a stream where they stopped so Yani could fill some of the drinking gourds. As she worked Deet paced restlessly.

"I think I will leave you for a while. I have been seeing many deer signs since we entered the forest and I have a taste for venison tonight," he finally said.

"You know the first camp site. We will wait for you there. I think Yani can get a fire going tonight, can't you, Daughter," said the Knapper. "We'll have it all ready to cook a tasty piece of venison when you get there."

"Of course, I can see to the fire," smiled the girl. "Just be sure to bring home something to cook on it. I have a taste for venison, too. Jerked is good but fresh is so much better."

As the hunter moved off into the forest, Yani and the Knapper set out toward the campsite. The days had toughened the old man and he was walking more easily if a bit slower than his old pace. He leaned more heavily on his walking stick and his limp was more noticeable but other than that he was managing well.

"What villages will we visit on the northern journey," asked Yani. "Any that we have been to before?"

"I don't think we will stop at all the villages I usually do. I had thought of visiting my village but it is too far to the east. It would add many days to our journey. I was thinking though that you might like to stop in your village to see your family. It is on the most direct route to the sea."

Yani stopped in her tracks. She hadn't thought of the possibility of seeing her family. Why, she scarcely thought of them at all anymore. She was with her family- Knut, and Wolf and even Deet, seemed more like family than her true mother and father. But, then she thought about her young sisters and mother and decided it would be good to see them. She was not sure that she wanted to see her father. Her feeling toward him were so mixed up.

"I guess, it would be nice to see them. I could tell Mother about her family. I would like to see my sisters….." Her voice trailed off as she resumed walking.

"And your father?" asked Knut.

"I am with my father," answered Yani as she moved ahead of the old man and Wolf.

The Knapper decided not to pursue the issue at the moment but knew it would have to be addressed before they reached the village of Yani's family. For a while they walked in uneasy silence, each traveler wrapped in his own thoughts.

Finally, Yani broke the silence. "You are my father. The man that sold me to you never really wanted me. He needed a son and I was a disappointment to him. I do not hate him. At least not any more, because if he had not given me to you for the blades, I would still be living in the village or perhaps married off to some old man in another village who would treat me as badly as my father treated my mother. My father did me a kindness by giving me to you, but he does not know that he did."

"Your gentle wisdom has always pleased me, Daughter. Your mother will be gratified to see that her daughter has grown into such a fine young woman."

"I will be glad to see Mother but, I think, I would like to see my sisters most. I am sure they have grown since I left the village. Do you think they have forgotten me?" she asked.

"No, Daughter," replied the old man. "I am sure they think often of their sister."

"I hope so," whispered Yani.

Chapter Four

Three days later they entered the first village. They stood on a rise looking down into a wide river valley. All around the village were large fields that showed signs of cultivation. The houses were built of stout logs and Yani marveled at the number. She had never seen so many houses in one place. At one end of the village there was a small house off by itself. Smoke billowed out of it and as they approached, a loud clanging could be heard coming from that direction.

"What do you suppose that strange sound is?" Yani asked as she helped Knut down a steep part of the trail.

"I don't know," wheezed the old man. "But, I plan to find out. This village has changed much since I was here four years ago. How could they have plowed such vast fields and cut so many tree to build those houses in such a short time? Why, to cut one tree the size of those takes days. First you must gird it to stop the sap from flowing. Then when it has started to die and the wood is brittle, you can begin chopping through it. Something very amazing has taken place here."

That night as the men sat around the fire of the village elder, they learned the mystery of the sudden change. Deet turned the strange spearhead over in his hands looking at it in wonder.

"It is like no rock I have ever seen," he marveled. "The edge is much smoother. There are no chip marks at all. How can it have been sharpen with no chip marks?"

He handed it to Knut who also examined it. "This has not been chipped or flaked." He turned the blade over in his hands thoughtfully for several moments. Slowly recognition registered on his old face and he nodded. Leaning over to his pack, he removed his fire starter pouch and took out the flint. He sharply rapped the flint with the strange blade and sparks flew out from it. "As I though, it is the essence of the fire stone. But, how did you remove it from the rock it was living in?"

"You have called it correctly. It is the essence of the firestone. It can be released by using a very hot fire. The essence becomes liquid and flows out of the rock where it can be caught in a hollowed out rock much like a grindstone. It can then be pounded into blades or axes or, best of all, plowshares. It is stronger than wood, antler or flint and when it becomes dull you need only rub it against a dampen stone to bring the edge back. See," said the elder as he spit on one of the stones around the fire pit. He rubbed the edge of the spearhead against the stone working it in a circular motion. After a few moments, he handed the point to Deet, who gingerly rubbed his finger across the edge.

"Ouch!" he cried putting his finger to his mouth. "It cut me!" He held up his bleeding finger for the others to see.

"I said it would be sharp," chuckled the elder.

"Deet, must always learn things the hard way," said Knut, shaking his head. Then he added with a frown, "It is good that I am so old. I think this new type of point will soon replace the need for my blades."

"I am afraid that is so, my friend," replied the Elder. "I do not think that many in this village will trade with you this season. But there are still other villages that do not know the secret of releasing the fire stone essence. You will still be needed there for as many years as you have left. But, you are right the knowledge will soon spread and then...."

"Then a knapper will no longer be needed," Knut finished for him.

"But now it is late and we must all sleep. There will always be a place for you around my fire pit, Knapper, even if I don't need your blades."

"Thank you, my friend, but I fear this is my last journey to the south," replied the Knapper.

"Then I shall miss your company until we meet on the Other Side," said the elder. "But I think that will be only a short wait," he added with a grim smile.

The Elder had been right about the trading in his village. Few in the village wanted flint blades with the new fire stone blades available. Yani had carried out most of the trading that was done but it was with the medicine woman of the village and not for blades. They had shared herbs and knowledge late into the night as the men had discussed the new innovations in weapons and tools. As they left the village, sadness enveloped the old men. They both know they would not be seeing each other in this world.

Chapter Five

It was threatening snow when they neared Yani's village many days later. The going had been slow and the trading not nearly as good as in most years. In several of the villages they found, although the knowledge of releasing the essence of the firestone had not been discovered, trading for it had. Even Deet had given into temptation and had traded a fox fur for one of the new spearheads shortly before leaving the Village of the Firestone. He had guiltily carried it in his pouch for several days after leaving the village. One night as they had sat around the fire, Knut finally said, "Deet, don't you think you should at least try out that new spear point? It seems a waste of that fox pelt to not use it."

"I didn't know that you had seen me bartering for it," replied a sheepish Deet. "I don't think it will be as good as your blades but I at least wanted to try it out. Then I got to thinking it might hurt your feelings and well, I just..." Deet hung his head as he ran out of words.

"Deet, I am not vain enough to think that my blades are the only way to kill an animal. The new points are much better than a flint. Just as the flint is much better than a fire hardened wooden point. It is a good thing, use it." It was that spear that Deet was carrying as they entered the village.

Yani had mixed emotions about seeing her family again after all this time. How would they react to seeing her? Would they be glad? Or would they resent her happiness. Now that she was actually approaching her village, she found herself overcome by waves of nostalgia. Each familiar place she came upon was like seeing a long lost friend. She slowly walked across the meadow where she had been gathering spring greens when the Knapper had first seen her. The contrast between the gentle sunlit meadow and this stark winter landscape was as different as that between the timid little butterfly dancer who had left the village and the assured young wolf tamer who was returning.

Sensing her need to be alone, Knut and Deet hung back. Yani, with Wolf by her side, crossed the meadow toward the village. As they approached the first house, a girl stepped from the shelter. Hesitantly, she approached Yani. When she was within a few arm's length from the girl and wolf, she stopped. "Yani?" she asked, "Is it really you or another dream? I fear it is a dream since you are walking with a wolf. But, you look so real."

"Dami? Can this grown up girl be my little Dami?" asked Yani, tears welling in her eyes. Opening her arms, the younger girl fell into them, wrapping her own around Yani's waist.

"Oh, Yani, it is not just another dream! You have come home at last. I knew you would. Mother said that you were probably dead and that I would never see you, but I knew better. And now that you are back, Father will have to let you stay, won't he?"

Holding her younger sister against her chest, she looked across the meadow to where the Knapper and Deet were standing. Yani was torn with conflicting emotions. Across the snow covered meadow stood the two men she knew cared for her deeply. Behind her was the mother and sisters who see felt sure also loved her. As she rocked her sister, an angry cry from the village broke the spell of the moment.

"Dami!" shouted an angry male voice. "Get away from that stranger. She has a wolf with her. I should take a switch to you, girl. Get back with your mother and sister. They need your help." Turning his wrath on Yani, he said angrily, "Get that beast away from our village. We have a valuable flock of sheep here and they are not food for wolves. Go back to the forests where you belong."

As Yani look speechlessly at her father, the Knapper and Deet joined her. "Well, Gret, I see you have not changed since we last met. But is appears your daughter has. Or, should I say my daughter?"

Looking from the Knapper to Yani, Gret's expression changed from anger to wonder then to a look of cold indifference. "Yani, your mother will be happy to know that you still are alive. She is at the house. She will want to say hello to you before you move on." And with that he turned and walked away.

"Father," started Yani, but her voice trailed off as Gret's back receded into the forest at the edge of the village. Big white flakes of snow started to fall as the Knapper moved close to Yani and put his arm around her shoulder.

"Come, Daughter," said Knut. "There are many hearths that will welcome us in this village. You will be able to spend as much time as you would like with your mother." Looking at the sky, he added, "And I have no intention of attempting to move on in this. I am too old to travel in snow storms."

Dami took Yani's hand and lead her toward their home. "It's all right, Yani, I am sure Mother will make him change his mind when she sees you. He will let you stay. Especially when he see this snow. Don't you like the way it looks? But, it is so cold. Oh, just wait until you see Cali. She is almost as tall as I am. Where did you get the wolf? Oh, and your dress, it is so soft," prattled Dami as they entered the village.

"Hush, now," chided Yani. "I will tell you everything but slowly." She stroked the girl's hair when they stopped before the house. Yani looked at the excited girl and smiled sadly. In her heart she knew that she would be leaving again in a day or two. She knew her sister would be disappointed but her life was no longer here. She was not that little girl who left this village in misery two springs ago. Taking a deep breath she lifted the skin across the door and went in to meet her mother.

Chapter Seven

The fire in the hearth was throwing soft shadows against the loft of the village elder's house as Yani lay curled beside Wolf on her bearskin on the dirt floor. She listened to the rhythm of the sleepers around her but she could not drift off. Her mind was awhirl with all the emotions and memories of the day. She could still see her mother's face with that look of fear then joyful surprise when she had looked up from her cooking and had seen Yani in the doorway. Yani had shyly entered what used to be her home, unsure of the welcome she would receive. The warm hug her Mother had given her left no doubt that she was glad to see her. But, the joy in her eyes was soon replaced by anxiety as her mother glanced toward the door. Yani did not need to be reminded that her father would be back soon and demand his supper. Yani had quickly joined her mother at the hearth. As they had worked, Yani had begun to tell her mother of all that had happened since they last were together. She had just started to tell of her mother's village in the Mountains That Are Always White, when Deet had lifted the skin over the door and stuck his snow covered head in.

"Yani, the Knapper has asked that you come to the elder's house now. He needs your help. You can finish your visit tomorrow," he had said with a meaningful glance over his shoulder.

Yani had been reluctant to leave but she had known that Deet had been warning her that her father was on his way. So, giving her mother a quick hug she had followed Deet to the elder's house where she now found herself tossing restlessly.

Why did her father hate her so? Had she been such a terrible daughter? She asked herself. Wolf sensed her unrest and whimpering softly laid his big paw across her chest. Smiling at him, she scratched his ears then curled up around him. Soon the night sounds and the crackle of the dying fire, added to his warmth, lulled her to sleep.

The next morning she walked out into a world of sparkling white. The storm had continued through the night blanketing the village and the surrounding forest with a thick layer of snow. With Wolf at her side, she walked through the waking village. She had her water basket on her arm as she headed for the sheepfold. Sensing Wolf's interest as she approached, she reached down and rested her hand on his head. Kneeling so she could look at him face to face, she said, "Wolf, these animals are not food. These are my friends. Do you understand me? I hate to tie you up but you must not go near these animals. Father would love to have an excuse to kill you and if you go near the sheep he will."

Wolf cocked his head to one side and whined. "Stay!" commanded Yani as she approached the fold. Looking back she saw that he was sitting where she had left him but with a look on his faced that said, "Can I come now?" Looking over the woven fence of the fold, she saw that the flock had indeed grown since she had left. By the looks of some of the ewes there would be more new lambs in a few weeks. Knowing that Wolf would be sorely tempted to make an easy meal of the sheep if given a chance, she decided that it would be wise for them to move on as soon as the Knapper had rested and completed his trading. Until then she was going to have to keep a very close eye on Wolf.

When she had filled the basket with fresh snow from the edge of the meadow, she and Wolf returned to the elder's house. After she had put the basket of snow to melt near the fire, she took Wolf's harness from the top of her pack and slipped it over his head. "I hate to do this when you have been so good but I am afraid you will forget that you are not a wild animal any longer. It will only be for a couple days at the most." Saying this she looped a rope through the harness and wrapped it around the pole by her pack. "I know that this won't hold you if you want to go but it will remind you to wait for me. At least, I hope it will," she whispered.

After she had made sure that the men had their breakfast, she took Deet aside. "Are you going into the forest to hunt today?" she asked.

"Yes," he replied with a grin. "Is there anything that you would like me to kill for you? I may not be as good at filling you request as Wolf but I will try." Shaking his head, he added. "I will never forget how he brought your that deer back in the cave across the Steppes."

Blushing at the teasing, Yani reply, "Deet, please be serious. I am afraid for Wolf."

"Yani, I think Wolf can take care of himself. Why would you be afraid for him?"

"It is the sheep," Yani began.

"The sheep! I think Wolf is safe from them," laughed Deet. Seeing the look on Yani's face, Deet said gently. "Yes, I see what you are thinking. I'll take Wolf with me and be sure that he doesn't wander off too far. They must be a great temptation to him."

"Thank you, Deet," replied Yani softly.

As the Knapper bartered his points, Yani continued her visit with her mother and sisters. It was nearly sunset when she rose from the spinning they had been working on to return to the elder's house. They had had a good visit but Yani knew this was no longer her home. As she ducked through skin covering the door, the wind that brushed her cheek was not the cold north wind of the night before but a soft southern breeze. This, she knew would soon melt the snow. As she crossed the commons in the center of the village, she felt the dampness seep into the old summer moccasins that she had been wearing in the village. She hoped that the Knapper was ready to move on. Now that she knew this was no longer her home, she was eager to be back on the trail going toward the sea. As she walked across the common past the well, she remembered the next village was that of Lamu and Birg. Automatically, her hand went to the golden stone with the butterfly that Birg had given her. Yes, she was ready to move on.

It was only Yani's mother and sisters who came to bid them goodbye as they left the village with the sunrise. She gazed around the village and the forest's edge to see if she could catch a glimpse of her father. Seeing no sign of him, she turned back to her mother and sisters. With a sigh, she hugged her mother again and tasseled the girls' hair then squaring her shoulders followed the men down the path. At the other side of the meadow, she turned for one last look at her village and saw that her mother was still standing where they had parted. With a final wave, she turned and returned to the village leaving Yani to her journey.

Chapter Eight

By midmorning the snow had completely melted and a warm soft breeze was quickly drying the land. The rest had revived the Knapper but by midmorning his energy had again begun to flag at an alarming rate. When they emerged from the forest, Deet, seeing his haggard faced, suggested they rest. Gladly, Knut dropped to the ground with a sigh. Yani took some dried venison from her pack and handed a piece to each of the men. Knut chewed on it with little interest and soon nodded off. As Knut dozed leaning on his walking stick, Yani shifted some of the load from Wolf's trailing pack to her basket. Guessing her intent Deet silently added some of the load to his pack also. When they had the trailing pack nearly emptied, Yani touched Knut on the shoulder. "Father, the way is flat for now. It would be easy for Wolf to carry you here and that will help you save your energy for the climb across the mountain."

"But, I can..."began the old man. Then he stopped and smiled up at her, "As always, my wise daughter is right. I will ride while it is level and an easy trail. Later I can prove how able I am."

Yani helped the Knapper to the trailing pack and when he was settled, tucked the bear skin close around him. Wolf looked over his shoulder with interest at the change in his load. As they started down the trail, he glanced back a few times but soon lost interest in the old man that he carried. Knut soon was dozing despite the occasional bouncing of the trailing pack as it bumped over rocks in the path.

They camped that night by the brook where Knut had made Yani the moccasins for her bruised feet on their first journey north. *Could it be only two years since that first tearful, terrifying day on the trail,* thought Yani as she went about preparing a meal for the men. She had released Wolf to hunt and was amazed to see his bountiful energy. Her shoulders ached from the extra weight of the pack, but she realized that

Knut weighted much less than then what she had carried. *No wonder he has so much energy. What he is pulling weighs not much more than a hare,* she thought with a sigh.

Later that night, when Knut was asleep by the fire, wrapped snugly in the bear skin, Deet came over to Yani. "Sit here in front of me, Yani," he commanded when he was settled on a large rock near the fire. "I can tell that pack was much too heavy. Let me rub your shoulders so they won't be so sore tomorrow."

"I am fine," said Yani as she continued to repack the cooking things. Deet watched with a patient smile until she lifted the pack to move it away from the fire. She winced and quickly set it back down.

"Yani, let me help your shoulders. You still have many days of carrying ahead of you and I am not sure how many of those days Knut will be able to walk. He is weakening more rapidly than he wants to admit to us. Now, come here," he finished using a stern tone that Yani had never heard from him. Meekly, she walked to his side of the fire and sat down on the ground before him.

As soon as she was settled, Deet began gently kneading her aching shoulders with his strong hands. At first the rubbing hurt so badly Yani wonder how this could possibly help, but soon the knotted muscles began to relax. As they did, so did she. Soon her eyes drooped closed and she let her mind drift to the days that lay ahead. She was seeing the trail leading toward the mountain when it began to blur and be replaced by the trail through the beech forest. She emerged at the top of the cliff where she heard the gentle lap of the water and the quarrelsome mewing of the gulls. She drifted from place to place at their seashore home only to settle by a sun warmed rock jutting from the sand. She could feel the warmth of the rock against her cheek and the breeze gently brushing her hair from her face. It was so peaceful and comfortable that she felt she could go on forever sleeping on the warmth of this rock. As her mind paused at the word *sleeping,* she came

224

awake with a jerk. Her head rested on Deet's strong thigh and he was brushing the hair back from her face gently.

"I'm sorry, Deet," she stammered as she clambered stiffly to her feet. "But is felt so good and I was so relaxed that I must have fallen asleep."

Reaching out and taking her hand, Deet turned her around and putting a finger over her lips said, "Yani, you are exhausted. I know you did not sleep much in your village and then carrying twice the load today. Of course, you fell asleep. Now get your sleeping cloak and settle down for the night. I'll see to the fire."

Smiling her thanks Yani pulled her deerskin cloak from the top of her pack and curled up by the fire. Soon the rhythmic rise and fall of the deerskin told Deet that she was asleep. But sleep was slow to come for him as he sat by the fire and watched the sleeping girl.

Chapter Ten

Yani awoke to the sound of birds in the trees above. She looked up to see a cedar waxwing in the branches above her head. Dreamily, she wondered if that was the same bird that had sung her from her sleep on her last stop near here. After all, that campsite had been just over the mountains from here. *Do cedar waxwings go south for the winter?* she wondered. *Do they stay in one place or do they travel around like me?* Opening her eyes, she saw sunlight glistening through the branches promising a good day for travel. She knew it would be a difficult day with only a brief stop at the top of the mountain for a noon time rest. If the wind and sun were favorable, it would help. She knew also that an early start would be essential if they were to make it across the mountain in one day with Knut in his weakened state. She sat up and stretched, then stood up and folded her deerskin tucking it in her pack before beginning to make their breakfast.

Deet was unusually quiet as they started up the mountain. Yani's pack felt almost empty after the heavy pack of the day before and she was soon helping Knut as they began the climb up the mountain. By midmorning she began to wonder if they would be able to make it to the top at all let alone in one day. Knut was moving more and more slowly. When they stopped for a rest, Deet motioned Yani off to one side just out of Knut's hearing. In a quiet voice, he asked, "Do you think Wolf would be able to carry my pack as well as the load he has now if we move some of it over to your pack?"

"Probably," said Yani. "But why? Have you hurt yourself?" she asked, alarm creeping into her voice. The idea of having the Knapper and Deet both unable to travel frightened her.

Chuckling, Deet replied, "No, I am fine. But if I have my pack on Wolf's trailing pack I can carry the Knapper." Glancing his way, Deet continued, "I don't think he will be able to climb the rest of the way. His

226

color is not good. Look at how gray his face is. And it will be just as difficult going down the mountain."

Nodding, Yani moved silently to the trailing pack and began to rearrange the load to make room for Deet's pack. When Knut realized what they had planned, he objected, but rather weakly. It did not take much to convince the old man that this was for the best. With the old man perched on Deet's broad shoulders, they continued the journey, reaching the camp on the other side of the mountain just after the sun had set. As they made camp by starlight, the Knapper dropped into an exhausted sleep.

The next day they moved slowly down the river valley, matching their pace to that of the Knapper. Even moving at a slow pace, they were forced to make many more rest stops than they normally would have. The way was too rough for Knut to ride on the trailing pack and since he insisted on walking here, Yani and Deet felt they should let him. There was plenty of water. The game was also abundant, so Deet took advantage of the frequent stops to slip off into the forest to hunt. By evening he had several squirrels to add to the cooking pot.

When the trail flattened out again early the next day, the old man again returned to the trailing pack. For the rest of the journey, he spent much of each day riding. He would begin the day's march leaning heavily on his walking stick and shuffling slowly along beside Yani. Nonetheless, by midmorning his stamina would fail him and he would return to his place behind Wolf. After the noontime rest, he would again walk for a short time but each day he walked less and less. He was dozing fitfully behind Wolf when they at last neared the Village in the Marsh. It was late afternoon when they approached the edge of the Marsh and looking back at the sleeping figure beneath the bear skin Yani wonder how she was to lead them across the causeway to the village. She rubbed the amber on the cord around her neck absently as she pondered the problem. *If we call out loudly, could we be heard all the way to the village?* she wondered.

They had just topped the last gentle rise before the trail turned to skirt the marsh, when Yani noticed a curl of smoke drifting up from a small fire. As they neared the fire, Wolf began to growl softly. Deet motioned for Yani to stop as he advanced toward the fire. Yani anxiously searched the reeds at the edge of the marsh looking for the builder of the fire. Just before Deet reached the fire, a young hunter rose up from the reeds. He lifted his spear but did not throw.

"Is this the welcome you give travelers in your village?" Deet asked angrily. "I had been lead to believe we could expect a warm welcome here. I see I was wrong."

Turning on his heel Deet retraced his steps to where Yani waited. "Come on Yani, let's go. I know when I am not welcome," said an indigent Deet.

Before Yani could respond the hunter let his spear fall and cried, "Yani! But where is the Knapper. And what are you doing with a hunter and a wolf?"

Yani searched the face of the young man as he came forward now smiling broadly. Although he looked familiar, she couldn't put a name to the face. She had only met a few of the young hunters in Lamu and Birg's village but could remember none of their names. It was apparent that this one knew her. It was perplexing. Why would a hunter of the village have remembered her name when she could not even remember his face. She had been just a slip of a girl when they had been in the village a year ago. Reading her thoughts, the young hunter pointed to the amber that Yani was worrying between her fingers. "I see you still have the butterfly I gave you when we last met. And a new dress to match the stone it was in."

A smile of recognition warmed Yani's face. "Birg, you have grown. You are no longer the greedy boy who ate all the duck."

228

"And I see you are no longer the well behaved daughter of the Knapper who knew when it was proper to hold her tongue. You seemed to have become a sharp tongued woman," he retorted but with a broad smile.

Deet cleared his throat to remind them of his presence and said, "If you have finished with your welcoming speeches, I think we should figure out how we are to get the Knapper across to the village."

"The Knapper? But why is he not with you? Why would he need help getting across to the village? Is he ill? Where did you leave him? Is he far behind?" asked a bewildered Birg.

"Birg, he is here," said Yani gesturing toward the trailing pack. "He is too weak to walk. I have some herbs that may help him regain his strength but first we must get him to the village. He needs to rest and more nourishing food than trail fare."

"The hunter's wolf is carrying him?" said Birg in wondered. Turning to Deet he asked, "How did you train a wolf to do that?"

Deet gaffed at the indignant look on Yani's face, quickly saying, "If you want to know how Wolf was trained you will have to ask Yani. She is the one who did it. I would never be brave enough to take on a full grown wolf."

"Yani!" exclaimed Birg. "Yani trained the wolf? How could a girl…."

"If you two don't mind, Knut needs to get to the village," said Yani. With the color rising in her face, she turned on Birg adding, "And just why is it so astounding that I am the one who trained Wolf? I see you have many things to learn about girls, Birg Who Eats All the Duck."

As they faced off Wolf whined and the old Knapper moaned in his sleep. Yani quickly broke off and ran to his side. One look at his gray wane face told her that he needed to be moved to the village quickly.

"Can you carry him?" Birg asked turning to Deet. "I will lead the way and help Yani with the packs." Then looking at Wolf he added, "What about him?"

"Wolf will be fine," said Yani. "When I release him he will hunt for a while then come and find me. Will the trailing pack be safe here by your fire or should we come back for it tonight?"

"It will be fine here if we cover it with reeds. Now, Deet, is it? If you will give me your pack and pick up the Knapper, we can go. When you walk over the causeway be sure to place your foot exactly where I do. The way is not wide and it make many turns."

When they were nearly across the causeway, Yani heard a cried from the village and a young woman came running toward them. "Yani! At last! We have been watching for you from since the last full moon! Birg has camped on the other shore for days, he has been so anxious to see you!" a much grown Lamu babbled. "Oh, but I wasn't to tell you that, was I?" she added with an impish grin.

"Sisters! They are a vexation to the spirit. Can you for once be quiet? Can't you see the Knapper is ill? Run and tell Mother so she will have a bed ready for him," growled Birg, his face flaming.

"Oh," said Lamu, "Is he very ill?"

"Just go!" With that Lamu turned and ran toward their house as the travelers left the marsh and entered the village.

Chapter Eleven

That night after Knut had finished the last of the herb tea Yani had brewed for him, she helped him to the sleeping bench and saw that he was warmly covered. Then she return to the fire and sat beside Lamu to at last visit with her friend. As she settled by the fire, Lamu asked, "So, Yani, what wonderful tales do you have to tell me this time? Did you find your mother's family?"

"Lamu, it has been a wonderful journey but very hard also. But the first story I must tell is about Wolf since he will probably be arriving at any time."

"Birg told us about the wolf that carried the Knapper here. Did you really train him by yourself?" asked Lamu. "Birg still doesn't believe a girl could train a wolf. I told him that if any one could, you could and he just mumbled something and walked away."

"Let her tell her story," chided Honi.

"I will," replied Lamu, "but I wish she would hurry up."

Smiling, Yani launched into the tale of how Wolf came to be with them. As she was beginning the tale Birg slipped quietly into the house and took a seat across the firepit from her. Pretending not to be interested to all, it was clear he was listening to everything she said. As she finished she heard a whimper from the door. "I think that's him now," she said as she got up to go to the door. Just outside was Wolf, wet and muddy from his swim across the marsh. "Look at you, Wolf. You are going to have to sleep outside tonight. I am not sharing my bed with someone that muddy and wet. Stay, Wolf."

As Yani dropped the skin flap back over the door, Lamu giggled and called to Birg across the fire. "You must remember that Birg. Yani will not share her bed with you if you are all muddy and wet."

"And you, little sister, will find that no one will share their firepit with you if you do not learn to stop your constant chatter," retorted Birg.

"What do I care about sharing a firepit? Men are just big ugly boys," sputtered Lamu, her face turning red in the firelight.

"Both of you stop your teasing before your chatter wakes the Knapper. He is sick and needs his rest," scolded Loki. "Yani, you must be tired, too. It's late and tomorrow is another day."

During the night Yani went to check on the Knapper often but each time found that he was sleeping soundly. As she settled back down in her sleeping robe after one of her trips to check on him, she felt she was being watch. Looking across the room, she saw Birg's eyes on her. When she looked his way, he smiled at her before rolling over to return to sleep.

They stayed in the Village in the Marsh for ten days while the Knapper regained his strength for the final leg of the journey home. Each day Yani helped with the chores of the hearth and soon began to feel like a member of the family. Each evening Birg silently watched her from across the fire.

On the morning of the eleventh day as the Knapper said his good-byes, Yani had taken Wolf across with Birg leading the way before returning to say her goodbyes and collect her pack. It had been an uncomfortable walk with many unsaid things hanging between the two young people. As they had waded through the water Birg had turned to Yani and had asked, "Why must you go? The Knapper is old and will not live much longer and if you were here we could help take care of you."

She knew he had meant it kindly but nonetheless she had snapped at him. "I don't need anyone to take care of me! And I am capable of taking care of my father as well. He wants to return to his home and that is what we will do."

He had turned away and walked so fast that Yani had had trouble keeping up. After leaving Wolf on the shore, she followed Birg back in an uncomfortable silence. She had wanted to apologize to him but the rest of the morning he had avoided her.

As they prepared to leave the village, Birg offered to help with the packs. Deet once again was to carry the Knapper across the causeway but this time he was not as docile about it. "I am not a child to be carried," Knut insisted, when they got to the edge of the water. "I am capable of walking. Why are you treating my like a helpless old man."

"You are a helpless old man," laughed Deet.

"One that is capable of falling in the marsh and getting all wet. And, of catching a chill and then becoming sick with a fever," said Loki. "Please, Knapper, let Deet carry you. You still have a long journey and there will be plenty of walking for you without wading across the marsh."

Sighing, the Knapper allowed Deet to hoist him onto his back and they started out across the causeway. Yani would have liked to have talked to Birg as they crossed the causeway but he walked ahead of Deet so there was no way to get near enough. Sighing she decided she would never understand boys and their strange ways.

When they arrived at the firepit Birg had been waiting at when they arrived, Wolf was obediently waiting. He nuzzled her side as she checked the harness and trailing pack. It seemed to be in order. Even though they come back and had wrapped it in a deer skin and weighted it down with rocks, she was afraid that some animal may have found it and gnawed on the leather thongs of the harness. As she prepared to harness Wolf, she looked again for Birg. When she saw that he was headed back toward the causeway, she dropped the harness and ran after him. She caught up with him just as he started to reenter the water for the wade back.

"Birg, please, wait," she said grabbing his shoulder.

He stopped and turned to face her. The hurt look on his face brought tears to Yani's eyes. "Birg, please. I am sorry I was rude to you. I know you and your family only want to help but I must take Father home." Yani looked down at her hands then off to the horizon toward the sea before turning to meet Birg's eyes again. "He's dying," she said in a sad soft voice. "He wants to die there with the sound of the sea in his ears. Don't you see? I have to take him back."

"Then I'll come with you," offered Birg. "I am a good hunter and I can…" Seeing the storm of protest rising in Yani's eyes, he stammered to a stop.

"Thank you, Birg, but I can take care of him myself. We have Wolf to protect us and Deet will see us there," said Yani. "Please do not be angry with me."

Birg looked at her for a long time before he smiled. "I will come if you need me."

"But how will you know if I need you?" smiled Yani. "I can't call loudly enough for you to hear me."

Giving her a long searching look, Brig said, "I will know." Then he turned and retraced his steps across the causeway. She watched until he reached the other side of the marsh. As he stepped from the water, he turned and waved. She returned his wave then hurried back to the task of harnessing Wolf.

Chapter Twelve

The journey north was slow. The day began with the Knapper walking beside Yani in his unsteady shuffling pace. When he could walk no further, they would stop and rest before resuming the trek with him dozing on the trailing pack. He would nap for a while then again walk until his strength failed him. Therefore, what should have been an easy two-day walk became a three-day struggle. The last day the Knapper spent nearly the whole way on the trailing pack. Yani's back ached from the added weight of her pack but unlike that first time she had approached the beech forest, this time she was going home. When she saw the naked branches of the beech forest, gray against the horizon, they were a welcoming sight. Since they were arriving a moon earlier than they had when she first had come with the Knapper, the buds on the trees were just beginning to open showing misty wisps of yellow green here and there.

The sun was setting as they started into the forests but the lack of leaves and Yani's familiarity with the path encouraged them to press on. Deet was hesitant to let Yani lead but the Knapper raised up on the trailing pack and said, "She knows the path. If you lead you may well walk off the cliff in the twilight. Let her lead."

So it was Yani who lead the way along the path and showed Deet the way down to the beach. When he looked at the steep climb, he said, "Tonight we camp here. There is time enough tomorrow to go down."

"But, we are almost home," started Yani. "It is just a little way now. I could walk this trail with my eyes closed!"

"Yani, I will have to carry Knut and I am not going to try that in the dark. We camp here and go down tomorrow."

So they spent the night on the cliff, listening to the mewing of the gulls and the crash of the surf on the beach below. Yani woke with the morning sun warming her face. She laid wrapped in the old deer skin that had been with her so long and a feeling of peace spread through her. She was home.

Chapter Thirteen

As soon as the Knapper awoke, Deet helped him to his feet and started to pick him up for the climb down the cliff.

"I can walk down by myself, " he protested. "I just needed the sea air to make me stronger. Go before me so I can steady myself on your shoulder, but I don't want to be carried."

Glancing over Knut's should at Yani, he saw that she nodded agreement. So leaning on his walking stick and steadied by Deet, the old Knapper returned to his seaside home. Yani, with Wolf at her heels followed them down the winding path to the beach below. The tide was at its lowest as they walked along the shore in the early morning mists. Automatically, as they walked along, Yani looked for usable nodules for her blades. She knew that any blades that they would trade in the future would be of her making.

When they finally reached the base of the shelter, she reached up taking hold of the vine and pulled down the ladder. Knut rested on a flat rock as she scrambled up to open the shelter and make it ready for the exhausted old man. From the edge of the shelter, she called back down to Deet, who stood gazing out to sea, "Deet, don't drink that water. Go to the spring back there."

"Why not drink from the sea?" he asked. "There certainly is enough of it."

"You may if you wish but remember where the spring is," Yani called as she turned to the shelter. Soon she heard Deet cough as he spewed the seawater from his mouth. "Why didn't you say it was salty?" he yelled up to Yani as he headed for the spring.

"I told you not to drink it," she called back down to him. "Some people just have to learn the hard way." Yani laughed as she rolled up the mats covering the sleeping bench and lifted the baskets piled there on to the floor of the shelter.

Climbing back down to the beach, she saw that Knut had curled up in the bearskin and was sleeping soundly in the sun. Deet was coming down the path from the cliff with one of the packs as she reached the ground. Taking the pack from him, she asked, "Would you mind looking for drift wood on the beach for a fire while I unpack this? I think the acorn meal is in here and I want to have a good porridge ready for Father when he wakes up."

"Just for the Knapper, or can I have a bite or two of it?" asked Deet pulling a pathetic face.

"Deet, can't you ever be serious? Of course you will eat, too. If I know you, more than Father and I put together. But none of us eat until I have wood and a fire built." Turning to her pack once more, she mumbled, "But first I need to find the acorn meal. And, now where did I put that pot? I must I left it up in the shelter someplace. If I can't find it I will have to go back up the trail to get that new one we traded for after the village with the firestone spear heads."

"Firewood," muttered Deet, as he started down the beach leaving Yani to her sorting.

When he returned a short time later, Yani had made several trips up the ladder to assemble the cooking things she would need for the morning meal and had water from the spring ready to heat. As she stood waiting for Deet, her eyes scanned the waves. It was so good to see the sea again with its little white capped waves breaking here and there like watery sheep in a blue-green meadow. As she watched a huge black tail emerged from the waves pointing skyward before falling back into the sea with a splash.

"Deet, look!" she cried. "There! A whale fish! Watch! Maybe it will wave its tail at us again."

Deet turned to look in the direction she was pointing, but all he saw was the great expanse of water. Finally he turned to her and asked,

"Are you sure you saw a whale fish? How can anything that is as big as you say it is disappear that fast?"

Yani laughed and replied, "Wait. If you watch you will see one too. Then you will believe me when I tell you how big they are."

By evening they had the old Knapper settled once more in the shelter and all the trade goods carried down the cliff. Yani had begun to store them in the baskets she had left behind when they went to the south. The only problem seemed to be Wolf. He could not climb the ladder. He was unhappy not being able to sleep by Yani and she missed his warmth. The new sounds and smells of the beach seemed to frighten him. Finally after listening to him whine for what seemed like forever, Yani carried her old dress down the ladder and laid it on the beach.

"Wolf, you have to sleep down here. You are being such a big baby. There is nothing here that will hurt you. You have enough to eat and the spring is right there for you to drink from. Now be quiet please."

Wolf watched her climb back to the shelter with a pathetic look on his face. After a few pitiful little yaps, he settled down with his head on Yani' s old dress, comforted by her smell. As the sun dipped behind the cliff, the three friends settled down for their first night together by the sea.

Yani soon slipped into a comfortable routine of caring for Knut as well as the ordinary chores needed to provide for them. She would rise early to have the herbal tea brewed for him when he awoke. He never complained but the tight expression on his old wrinkled face told her all she needed to know of his pain. While he drank his first bowl of tea, she prepared their breakfast. Then she would get Knut settled in the sun at the mouth of the shelter. As he dozed there she went about the business of fishing or looking for mushrooms and berries in the woods. Deet had helped her build drying racks that were soon full of an assortment of mushrooms and sweet wild strawberries drying in the sun.

She showed Deet how to stretch the nets in the water and he was soon bringing in huge catches of fish. The smoking fire was never empty, promising plenty to eat during the summer and into the coming winter.

Chapter Fourteen

And so, the days lengthened and the leaves of the beech trees turned the dark green of summer. With the longer days, restlessness over took Deet. He spent many hours walking the beach until one morning when Yani awoke, she saw him sitting by the edge of the shelter with his pack at his side.

"Are you leaving, Deet?" she asked quietly.

"Yani," he started but then looked off out to sea. After a long uncomfortable silence, he continued, "Yani, I must. I am a hunter and a wanderer. I have never stayed this long in one place. I had hoped to be here to take you back to the Village in the Marsh when the Knapper crossed over but it seems the sea and your good care has made that unnecessary. So.." and again his voice trailed off.

"Deet, I will miss you. But I do understand. Just remember you are always welcome here."

So as the old man slept, Deet shouldered his pack and climbed down the ladder and up the cliff to return to his wandering life. Yani watched him go, wondering if they would ever meet again. She turned sadly away as he disappeared into the forest and began to prepare for the day.

One morning in late summer, Yani awoke to find Knut sitting on the bearskin gazing at the lightening sky. "Are you hurting, Father? Is the tea no longer helping?" asked an anxious Yani.

"No, child, the tea is working as well as one can expect," he said with a sad smile. "Today I have special work for you."

"What do you need, Father?"

"I want you to go to the end of the cliff and gather reeds for a basket. It must be a large basket. As large as a man is tall. Will you do that for me?"

"Of course, Father, but why would you need so large a basket?" asked Yani.

"When the time comes for its need, I will tell you. But for now, will you do as I ask without questions?"

Chastened, Yani replied, "Yes, Father, I will do as you ask." Tears stung her eyes as she began preparing the tea for the old man's breakfast.

Seeing her tears, Knut said, "Yani, come here." When she was kneeling at his side, he took her young face in his trembling wrinkled hands. "Yani, don't cry. It is not necessary that you know now. The time for knowing will be here soon enough. Then, I will tell you. Do you trust me in this thing?"

Yani hung her head and wiping tears from her eyes, whispered, "Yes, Father. I am sorry."

"There is no need to be sorry, Child. You have done no wrong."

When Yani returned with the reeds later that day, the Knapper showed her how he wanted the basket made. Under his direction she worked on it the rest of the afternoon and well into the evening. It was a long narrow basket nearly as long as the Knapper was tall. At each end he instructed her to form the reeds into a tall point. The top of the basket was rounded over until only a narrow opening three hands across ran its length allowing access to the inside. Late the next day, she had the tightly woven basket completed. When she was done, the Knapper asked her to coat the outside with pitch.

As the pitch dried, Yani stood back to look at her handiwork. "It looks like a boat!" she exclaimed. "Just like a small version of the ones the Seapeople ride in! Is that what is it, Father, a boat? But it is so small?"

"Yes, Child, it is a boat of sorts. And it is just the right size for the journey it must take. Now come and sit with me. I am weary and would like to hear you recount the journeys we have taken together."

242

Late into the night the old man and the girl sat by the fire in the cave shelter talking of the villages they had visited and their short happy life together.

Two days later Knut surprised Yani by asking her to help him climb down the ladder to the beach.

"But, Father, you are so weak yet. What if you are not strong enough to climb back up?" she asked.

"Then I will sleep with Wolf. He has been lonely since we got here. Come, girl, help me down or I will have to jump."

A troubled Yani rushed to his side fearing the confused state that some old people develop had taken hold of the Knapper. Seeing her expression, Knut laughed, "I am not becoming foolish, Yani. But I must go to the beach today. It is time." As he finished, he reached out and gently stroked her cheek. "Come, my Yani, help me down."

When he was safely on the beach, he sent her back to the shelter to get the strange basket. "Now place it by the spring above the high water line. I think that you will need it very soon." When she had placed the boat by the spring, she returned to stand by him. "Come and sit by me and I will tell you what the strange basket is for."

Yani sat on the bearskin facing the old man. He picked up her firm young hand, looking into her eyes. "Tonight the wind will change and by morning it will be blowing from the west. It will be a strong wind that will carry the drift wood and seaweed far out to sea. When morning comes, my beautiful golden butterfly, I will no longer be with you. My spirit will have followed the paths of my ancestors to the Otherside." Seeing her look of denial and tears forming in her eyes, Knut quickly continued. "Yes, Yani, it is time. I am ready. I am old. I have lived a long good life. I have taught you all that I can and I know you can fend for yourself. You can also go to Loki and Hawn in the Marsh if you choose. We spoke of it when I was there and they told me to tell you that you are a daughter of their hearth. The choice is yours."

243

Tears stream down Yani cheeks and she shook her head trying to deny what she knew must come to pass. "Father, no, I will find new medicine plants. I will make you well. Wait, I will get the bag of herbs. I know there must be something that I can try." Knut pulled her back down as she started to rise to fetch the bag.

"Yani, stay. There is nothing that you have that will help me. I have known for days that the end is here. The tea no longer eases the pain. I am ready and were it not for my sorrow at leaving you, I would be eager to go. So, dry your tears, Child and let us spend our last night together recalling our joys. It is not a time to dwell on sorrow.

"But first I must tell you how it is to be tomorrow. When my spirit has gone from my body, you are to put me in the basket-boat. Then you are to push the basket into the sea and wade out with it until it is beyond the breakers. With the strong west wind to pull it out to sea, it will carry me way. That is the last task I ask of you. I want my body to go to the sea that I love. Will you do as I ask?"

"Yes, Father," whispered Yani.

"Now let us talk of pleasant times. Let me tell you again of that first sight I had of you. A golden child dancing with golden butterflies against a forest of green and a sky so blue it hurt your eyes. I thought you were the most beautiful of all the golden butterflies."

And so, they talked far into the night. When the stars were beginning to fade from the sky to make way for the coming dawn, the wind shifted and carrying the musky smell of the forest down to where the woman-child slept. As the last of the stars blinked out in the soft pink light of the morning, the old Knapper made his last journey following the starlit trail of his ancestors.

Yani woke to the wet tongue of Wolf against her cheek and the morning sun shining on her face. For a moment she was disoriented, unable to recall where she was. Then she remembered the previous night. Coming quickly to her knees, she looked to where the old man

244

lay. Picking up his icy hand, she knew that he had gone. Gently, she laid it back upon the beach and buried her face in Wolf's soft fur and wept. Soon the keening of the wind through the beech trees reminded her of her last promise to the man who had become her father. Wiping her tears with the backs of her hands, she sadly dragged the basket-boat to the water's edge. Then she returned to the Knapper and gently lifted him into her arms. Carrying him to the basket, she laid him gently inside, turning him on his side in a sleeping position. She was shocked by how light and fragile his body had become. Pulling off her dress, she pulled the basket into the waves and waded into the cold sea, pushing it beyond the breakers. When the water reached her shoulders, she gave the basket a strong push sending the Knapper on his last journey. She watched it slowly float toward the morning sun until it was a mere speck on the horizon. Then she turned and let the waves push her back to the beach.

Pulling her dress over her head, she walked to the bearskin and fell upon it. Long painful sobs racked her body. Wolf alone heard her grief.

Part 6
Home by the Sea

Chapter One

The sun had disappeared behind the beech forest when Yani woke from her exhausted sleep. She shivered as the evening breeze brushed her damp dress. Wolf, who had been watching from the spring, came to her side. She wrapped her arms around him and rested her head against his back. "Oh, Wolf, what must I do now? I don't want to go back to the Village in the Marsh. But can I live here alone? What if the Seapeople come? What should I do, Wolf?" she asked looking toward the shelter she had shared with the Knapper. "How can I climb back up to our home if Father is not there?"

Yani was still sitting there when the stars began to light the sky. As she watched the fires of night blink on a shooting star flashed across the heavens. Just as its tail streaked across the blackness, Yani whispered to Wolf, "I wish Father had told me what I should do when he was gone." She buried her face in Wolf's soft coat and again the tears stung her eyes. This time, they were tears of frustration and self-pity.

Morning found her still on the beach curled up around Wolf for his warmth and comfort. She sat up stiffly and after long moments of hesitation, she stood up and walked to the ladder. When she pulled herself up onto the ledge she and Knut had shared so happily, she was overcome with a wave of loneliness. She stood for a moment more before beginning the task of removing the Knapper's things. She knew it was bad luck to have the personal items of a person who had passed over in your home. *Why didn't I put them in the basket-boat with him? How will he manage on the Other Side? I have failed him in the last duty of a daughter,* she thought. Tears again overflowed her eyes and rolled unchecked down her cheeks. "I am sorry, Father," she whispered. "How can I make up for this terrible failure?" As if in answer to her whispered plea, the breeze ruffled the reeds left from the basket, sending their chaff up into her face. Yani sneezed as it tickled her nose and she looked at the bundle of reeds where she had left them to use later.

"That's what I must do!" she cried. "I can make another basket-boat and send it on to you. Then you won't be without the things you need to be comfortable." Snatching up the bundle of reeds, she took a large handful and laid them in the stream to soak. Having a task to focus on took her mind off her sorrow and she was soon working busily. By the time the sun had reached its highest point, she had another basket-boat ready to be sealed with pitch. As it dried in the sun, she began to gather all the things she thought the Knapper would need on the Other Side. She put in a deerskin sleeping cloak, his extra moccasins, acorn meal, a spear with a fresh point and a pouch of dried berries. The last item she picked up to add to the pile of his belongings was the small pouch containing his firestone. She hesitated holding it in her hand. She knew she would need it to start a fire if the one in the firepits were ever to go out. She also was reluctant to part with all of Knut's things. Even though she knew it was bad luck, she hung the pouch around her neck.

By evening she had the basket-boat ready to send on its way behind the Knapper. Once again she waded into the breakers and when she was shoulder deep, she gave the basket a shove letting the evening breeze catch it and push it out to sea.

Tired but more content now, she climbed to the shelter and lay down on the Knapper's bed for the night. She watched the stars dot the sky and then fade as a fog moved in to hid their bright twinkle. The moon had risen high in the sky making a pale circle of light though the fog and still she could not fall asleep. Below on the beach, she heard Wolf whine in his sleep and she wished he were here with her to curl up around for comfort and warmth.

Finally she got up and taking her sleeping cloak climbed down the ladder to the beach below. Going to where Wolf lay by the spring, she curled up on the ground next to him. With his warmth for comfort, sleep finally found her.

Chapter Two

When she awakened the next morning, she lay for a long time watching the sun light the eastern sky. She wondered if Knut had found the basket-boat that she had sent to him. *Are you cold and lonely like I am? Can you see and hear me from the Other Side? Did I send enough for you to eat? Do you eat on the Other Side?* As she pondered these things the growling of her stomach reminded her that she had not eaten since the night before the Knapper died. She stood up and climbed to the shelter where she began to prepare her breakfast. As she worked she heard Wolf bark as he chased after a rabbit or a squirrel in the forest above. *If only Wolf could climb the ladder,* she thought. *I wouldn't be as lonely if he were here with me. What if he is off hunting and the Seapeople come? Can I trade with them? Or must I run and hide.*

The memory of hiding from the Seapeople reminded Yani of the hiding place in the tree. *If I were to live there I would be safe from the Seapeople and Wolf could live with me again. It would also be warmer when the winter comes.* "Yes, that is what we will do!" cried Yani. "As soon as I eat I will move to the tree."

Yani ate quickly and began to gather the things she would need to live at the top of the cliff. She put them into baskets to carry down the ladder to the beach. Soon she had the things she wanted to take collected into a pile at the base of the cliff. She called to Wolf who came loping up the beach to her. She knelt beside him to put the harness over his shoulders. He obediently sat there while she tied the poles in place then loaded her belongings on to the trailing pack and lashed them in place.

"Don't worry, Wolf, this time we don't have far to go. It's just to the top of the cliff and a little ways into the woods. Then tonight we will have a new home where we can sleep together. Would you like that

Wolf, to share my sleeping cloak again," she prattled to him as she worked.

When they reached the top of the cliff, Yani had to think a while before remembering where the hiding place was. The forest had changed over the years but finally she found the path leading to the hollow tree. Following it she soon found the opening behind the ferns. Kneeling, she clear them away.

"Well, Wolf, here it is," she said pointing to the opening at the base of the huge tree. "Let's see what it looks think inside." Bending down she crawled into the tree and sat up. It took a moment for her eyes to become accustom to the gloom of the hollow space but soon she could see. Her first thought was that she had a lot house cleaning to do. It looked as if a whole tribe of squirrels had spent the winter here from the number of nut hulls that were littering the floor. She crawled back out of the tree and untied the trailing pack from Wolf. She slipped the harness over his head telling him, "You might as well go off and hunt because I have a lot of work to do before our new home will be ready. You could bring me back a rabbit since Deet is not here to do it for me." Laughing, she broke off a twiggy, leaf-covered branch to use to brush the debris from the floor of the tree shelter. She worked diligently until the floor was clear of hulls and sticks. When she was satisfied, she began to drag the bundles from the trailing pack into the tree.

By late afternoon, she had the tree converted into a snug home. Looking around, she was happy with what see saw. *This will be a good place. Wolf can get in and I am safe if the Seapeople come.* She wiped the sweat from her forehead and looked at the fire pit. *I think I will make another one on the outside to use for the summer. It will be good to have a fire in here during the winter but for now I will cook outside.*

Yani took her basket to the brook and gathered as many large flat stones as she could carry. Lugging them back to the tree, she raked the leaves away in a large circle and scooped out the earth to form a

251

shallow depression. Around this she made a ring of stones piling one on top of another until she had a pit that would keep the fire from spreading, catching the leaves around it on fire. She then gathered sticks and twigs from the forest floor and piled them near the fire pit. That done she went to the brook once more and brought a basket of water. She had only to make the fire to be prepared to make her supper.

She put tinder in the bottom of the pit and then built the small pyramid of twigs as Knut had taught her to do. When all was ready, she retraced her steps to the shelter below and using as stick raked some of the hot coals into the pot she had brought back with her. Holding it gingerly, she hurried back up the cliff to the tree and carefully emptied the hot coals into the pit being careful not to disturb the pyramid. Using the stick, she pushed the hot embers against the tinder and soon the twigs had caught fire. She added larger branches to this until she had a nice fire burning.

When the sun began to set, Yani and Wolf crawled through the hole and into the shelter of the tree. Yani curled up in her sleeping cloak and was soon sleeping soundly with Wolf by her side.

Chapter Three

Yani and Wolf soon fell into a pleasant routine in their new home at the top of the cliff. Their days were taken up with gathering flint nodules for blades, fishing and gathering medicine plants. Always, Yani kept a wary eye on the sea. The Knapper had said the Seapeople never failed to come for his flint blades but there had been no sign of them so far this year. Perhaps she worried for nothing.

It was late in the afternoon when the beech nuts were beginning to fall that Wolf stopped in the trail ahead of Yani, the hair raised along the back of his neck. Yani look in the direction he was looking but could see nothing to give alarm. His quiet growl told her there was danger although she could not see what. Backing into a nearby thicket, she knelt in the protection of the foliage. Wolf followed her, crouching, ready to attack if need be. As they waited, a shape appeared on the path ahead. Moving stealthily toward them was a man. A tall man wearing the blue and red paint of the Seapeople. He would walk a few steps along the trail then stop and look at the ground. As he neared, Yani held her breath lest he hear her breathing. When he got to the thicket where they were hiding, he stopped and looked straight at her. Yani sat frozen, prickles of fear running down her back. Wolf, though silent was tensed, ready to spring at any sign of aggression. They remained locked in silent confrontation for what seemed ages to Yani when the Sea Man spoke. Yani could not understand his strange tongue but she knew that her hiding place was known. To her surprise, he turned and walked a few steps away and dropped down at the base of a tree, leaning back against it. Again he spoke and motioned for her to come join him. He then began removing goods from his pack and placing them on the ground in front of him. When he had an assortment of items laid out, he pointed to the blade on his spear and held up four fingers. He spoke some more, pointed to his knife and held up two fingers. He then stood

253

up motioning toward the sea. He waved in her direction before turning on his heel and heading back down the trail toward the cliff.

When Wolf had relaxed telling Yani that is was safe to emerge from the thicket, she walked over to look at the assortment of items that the Sea Man had left. Pondering what she should do, she fingered the soft white fur that lay among the things. That alone was worth more than the blades he had requested. Making her decision she walked quickly to the tree and selecting the blades that he had indicated as well as several more. She slipped the blades into a pouch and started out of the tree when she spotted her herbs dying above the doorway. Turning back she added a pouch of dried mint and fennel to the assortment of blades.

When she got back to the place where the Sea Man's goods lay, she chose the white fur and a bag of the rich fat that the Knapper had told her came from the whale fish. Then she laid the blades and the herbs on the ground in their place. She was just rising to go when Wolf once more bristled and growled. There standing by the trail was the Sea Man. Wolf took a menacing step toward him but Yani called him back. "Wolf, stay," she said calmly. Then to the Sea Man, "Here are the blades you asked for. This," she said holding up the mint, "is good for the stomach." Then she pointed to her stomach. "This, " indicating the fennel, " is good for coughs." And she coughed.

The Sea Man nodded that he understood and then asked something else. Yani shook her head with a puzzled expression. Again he asked the same thing but when he saw that Yani did not understand, he scrunched his body and began to walk down the path with the shuffling gait of the Knapper. With a look of understanding, then sadness, Yani pointed skyward and waved her hand indicating that he had crossed over. Again the Sea Man nodded that he understood. He walked the few steps that stood between him and the trade goods. Yani and Wolf watched as he picked up the blades that Yani had put out for

254

him. Looking closely at them, he pointed at her. Not sure what his reaction would be to a woman breaking the taboo of touching weapons, she just stared back in apprehension. Again the tall Sea Man pointed from the point to the girl. They stood there with their eyes lock as the birds warbled in the trees overhead and the sea breeze rustled the leaves. At last, Yani nodded. Again he looked from the blade to the girl. Then a broad smile broke across his face. He pointed to the blade and to the girl several times as he continued to talk rapidly to Yani.

When it appeared that he had finished with the topic of the blades, he turned his attention to Wolf. Again he asked Yani a question. Then he pantomimed petting Wolf. Yani reached down and stoked his head gently. The Sea Man nodded vigorously and pointed to himself. Smiling Yani nodded. The Sea Man quickly knelt by Wolf, who bristled and began to growl. He drew back, looking at Yani. "Wolf, be nice," Yani said. "He wants to be your friend."

The tall man looked at Yani again and when she nodded, he again knelt by Wolf, this time more slowly. Wolf allowed him to stroke his fur and scratch his ears all the time keeping a wary eye on him. When the Sea Man stood again, Wolf sniffed curiously around his knees and ankles.

After an awkward silent, the Sea Man pointed to himself and said "Jorg." He waited a moment and repeated it. Then he pointed at Yani and raised his eyebrows in question. When Yani didn't respond, he repeated the procedure. This time after he had pointed to himself and said "Jorg" he pointed at Wolf and haltingly said, "Wolv". Again he pointed at Yani and raised his eyebrow. Smiling, Yani pointed to herself and said, "Yani". She then pointed at Wolf and repeated his name. Jorg repeated both their names and smiled. They stood looking at each other for several moments before he turned on his heels and started off down the trail toward the cliff.

"Well, Wolf, we have met the Seapeople and they are not as terrible as they seemed. At least that one was not," said Yani as Jorg disappeared into the forest. "Actually he was rather handsome. I have never seen such blue eyes. And he's so tall.

Chapter Five

Many days passed after the meeting with Jorg in the forest. The trees had shed their leaves and the days were getting shorter. Yani had a good supply of dried fish, acorn meal and dried berries in her home in the tree. Each day when she went to the beach, she gather what driftwood there was and now had a large pile of it at the base of the cliff by the trail. Knowing that the nice weather would not last much longer, she took the trailing pack from where she had leaned it against the tree and laid it out on the ground. Then she fetched the harness from inside the tree and called to Wolf.

She put the harness on Wolf but carried the trailing pack over her shoulder as they made their way down the cliff to the pile of firewood on the beach. There she tied the trailing pack in place. When she had the trailing pack loaded with driftwood, she stood eyeing the cliff path. "Wolf, I am afraid that if you try to go up that way the load will tip and you will fall." Looking down the beach to where the cliff dips to sea level, she continued, "It's much farther but the climb back up is much less risky. I think you can remember how to pull a load, can't you?"

Yani picked up her carrying basket she had fill with odds and ends from the shelter that she had decided she might need during the winter and they started off down the beach.

It was late in the afternoon when they finally had the firewood stacked by the tree shelter. Looking at it Yani realized that there was not nearly enough to keep her warm during the coming winter. "Wolf, I think we have much work ahead of us. This will only last a couple moons. Tomorrow, we begin to gather wood from the forest, too."

The next days were spent in searching the forest floor for dead falls that were not too rotten to give off heat and scouring the beach for more driftwood. In the evening of the first day of wood gathering, Yani had sat by the fire and sharpened and hardened the ends of two stout branches. The next morning she used a stone to hammer them into the side of the tree just above her shoulders. When they were deeply embedded into the tree, she had two pegs that extended out the length of her lower arm. The next day as they were looking for wood she cut lengths of grapevine and stripped them of their bark. She then took the vines and wove them back and forth between the pegs to form a hammock. Selecting some of the hardest dead fall and an assortment of driftwood she filled the hammock from her supply by the tree. Satisfied that now she would have dry wood to keep her fire going even in the bitterest blizzard, she smiled with contentment.

"Well, Wolf, I think we are ready for anything. We have food, firewood and a snug house. I have herbs to take care of any sickness we might have. Now all I have to do is collect enough flints to work on over the winter. But there is time for that tomorrow."

Chapter Six

The first frost had long since killed the summer plants when Yani was walking on the beach late one afternoon. She was basking in the gentle warmth of the sun and thinking how strange it was to have this warmth so late in the season, when she heard a rumbling of thunder in the distance. She looked out to sea, the direction from which storms usually come, but the sky was clear and blue. She continued to look for flint nodules for the blades she would make, when Wolf began to whimper. Again she looked at the sky but saw nothing to cause alarm. "What is it Wolf? I can feel the energy in the air, too, but the sky is so blue. It does feel like a storm but there are no clouds or wind."

As she spoke the hair on her arms began to stand up as it sometimes does after being rubbed against fur. Looking around Yani saw a huge black rising above the beech forest. As she watched a cold wind swept up the beach and a steak of lightening split the sky. "Come, Wolf!" she cried and started to run toward the cliff path. The storm broke in full fury just as she and Wolf clambered to the top. They raced along the trail in the midst of pelting hail. A tremendous flash of light blinded Yani and was followed immediately by a deafening peal of thunder. When she rounded the trail and her tree finally came into view, she stopped in horror. The top had been split away by the lightening and fingers of orange flame were licking at the branches. Frantically she crawled into the tree and began dragging her belongings out into the clearing. Ashes from the burning tree began to shower down onto her shoulders but she took no heed of their sting. She dragged several loads out into the open and was starting back in for the next when the top of the burning tree crumbled cascading down filling her home with flames. "No!" screamed Yani. "Oh, please, no!" She dropped to the ground rocking back and forth as she cried.

Through her tears, she spied her pile of firewood at the side of the tree. She scrambled to her feet and began throwing it as far from the smoking tree trunk as she could. Flames licked up from the interior of the tree sending a huge column of smoke into the blackened sky. When the growing flames stopped her for trying to save the wood, Yani collapsed in tears on the ground and sat there as a cold rain began to fall. Trembling from cold, fear and frustration, she listened to the raindrops sizzle as they came in contact with the fire. Wolf came to her side and gently nudged her arm. Turning to him, she wrapped her arms around him and sobbed. "What are we to do now, Wolf?" As she cried her fingers strayed to the piece of amber around her neck. "All our hard work, Wolf, and it's gone." Shivering, she looked at the meager pile of things she had been able to save before the tree had collapsed. "At least the trailing pack poles were not lost since I put them in the cliff shelter for the winter. So what do I have?" she asked as the rain changed to snow. Pulling the bearskin around her shoulders, she numbly filled her carrying basket with things to take to the cliff shelter.

Yani had made four trips through the snow to the top of the cliff to bring firewood and the rest of the things she had saved when the ice on the trail made the footing too dangerous to risk another trip. She was soaked to the skin and shivering when she was faced with the most difficult problem. What was she to do about Wolf? He could not climb up and he was too heavy for her to pull up with a vine. As she looked from the shelter to Wolf, he gave a bark and loped off down the beach. Resigned to spend the storm without her friend, she turned back to the base of the cliff.

Climbing the ladder into the shelter, she began to prepare it for the coming night. As the wind whipped around her, she slide one of the trailing pack poles from the grapevine webbing. She took a piece of driftwood and threaded the loops over it pushing them together before tying it to the other pole. Then she drove the trailing pack poles as deeply into the chalk floor as she could, one at either end of the shelter. After that she lashed the woven drying mats to the poles creating a wind block. With protection from the wind, she prepared to build a fire. Going to the back of the shelter, she gathered some of the dried reeds left from the basket-boat she had made for the old Knapper's final trip. To this she added some small pieces of driftwood. Soon she had a fire blazing in the fire pit that drove off the worst of the cold. Gathering up all the mats she had, she tied them to the windbreak until it was several mats thick. Curling up in the bearskin on the sleeping bench, she began to cry softly. Rubbing the butterfly stone between her thumb and forefinger, Yani finally drifted into a troubled sleep with the sea crashing on the beach below and the wind howling in the beech trees above her.

Chapter Seven

The winds raged all that night and the next day. Sometime during the second night the keening of the wind in the trees changed pitch and the following morning Yani was awaken by the impatient bark of Wolf. She lay on the bearskin listening for the howl of the wind but it was strangely silent. Finally, she opened her eyes and sat up. Immediately she felt a throbbing in her head behind her eyes. Standing up she began to sneeze. "Wolf, please be quiet" she mumbled as she stirred up the coals in the fire pit and added wood from the dwindling pile. "Alright, I am coming," she said as she walked to the wall of mats that separated her from the outside world. Pulling one of the poles from the hole in the chalk floor, she lifted it to one side and looked out. She saw Wolf frisking in the snow that covered the beach to the high tide mark. Despite the miserable throbbing in her head, she smiled at his antics. He ran to the edge of the water and waited as a wave moved forward. Just ahead of it, he ran back though the snow to circle around again daring the wave to catch him.

Taking the water basket, Yani walked to the edge of the ledge and filled it from the spring. When she returned to the shelter, she was shivering violently. She filled one of the clay pots that she had managed to save and set it in the fire to heat. Pulling the bearskin tightly around her, she opened her medicine bag and looked for the dried fennel to brew some tea. She added more wood to the fire in hopes of chasing off the chill and pulled Knut's old deerskin from under his sleeping bench and wrapped that around her feet.

What am I to do if I get really sick here all alone, she thought. She rubbed the golden butterfly stone absently. She thought of Loki and the Village in the Marsh. If she were in the village, Loki would brew her some good tea. She would be in a warm house with plenty to eat and Wolf could be sleeping by her to keep her warm. A tear trickled down her cheek as she took the tea from the fire and began to sip it. Soon the warmth of the liquid spread through her body warming her. She curled up near the fire and fell into a feverish sleep.

Sometime later she heard Wolf barking again but this time it was not his playful yap but a challenging growling bark. Yani tried to arouse herself to go to see what had disturbed him but her fevered mind refused to respond. During the night, she opened her eyes to see the troubled face of Jorg looking down at her. The flickering fire cast his tall shadow on the back of the shelter as he brought her warm sweet tea that soothed her aching throat. He said something as he leaned over her but she did not understand. She tried to answer but the words seemed to stick in her mouth. She felt his strong hand behind her head lifting her up as he held the bowl of tea to her lips. She drank and then drank again before he laid her back on the bearskin and tucked it tightly around her. As she drifted in and out of consciousness, she expected to see Jorg blue eyes looking down at her each time but he never again appeared. *Perhaps I only dreamed it*, thought Yani during one of her waking moments. *Fevers do bring on strange dreams. But it was so real. I can even remember the feel of his hand against my head.*

Much later she heard Wolf's barking again but this time it was a welcoming bark. She smiled and thought, *Jorg must be back.* She dozed again until she was awakened by Birg's voice talking to Wolf. *Oh, good,* she thought, *I don't have to wake up. Birg will take care of whatever is bothering Wolf. Maybe he will know Jorg's language so he can thank him for me.*

Later she opened her eyes and the flickering of the fire again cast a tall shadow on the wall of the shelter. Watching the dancing movement of the shadow, she whispered "Jorg? Did Birg talk to you? Where is Wolf?"

A cool hand touched her forehead and a soft voice said, "Rest, Yani. The worst of your fever is over but you are still weak. I need to

263

get you back to the village where Mother can see to you. We have a long hard journey ahead of us tomorrow."

Yani's eyes focused on the worried face of Birg. "Birg, you came. I rubbed the butterfly stone and you came. Did you talk to Jorg?"

"Yani there is no one else here. It is only the fever," brushing the hair back from her forehead, he continued, "I said I would come if you needed me, didn't I? Here, let me help you drink some tea. I found the pouch of fennel by the fire and have brewed some more for you. I think that is the right herb for the coughing sickness. Tomorrow I am going to try to get Wolf to let me put the harness on him and we will take you to the Village so Mother can make you well. But now you need to sleep.

Chapter Eight

When next she woke, it was to find Birg curled up across the fire pit from her sleeping soundly. She sat up slowly, expecting the pounding to return to her head. She still had tightness in her chest and a stuffy nose but that was all. She checked the water basket and found that Birg had filled it before he went to sleep, so filling the clay pot, she brewed fresh tea.

When Birg woke later in the morning, he found Yani sitting by the fire wrapped in the bearskin. "Good morning," she smiled.

He smiled back then yawned and stretched. "Well, from the looks of you, I made this trip for nothing. I expected to have to wrestle Wolf into submission so he could drag you back to the village."

They sat in uncomfortable silence and watched the fire until Birg said, "You are still coming back to the village with me but I think you may be able to help me get Wolf harnessed."

"Birg," protested Yani, "I can stay here by myself, really."

"Yani, please, don't fight with me over this. Mother said she would skin me alive if I were to come back without you. And when she hears that you have been sick, I would really be in trouble. Do you want me to be banished from my home because you're a stubborn girl?" Although his voice held a teasing quality Yani knew he was going to stand firm on this. "And, Lamu, said to tell you she has a secret she wants to share with you. Some secret," he snorted, "that magpie has told everyone in the village that would listen."

"So, why don't you tell me what it is," asked Yani, "if everyone knows it anyway. That way I don't have to go back to hear her secret and you don't have to tell your mother I have been sick. That can be our secret."

At this Birg smiled wickedly, "I think I will make you come back to the village to find out Lamu's secret. After all Lamu would be

265

mad if I were the one to tell you. And what kind of son would have secrets from his mother? Why, Yani, that is asking me to lie to her. When she asks how you are what am I to say?"

"Oh, Birg!" laughed Yani. "Would you tell Lamu's secret if I promise to go with you?"

"I'll think about it. But let's get started packing. When we are all packed to go and through the beech forest I'll tell you."

"Why not now?"

"Because," answered Birg, "this way I will be sure that you will go with me."

"Are you saying you don't trust me?" asked Yani indignantly.

"I'm only saying that I don't want you to change your mind. After all I would miss Mother's cooking if I had to take up with Deet and roam the forests." Birg ducked as Yani throw a basket at him.

When they had all the things that Yani would need packed in baskets, she was beginning to tire so Birg suggested that they wait and leave at first light the next morning. With Birg's help, Yani fixed a pot of acorn porridge and as they ate, she told Birg what had happened since she left the village, ending with the fire. When she had finished they sat in silence.

Why did I leave out the part about meeting Jorg in the forest and trading with him? Yani wondered. *But, for some reason I know I should not tell him that.*

Chapter Nine

"Yani, you could have been killed. Why didn't you come to the village as soon as Knut crossed over? You know you are like a daughter of our house. You would have been safe and warm."

"But this is my home, Birg," replied Yani. "I love the sea. And, if the lightening had not struck the tree I would have had all that I needed to be comfortable over the winter."

"Yani, you do see that you must come back with me now, don't you?" asked an anxious Birg.

"Yes, I suppose so," sighed Yani. "But just until spring. Then I am coming back here so I can find a good place for Wolf and me before next winter."

With a look of relief, Birg said, "When spring comes we can talk about that. Now, let's get some sleep so we can get an early start."

The stars were still out when the two young people climbed down from the shelter the next morning. There was very little wind and the waves only made a gently lapping sound as they broke against the rocks on the shore. Yani whistled for Wolf as Birg pulled the poles for the trailing pack down from their place against the cliff. As they waited for Wolf to appear Birg helped Yani remove the driftwood and thread the poles back through the grapevine webbing. She had the goods she would take with her for the winter stacked on the beach. When she had the trailing pack loaded and ready, she whistled again. From far down the beach, she heard an answering bark.

"Come on, Wolf," she called. "We are going on a journey. Hurry!"

Wolf loped up to her and jumped up placing his big paws on her shoulders covering her face with wet kisses. "Stopped it, Wolf!" Yani laughed. Pushing him down she scratched his ears and rubbed his jowls. "Yes, I know, I missed you too. But you have work to do. "

Soon she had the harness in place and they were ready to start. Looking at the icy trail up the cliff, Yani said, "Birg, I think we should go down the beach and up the long way. I am afraid one of us will fall if we go that way."

Birg looked in the direction that she pointed and asked in amazement "You mean that is the way you get from the cliff to the beach?"

"Yes, that is the way from the beech forest to the beach. Isn't that how you came?"

"Well, no, I ah, actually I came," began Birg. Then he sighed looking very shamed faced. "The truth is I have no idea how I came. I knew that the Knapper lived by the sea and I had to find you. So I kept going toward the rising sun until I found the sea. Then I followed the sea. I had about decided that I was going in the wrong direction when I found Wolf. Or, I should say, he found me. It was Wolf who lead me here."

"Do you mean to say, you were lost!"

"I wasn't exactly lost since I knew I was by the sea but, well, I.."

"But, Birg, if Wolf lead you here why did he growl at you so?" asked Yani.

"What do you mean? Wolf, didn't growl at me. He was happy to see me."

"But I heard him growl at you when you first came. The night you fixed me the sweet strange tasting tea. And I meant to ask you, what kind of tea was that? It made the cough so much better."

"Yani, it must have been the fever making you dream. I didn't make tea other than the fennel tea you had left by the fire. And Wolf did not growl at me."

"Then who did he growl at? " muttered Yani.

They turned away from the sea where the cliff sloped down to meet the beach. They had easy going through the forest as the snow was

268

not as deep there. As they emerged on the other side they cut across the snow covered meadow until they reached the trail back to the village. Yani was able to keep a steady pace most of the morning but by midafternoon her strength was waning. Seeing this, Birg suggested, "You could let Wolf carry you for a while. Just so we could keep traveling while you rested."

Yani considered it while eyeing the heavy load that was already piled on the trailing pack then she shook her head. "He is carrying enough. And if I ride I will only get cold. The walking is helping to keep me warm." She smiled weakly at him and continued to walk. A little later when she stumbled Brig wrapped his arm around her waist saying, "Here, Yani, lean on me. I will help you." Gratefully, she accepted his help.

They stopped briefly at noontime for a rest and to eat. Birg checked the load on the trailing pack as Yani dozed. He had built a small fire to make a hot lunch thinking the warmth would give Yani the strength she needed to continue. He watched Yani as he waited for the snow to melt and for the water to get hot enough to add the acorn meal. The sky was clear and blue but the sun only gave off a feeble warmth. The temperature was pleasant now but he knew the clear sky would bring frigid temperatures when the sun set. A cloud cover, although it could also mean snow, would have held in some of the sun's warmth. When the porridge was done, he gently shook Yani from her sleep handing her a steaming bowl. Looking up she smiled her thanks. They ate in silence both feeling an urgency to be moving again.

The rest had revived Yani enough that they made good progress in the afternoon but as the sun faded from the sky so, too, did Yani's strength. As the sky darkened, Yani was again leaning on Birg for support. Knowing she was tired, he said, "I know you need to rest but is will be too cold to camp in the open. If you think you can keep going we can reach the Village shortly after midnight."

Yani smiled weakly and replied, "We must keep going. I can feel the chill in the air already. Will the wind pick up too?"

"It usually does in this kind of weather."

"Then we must keep going."

They continued to walk long after the sun had set. The way across the meadow was level and the starlight reflecting off the snow provided plenty of light for them to see their way. A narrow crescent moon was rising over the marsh when they finally reached the causeway leading to the village. Leaving their pack to collect later, they crossed the causeway with Birg leading and Yani following behind her hand on his shoulder for support and guidance.

Chapter Ten

Loki was sitting by the fire as Birg staggered in carrying an exhausted Yani. "Finally you are here. I felt that you would come tonight and I have been too restless to sleep. Here, Birg, put her down by the fire. I already have some water heating for tea."

Lamu, awakened by their arrival, stumbled over to the fire still rubbing sleep from her eyes. She wrapped a warm deerskin around the shivering Yani huddling close to her to add extra warmth. Loki glanced up from her search through the medicine pouch to see Birg heading for the door. "Birg, where are you going?" asked Loki. "It is the middle of the night!"

"I left Yani's things on the other side of the causeway when I unharnessed Wolf. I need to go back and bring them here," he said. "I don't know if I can carry them all," he added with a meaningful glance at Lamu.

Catching his eye, she quickly answered, "I'll come with you and help."

"Go ahead and help him," said Loki. "if you are sure that it can't wait until morning."

As soon as they were out of the house, Lamu began questioning Birg, "What happened to Yani? Where is the Knapper?"

"Patience, Lamu, I will tell you all I know but I have had a long trip today and need all my strength to make it back for the packs. I have had to practically carry Yani the last part of the journey."

They walked in silence across the causeway to the other side of the marsh where Lamu made sure she chose the heaviest of the baskets to carry back. When they got back to the house, Yani was sleeping soundly on Lamu's sleeping bench and Loki had a pot of stew warming on the fire for Birg.

When he was settled by the fire with a bowl of stew, she asked, "Now, Son, tell me, how it is?"

Birg sighed then began to tell all the things that Yani had told him of her time since she had left the village. The fire burned low before he finished and yawning staggered to his sleeping bench. Before Loki and Lamu had made it to their sleeping benches, he was softly snoring.

The next morning Yani woke to the mouth watering smell of venison stew. She rolled over to see Loki leaning over the fire stirring the bubbling pot. Stretching she rolled from the sleeping bench and joined Loki at the fire.

"Good morning, Yani," said Loki when she saw the girl. "I didn't expect you to be up this soon. Are you feeling better?"

"Yes, much," smiled Yani. "It is good to be at your fire pit again."

"Yani, you know I tried to get you to stay last spring. You should have come to us as soon as the old man crossed over. A young girl alone like that, anything could have happened. And from what Birg tells us it nearly did," scolded Loki.

"I know that I could have come here but the sea is my home. If you ever saw it you would know why I stayed. But I am glad to be here now," said Yani with a smile.

"And I am very glad that you are here," replied Loki coming to give the girl a hug.

"But not half as glad as Birg is," giggled Lamu from where she was sitting on her sleeping bench. "He moped around for weeks after you left. And all I had to do to send him into a black mood was to say how handsome I thought Deet was."

"Deet!' cried Yani. "He was jealous of Deet! Why that would be like being jealous of an uncle."

"I don't think Deet considers himself your uncle, Yani," said Loki. "And I think Birg is right to wonder what Deet's intentions are."

"I am not interested in any one's intentions," mumbled Yani.

"But I am," crooned Lamu. "Did Brig tell you I had a secret to share with you?"

"It is only a secret if no one else knows it, Magpie," said a sleepy Birg from his bench. "And in this case Yani is the only one in the village who hasn't heard it a dozen or so times."

"That isn't so," cried Lamu. "I've only told a few of my best friends."

"Who told their sisters and mothers and cousins and so everyone in the village knows."

"Oh, you," grumbled Lamu.

"So tell me your big secret so I will know, too," laughed Yani.

"I know who I am going to marry!" giggled Lamu. "He is tall and handsome and has the most unusual eyes. Green, like the reeds of the marsh in early spring. His name is Dev."

"But does he know he is going to marry you?" teased Birg.

"Mother," wailed Lamu, "make him stop!"

"Birg, let your sister alone," scolded Loki. "There is plenty of time to convince Dev that he wants to marry her. If we start saving otter pelts now, we should have enough to bribe him to take her before she is too old and wrinkled for him to consider."

"Oh, now you are doing it too!" squealed Lamu and she buried her head in the furs of her sleeping bench to block out the laughter.

Chapter Twelve

Yani was to hear much of the handsome Dev and how Lamu had first seen him coming across the lake "as if he were walking on the water. The sun was setting behind him making the water look like your butterfly stone only it was not hard like the butterfly stone," Lamu would whisper as they lay on the sleeping bench at night.

"And just when do I get to meet this wondrous Dev?" asked Yani one night as spring was beginning to creep into the marsh.

"Any day now," sighed Lamu. "He told Brig that he would be back to hunt the ducks that come to the marsh. And they should be returning soon."

This time it was Yani's turn to sigh but not in thoughts of a handsome man but in anticipation of the succulent duck meals that the spring would bring. "Lamu, how do you know that he is interested in you?" asked Yani. "Did you walk out alone to talk?"

"Well, no," replied Lamu haltingly. "But I am sure he is. Why else would he come all the way back to the marsh? His village is far. It lays across the hills to the east and by the Rushing River."

"Lamu, did you think that perhaps he comes back to hunt ducks?"

"Maybe, but he smiled at me often when he took the evening meal with us. I just know he is coming back to see me."

As Yani drifted off to sleep, she wished she were as sure as Lamu of Dev's intentions.

One morning as Yani lay listening to the waking sounds of the family around her, she heard the faint call of the wild geese as they winged their way north. Smiling to herself she knew that the ducks would not be far behind. And, with the ducks would come the marvelous Dev.

She turned over to look toward the fire pit to where Wolf had been sleeping when she went to bed only to see that once again he was gone. Lately he had been spending more and more nights away from the village. Yani frowned to think that he might be returning to the wild. Then she stopped herself. He had come to her on his own and so had always been free to return if he chose. After all it had not been too far from here that she had seen him for the first time. Perhaps he was returning to the pack. He may be lonely for his own kind.

Wolf did not return that night or the next. When on the third night he came limping into the house, Yani rushed to his side to see what was wrong. "Wolf, what have you done? Your foot has been cut badly and look at your ears! I think you have been fighting with something."

Going for her medicine bag, Yani said, "Let me see what I can do to fix you up." She took out a pouch that contained bear fat mixed with herbs and smoothed it over Wolf's many cuts. "Wolf, I think it is time we return to our home. I miss the sound of the sea and I can see that you are not content here either. We both are meant to live off by ourselves. As soon as you are healed, we will go back to the cliff. But, how will I tell Loki and Hawn after they have been so good to me?"

When Wolf's wounds had almost healed and the soft breezes of spring brought the perfume of early flowers, Yani finally approached Loki to tell her that she was planning to return to her home by the sea.

"Yani, we have always known that you would go back. It is not Hawn and I that will find it hard to understand but Birg," said Loki when Yani had told her of her decision.

Hanging her head, Yani hurriedly tried to explain, "I do like it here with you. You treat me better than my own parents did, but, how do I explain," looking up with troubled eyes she faltered to a stop.

"You do not need to explain to us. We understand. But, Birg, he will be more difficult. Yani, you know that he hopes you will agree to be his wife."

"I don't want to hurt him, Loki, but I am not ready to become a wife."

"I know, most woman aren't. But few have the luxury of making the choice not to be. When will you leave?'

"I think Wolf will be ready to travel in a few days. Then I will go."

Loki came to the girl and placed her hand on her shoulder. She looked deeply into her eyes and said, "Remember, Yani, you may always change your mind and return. If it is too difficult, do not let your pride stand in your way."

As tears formed in her eyes, Yani replied, "That is good to know. I will remember."

Chapter Thirteen

The next day the ducks returned to the marsh and that night for supper Yani feasted on the tasty meat that she loved. As they sat around the fire after the bones had been sacrificed to the gods of the marsh, Loki said calmly, "So Yani when are you leaving us to return to the sea."

Afraid to meet Brig's eyes, she answered, "I think, I must go in three days. Wolf will be healed by then and the spring is here. We have the ducks to prove it. Thank you for the delicious supper, Birg." As she said the last, she risked looking at him. The shock and anger she saw there hurt her.

"But, if you go now you will not get to see Dev," cried Lamu. "I thought you were staying forever. I mean I thought you and Birg," Before she could finish, Birg jumped up from his place by the fire and ran from the house.

Looking helplessly at Loki for direction, she motioned with her eyes for Yani to follow Birg. When she found him, he was sitting on a log near the marsh throwing stones into the reeds. She watched him for a while, collecting her thoughts, then she approached and laid her hand on his hunched shoulders.

"Birg," she said softly. When he did not answer she spoke a little louder. "Birg, please, talk to me."

"What do you want?" he said still not facing her.

Yani came around in front of him and knelt so she could see his face. "Birg, please understand. My home is by the sea. I must go back. That is where I belong."

"But, how will you live? Who will take care of you?" he demanded.

"I will take care of myself," laughed Yani.

"But, what will you eat? You can't live on acorn meal all the time."

"I won't live on acorn meal. I will have fish and rabbit and from time to time a deer. There are all kinds of mussels and shell fish, too," replied Yani.

"Oh, yes, I suppose you have trained Wolf to hunt for you. Or do you plan to kill these rabbits and deer yourself," sneered Birg.

"As a matter of fact, the answer to both your questions is yes. Wolf often brings me fresh kill. But, I can also hunt."

"Who ever heard of a woman who could hunt. The gods would not permit it. It is taboo for a woman to even touch a hunting weapon. Everyone knows that a spear that has been touched by a woman will not find its mark."

"Oh," said Yani quietly, "is that so. Everyone one knows this? Well, the spear that you are holding. Did you use it to kill the ducks we had for supper tonight?"

"Of course," said Birg.

"And it found its mark true enough?" asked Yani.

"Yes, but I don't see.." started Birg.

"And, who do you think made the point on your spear?" asked Yani.

"Why, the Knapper made it. I got it from him myself when he was here last spring. I traded a rabbit pelt for it," replied Birg.

"Birg, look at it closely. Is it like the others that you have gotten from Father?" demanded Yani. As Birg looked at the point a cloud of apprehension crossed his face. "Well, is it?"

"No, it's different. The edge is better worked. Father commented on it when he saw it, too. We thought that the old Knapper had found a new source of flint. Are you telling me that.."

"Yes, Birg, I am telling you that the reason it is different is that it was not made by Father."

"So if he didn't make it," pondered Birg. "Who did make it?"

"I made it." With that Yani stood up, turned on her heel and headed back toward the village.

Chapter Fourteen

Early the next morning, Birg left the house saying that he was going to go hunting and didn't know how long he would be gone. Yani followed him to the edge of the marsh and watched as he crossed the causeway. She stood watching until he had disappeared over the horizon, then she turned and walked back to the house. Entering she went to the shelf above the sleeping bench and lifted down her carrying basket. Sadly, she began to sort the things that she would take with her when she returned to the seaside.

Lamu came in as she was packing and plopped down on the bench. "I just don't see why you must go," she said. "Don't you like living with us?"

"It's not that, Lamu," said Yani. "It's hard for me to explain. My home is by the water. If you could only see it you would understand."

"But," protected Lamu, "how will you live? Who will take care of you?"

Yani laughed softly. "That is the same question your brother asked me. I think the answer I gave him hurt his feelings. Lamu, I don't need anyone to take care of me."

"But won't you get lonely?"

"I will have Wolf and besides if I do get lonely, I can always come back for a visit. Or perhaps I can rub the butterfly stone and Birg will come and bring you with him. Would you like that?"

"You don't really think that if you rub the stone, Birg will come do you?"

"No," giggled Yani. "But would you come for a visit anyway? Maybe you can have Dev bring you so I can see the wondrous Dev."

"Yani," said Lamu sadly. "I am going to miss you."

"And I will miss you." The two young women held each other, each thinking how different their lives had become.

The next day, Yani followed the causeway across the marsh and tied the poles of the trailing pack to Wolf's harness. Lamu and Honi had accompanied her this far helping to carry the bundles that she would pack on the trailing pack. When all was ready, Yani looked around one last time.

"He is watching from the marsh," said Honi with a smile. "You may not be able to see him but he is there. I know my brother. He has probably been watching every move you made for the last two days. And, Yani, he is probably where he could hear you if you talked loudly."

"Thank you, Honi," said Yani softly. "I will miss you." Turning to Lamu she gave her a fierce hug. Then turned to face the marsh and called out loudly. "Goodbye, Birg, I will miss you, too. Kill lots of ducks with that spear of yours and think of me when you eat them."

With one last look over the marsh, she called to Wolf and they started on their journey back to the sea.

Chapter Fifteen

They reach the cliff as the sun was setting behind the beech trees. Yani quickly untied the trailing pack from Wolf's harness and slipped it over his head. "You are going to have to fend for yourself again tonight, Wolf, but the first thing tomorrow I am going to figure out a way that we can sleep together. It is too near dark to bring all the things down the cliff now. Tomorrow will be soon enough."

A full moon was rising blood red above the sea, when Yani pulled the vine on the ladder and climbed to the shelter. The wind was beginning to pick up, so she quickly used the last of the driftwood from her woodpile to build a fire. She pulled her bearskin from her carrying basket and eating some jerked venison, she curled up on Knut's sleeping bench and was soon asleep.

She woke the next day to the sound of the surf and the salty smell of the sea. Yawning and stretching, she lay warm in the bearskin and thought about the problem of getting Wolf to her shelter. She knew he was too heavy to pull up in a basket, besides he would not want to be restricted to this narrow ledge. She let her mind wander to the lay of the land around the cliff. She pictured the ledge. The shelter was at the higher end so the water from the spring would trickle away from the spring and down the cliff face. That was the answer! She could cut a ramp from the beach to the low end of the ledge near the spring. Even though the chalk was soft it would take a while but she had plenty of time. The shelter would no longer be as safe but it would allow Wolf free access to their home. He could come and go as he pleased. She got out of bed and walked to the lower end of the ledge to see if it looked like her plan would work. Surveying the cliff face she decided it was a good plan. As soon as she brought the rest of the things from the top of the cliff, she would begin.

By noon Yani had carry all the baskets down the cliff and unloaded them in the shelter. Then she chose a large flint and chipped off a wide blade the size of her hand. She used the deer antler awl to shape it into a triangle with notches at the narrow point. She had cut a short strong branch before she had carried the last load down and this she attached to the blade at a right angle so that she could use it to scrap out the soft chalk cliff. When she had her new tool ready, she went to the end of the ledge and began chipping and scrapping away the chalk. Soon the work warmed her so that sweat trickled down her face and back. Wolf watched with interest for a while then wandered off down the beach to chase the crabs and play tag with the waves.

By the time the sun had dipped behind the forest, Yani had made a ramp twice the length of her body and wide enough for Wolf to walk up easily. Looking at the distance she had yet to go, she muttered to herself, "At this rate I will have it done just in time for winter."

After she had stirred up the fire and fixed a pot of acorn porridge for supper, she climbed down the ladder calling to Wolf. Together, in the light of a full moon, they walked the shore until the chill of the night air turned them back. Wolf whined as Yani started to climb the ladder to the shelter. Turning back to him, she knelt and scratched his ears. "Be patient, Wolf, I will have a way for you to come up soon," Yani promised.

Yani spent the Moon of Budding Trees scraping and chopping at the chalk face of the cliff. When the moon was full again, she finally had a ramp that ran low enough down the cliff that Wolf could jump onto it and run up to the shelter. That night for the first time, Yani and Wolf sat together on the edge of the ledge and watched a round orange moon rise above the sea. As the waves danced golden in the moonlight, Yani put her arm around Wolf, sighing, "At last we are home."

Made in the USA
San Bernardino, CA
17 October 2018